To all the faithful companions out there. Whether they are canine, feline, or equine, they enrich our lives with companionship and unbiased love.

"A guide dog is almost equal in many ways to giving a blind man sight itself."
   ~Britain's first recipient of a seeing eye dog, 1931.

"Everything has its wonders, even darkness and silence, and I learn, whatever state I may be in, therein to be content."
   ~Helen Keller

Chapter One

English countryside, fall 1803.

Lightning forked across the sky. A lone tree on the incline exploded. Static sparks crackled through the air. His mount shied and almost unseated him, but the squire pulled the frightened animal up and steadied it. A deafening wave of thunder drowned out all other sounds and the horse lost its nerve, rearing to paw at the heavens. The rider struggled to stay in the saddle and reined in his mount. He settled the gelding with a few unintelligible words and a hand along its neck. The sky opened, dousing him with torrents of icy water. He hunched against the weather and swiped his face with a shaky hand. Giving the horse its head he urged it on, its feet slipping and scrabbling for purchase in the muck. The animal stumbled, almost launching him from the saddle before regaining its footing and lurching the rest of the way up the slope.

The squire sawed on the reins as a dark figure separated from the shadows. He leaped from the gelding's back, great coat flapping in the wind, gray hair plastered to his head. Another flash of lightning lit the sky, followed by booming thunder. The animal shied, almost jerking him off his feet. Despite the skittish horse's reluctance he made his way to the man. "We must talk, for your pursuit of my daughter will end here and now."

The shadowed figure advanced toward him. "Old man, I have had enough of your refusals to see reason."

"You do not understand, boy."

The unidentified figure shoved him, causing the squire to lose his precarious stance. He landed spread-eagled, face up in the mud. With a groan he scrambled to one knee in the slop. "Please—"

Through Gypsy Eyes

KILLARNEY SHEFFIELD

CRIMSON
ROMANCE
F+W Media, Inc.

This edition published by
Crimson Romance
an imprint of F+W Media, Inc.
10151 Carver Road, Suite 200
Blue Ash, Ohio 45242
www.crimsonromance.com

ISBN 10: 1-4405-6666-6
ISBN 13: 978-1-4405-6666-0
eISBN 10: 1-4405-6667-4
eISBN 13: 978-1-4405-6667-7

"You will not keep me from what is rightfully mine, noddy old man," The younger aggressor raised his fist.

The squire reached up a hand to fend him off. "I must! Let me explain—" He tried in vain to stagger to his feet, but a second blow toppled him to the edge of the cliff. Again he struggled to rise. "Listen—" His second plea fell on deaf ears as the attacker's foot landed squarely on his chest. In desperation he flailed with grasping fingers, only to meet air as he tumbled over and over down the steep slope.

Delilah sat up with a jolt, her heart pounding against her breastbone. The mugginess of the stale air and the silken sheets beneath confirmed her rightful place in bed. She took a deep breath knowing she was safe, despite the fear the dream instilled looming as dark and endless as her future. Why this nightmare every night since her father's death? Was it some sick sense of need that made her unwilling to believe his fall an accident? There was no proof to the contrary. Her fingers curled around the hem of the sweat-dampened sheets as her heart protested. One day she would prove it wasn't an accident. Somehow.

Pushing the morbid dream out of mind, she donned her slippers. She tossed a simple peasant gown over her head and then tiptoed from her bedchamber. Sweat dampened her brow and the undersides of her breasts straining against the thin fabric. After easing the door closed behind, she paused to be sure there was no hint of movement in the hall. The mansion was silent as always at this time of night. With a grin of expectant pleasure she made her way along the corridor and then down the stairs when the familiar smooth banister met her fingertips. *So far so good.* It seemed a fool's errand to worry over discovery, for there was no one to question her mission except the servants, and they were easy to fool.

When she reached the main floor she trailed her fingers along the wall until they met the junction marking the servants' hallway and the way to the cook's garden door. *It is as easy as that.* She'd slipped from the house in the dark of night so many times over the last few years it was almost mundane, though each time still carried a little flutter of nervous anticipation. Once out the kitchen door she gave a low whistle. By the time she reached the garden gate he was there. The almost uncanny connection they shared told her.

She lifted the latch, stepped through, and held out her hand. A soft nose nudged her, a rumbled nicker confirming what she already knew. "Good eve, Jester." Sliding her hands up along the docile pony's face she reached for the headstall. After patting him she groped for the special harness he always wore, finding it with little difficulty. "It is far too hot for slumber, old friend."

Jester shook his head as if disagreeing with her when she shimmed onto his back. A gentle squeeze sent him down the path they both knew so well. The soft clip clop of his hooves resonated above the singsong of the crickets, and the breeze teased the hair from her clammy neck.

Delilah didn't need to see to know the route to take. Each step Jester took over stone and root and around turns was imprinted upon the map in her head. Somewhere above an owl hooted. She smiled. The sound was as predictable as the path she rode. The dark didn't frighten her. How could she be frightened of something she was so familiar with? Besides, any creature large enough to do her harm would avoid the pony, who was known to be protective. The rush of the small waterfall and odor of fresh, wet vegetation reached her before she noticed the tiny spray of mist the gentle cascade produced. It was much cooler and comfortable here in her secret place.

When the pony came to a halt she slid to her feet. He pressed against her legs to warn her of the stream bank and she patted him. "Thank you, Jester." He blew through his nostrils in response. Sometimes she swore he understood every word she uttered. It was a special bond they shared from being so close for so long.

Jester moved off a few steps when she pulled the dress over her head and dropped it to the grassy bank. She loved swimming naked in the water, finding it freeing somehow. Crouching, she felt for the edge of the bank with her toe before slipping into the cool water. With sure, even strokes she swam out into the middle of the deep pool and rolled over to float on her back. Her sigh carried on the whisper of a breeze as she relished the cool water against her flushed skin. *If only I could stay here in this pool forever.* The Indian summer couldn't continue much longer, however, and the crisp autumn season would soon begin in earnest.

The pony snorted and then nickered. She strained to hear anything beyond her own movement as she kept herself afloat. Was there a slight rustle in the brush? Stilling her movement, she paid closer attention. After detecting no further sound she closed her eyes, allowing herself to relax and float in the blissful rocking motion of the current. It must be a small woodland creature out to parch its thirst on such a stuffy night. There was nothing to fear from such creatures, she was sure. A soft splash gave her pause and she rolled over. Treading water she turned to face the opposite bank. Ripples rose, slapping her chest as if something waded in the shallows. She listened again. A rhythmic sloshing made its way toward her. Alarm quickened her pulse as she concentrated on the sound. "Jester?"

An answering nicker came from the bank behind her. She worried her damp lower lip between her teeth. *If Jester is yet on the bank, then what is in the water with me?* The unknown visitor slowed, treading water a few yards from her. By the noise it made she surmised it was large. Intuition told her it was not a mink or beaver come to fish. The fine hairs on the back of her neck began to prickle. Crossing one arm over her breasts and paddling with the other to keep afloat she inquired, "Is someone there?"

"I thought my eyes deceived me when I spied a fair maiden floating in this pool."

The unexpected baritone froze her movement. Delilah gasped, almost going under the surface of the water when she forgot in surprise to paddle for an instant. She scrambled for something appropriate to say under the circumstances. "I beg your pardon, sir? 'Tis most unseemly to disrupt a lady's swim."

He chuckled, a low, husky sound making her picture a large, muscular physique. "Ah, you are right; however, I have yet to determine whether you are a lady or merely a figment of my overtaxed imagination."

Heart thudding against her ribcage, she swam backward toward the opposite bank, struggling to appear calm and collected. The stranger could accost her here and no one would know to come to her rescue. *How senseless I have been. Surely Jester will be no match for a man intent on harming me.* Taking a deep breath, she gathered her courage. "I assure you sir, I am not a figment of anyone's imaginings, least of all yours."

"Hmm…" the preponderance followed her. "Perhaps then you are a woodland nymph out to temp any man who passes by to try your nectar?"

Her feet touched bottom, sinking into the sand. Before she could turn and make for the bank his hands were on her waist. To her horror he cradled it in a firm, yet gentle grip. "Release me sir, for you do offend a lady, not a nymph." She fought a growing sense of panic as he drew her to him.

His minty breath tickled her damp cheek. "You have flesh as any maiden. Do you taste as sweet as one, too?"

Anger and shock at his boldness brought her hand down with force to slap the surface of the water. He sputtered in response to the spray splattering his face. *Perhaps I might have the upper hand.* "Release me this instant or I shall scream and alert my maid who sleeps on the bank," she bluffed.

Despite the warning, he chuckled. "There is no maid, wood nymph, for I walked the whole perimeter when I spied you here."

Is his intent to take advantage of a lone woman and defile me? What am I to do? Summoning her little remaining courage, she tried to reason with him. "I say again, release me good sir, for my presence will be missed at the manor even as we speak." She grimaced at the tremor in her voice betraying her fear. He shifted, his mouth brushing her ear, and she gasped at the intimate contact.

"Ah, even so I would take a moment to test your lips to see if they are as soft and sweet as your voice," he whispered.

His lips claimed hers, causing her thoughts to scatter as he licked and nibbled her bottom one. The teasing, sensual sensation was so shocking and pleasurable she sighed, opening for him, forgetting her fear for a moment. When his tongue made contact with hers, she was jolted back to the seriousness of the situation.

She wrenched from his grasp with a soft cry and floundered to the pool's edge, his deep chuckles chasing her up the bank. For the briefest second she contemplated not pausing to find her gown, but the thought of giving him an unexposed view of her derriere stifled the thought. In haste she tapped the ground until her fingers found the edge of the material and then snatched it up, yanking it over her head. Her attempt to whistle for Jester resulted in a loud, puffing sound as air passed over her damp lips. A splash in the water drew her attention. She cocked her head to listen. Strong, rhythmic strokes moved away from the bank. Relief made her lightheaded with the knowledge the stranger was not in pursuit. Was she safe? Was his intent only to flirt and nothing more?

Jester's fuzzy coat slipped beneath her trembling fingertips, drawing her back to the present. She pulled herself onto his back with the aid of the special harness he wore. "Home, Jester."

"Good-bye, sweet wood nymph," the man called from the pool.

With a jab of her heels she urged Jester homeward, ignoring the stranger's taunt. Sticks stabbed and scratched her bare legs as the pony pushed through the brambles to the path. With a groan she realized her slippers remained behind on the stream bank. She bit her lip. *Well, I am not going to go back for them now, with him there. Who is he? What is he doing in my secret place?*

She arrived home sooner than she expected in her preoccupied state. After leaving Jester at the garden gate she hurried to her bedchamber. Once there she sat on the bed, drawing her knees to her chest, fingering the smooth stone wound with a lock of Jester's baby hair. The piece hung around her neck on a thin leather strap ever since she could remember. Rolling it between her fingers was comforting somehow. Her lips tingled with the memory of the stranger's kiss, and she traced her tongue along them seeking his minty flavor. *Why did he kiss me? Because he could? Because I let him?* Upon reflection she decided the kiss was intriguing. *If only he knew.* No one ever kissed her before and it seemed improbable anyone would ever again. There was no reason any man would desire her. After all, who wanted a woman locked in darkness?

Chapter Two

The desire to stay in the cool pool wilted after the mysterious maiden's retreat. Tyrone waded from the water and pulled his clothes on over his damp body. Perhaps he would take a detour into town, slake his lust with some ample-busted tavern girl, and arrive at the manor at a more civilized time. What would it matter if he delayed his arrival at Westpoint Manor by another hour or so? After all, his before-dawn arrival was bound to put the estate into turmoil. He grimaced. They were not the only ones who did not expect his appointment.

Tingling with annoyance he remounted his horse and turned it toward the main road. *Imagine, me, in charge of some spoiled miss.* He forced a deep breath through his pursed lips, the loud huffing sound causing his horse to shake its head and prance. He soothed it with his hand along its neck. Why did the king decide on him? Did the girl not have a living relative somewhere who could see her wed to some worthy lord right and proper?

This delay could cost him more than he wanted, for Miss Deval wouldn't wait forever. The thought of some young buck wooing away his prize grated on Tyrone's nerves. Then again, months spent courting the wealthy Miss Deval strained his temper. His hold on her affections was delicate at best. What if she fancied herself in love with someone younger or more handsome in his absence? A woman's affections were fickle and easy to sway with pretty words. Niceties were not his forte either. If he were to admit it, he harbored no feelings of love for the simpering beauty. Her shallowness in personality and temperament left him cold as ice.

He pushed the bitter thought aside. Her money and social position were all he needed from the marriage…and an heir of course.

With a grunt he shifted in the saddle, his buttocks sore and legs stiff from two days spent aboard his horse. He should have taken a coach; it would have been more comfortable though much slower. The king, however, insisted Tyrone get here post haste. He shook his head. Was the king fueling Tyrone's personal desire to carve a niche for himself in government, to further a royal agenda? Was Tyrone being used to attend an unwanted domestic problem? That was more likely he decided. Dealing with a modest squire's daughter would, after all, be beneath the monarch.

He flexed his jaw, which tightened with his vexation. The damsel managed these two months since her father's passing, or so he assumed, so what was the rush? Besides, from what he heard the wench was a veritable recluse. No one he questioned could recall seeing the girl since she was a small child. He pushed aside a heavy branch as his mount walked under it. Perhaps the girl was hideous or deformed. It would account for the former squire hiding his daughter away from the eyes of his peers. A man as rich as the squire shouldn't have struggled to find a match for the girl. A large enough dowry could buy any woman a husband. He frowned. Almost any woman.

His mind wandered back to the luscious vixen in the sheltered pool. He couldn't resist the seductive call of the gurgling water, its promise of relief from itchy sweat and trail dust much like a siren's song. Pushing through the surrounding brush as quietly as possible, he hoped to catch a glimpse of some tasty prey to take with him to the manor. A fresh kill might have appeased the stir his predawn arrival would cause. He had not expected to find a feminine shape floating atop the water just beyond the waterfall's cascade.

What was a woman doing bathing alone in a forested pool in the middle of the night? Perhaps awaiting someone, involved in some kind of forbidden lover's tryst? He recalled the waver in her voice when she called out to the pony on the bank. No doubt his presence frightened the lady, which he did regret. He chuckled. *Lady?* No lady he ever met would dare swim naked in a pool in the middle of the night. She was like as not a humble maid from the manor, affecting pretty speech for his benefit.

He drew a deep breath, remembering her subtle fragrance of honey melded with a tangy citrus overtone. The corners of his lips twitched into a ready grin. Her courage, slapping the water to splash him, both flabbergasted and intrigued him. No woman he knew would hold her ground in such a defiant manner. Despite her show of bravery though, her rapid breathing beneath his hands proved her nervousness. *Without question she is a very intriguing wood nymph.*

His tongue slipped from between his lips to recall her taste on them. *As sweet as her smell.* No, he couldn't have interrupted a rendezvous—her gasp of surprise was too pure and innocent to be an experienced seductress. He couldn't help but chuckle. In the minimal moonlight he caught a brief flash of her white, rounded derriere before a dark fall of hair concealed it and she faded into the shadows. His manhood throbbed and he tried to ignore it. Even if she was a simple maid, he could have not lowered himself to use force to slake his desire. Besides, it would bode ill for him if he were to misuse one of his new charge's servants.

The lights of the little town came in sight and he urged his horse on. The tavern was easy to find, for at this late hour it was the only building still lit against the dark. After dismounting in front, he tethered his horse to the hitching rail and headed inside.

A rowdy card game occupied the biggest table. The other three contained men either passed out face down or well enough into their cups they soon would be. He crossed to the bar and pulled out a stool to sit. "A pint of your best ale," he told the stoop-shouldered barkeep.

Without hesitation the man filled a glass and thrust it across the scarred counter.

Tyrone flipped him a coin. "Is there any entertainment to be had here?"

The barkeep tested the coin with his teeth before dropping it in the pouch around his waist. "I only got two girls, and one is taken fer the night."

"And the other? What of her?" Tyrone took a sip of the ale, rolling its smooth and rich flavor on his tongue.

"'Tis her night off." The man ran an appraising eye over Tyrone's well-made clothing. "But, I think she'll cut 'er bathin' short for the likes of you, my lord."

Bathing. Tyrone wondered if perhaps it was the same woman he encountered in the pool but then thought the better of it. No, the woman did not have the body language of a common whore. Still, not convinced, he asked, "Is she petite and dark haired?"

The barkeep frowned. "No, she's tall and fair haired, with breasts that'll make a grown man cry, my lord."

The pool was gloomy, but even so he was sure the wood nymph's breasts were small, though his inability to see more than her shape and the dark cascade of her hair might impede his judgment. The memory of her pert breasts as they brushed his chest made him shift on the stool. Shaking his head to dislodge the image, he picked up his glass and drained the contents before setting it down with a thump. It was assured he would never discover her name or see her again. "Maybe another time." His desire to bed a woman this night deflated, so he set out for Westpoint Manor. It would seem there was time to hunt for game to appease the estate's cook before he arrived after all.

Chapter Three

"Miss Daysland?"

Delilah turned from the piano. With effort she kept her expression neutral despite the maid's unwanted interruption of her music devotions. "Yes, Teresa?"

"There's a Lord Frost here to see you."

"Who?" Delilah frowned, trying to place the unfamiliar name.

"A Lord Frost, says he's the Earl of Merryweather."

It was customary for gentlemen to drop by to speak with her father on occasion; however, none ever requested to see her. Perhaps it was someone who only recently learned of her sire's death and wished to offer condolences. She turned back to the piano, settling her fingers on the smooth keys. "Tell him I am indisposed and send him on his way."

"Very well, miss, but I've the notion he'll not be pleased at being dismissed. If you'll pardon my saying so, he looks rather used to getting his way."

Delilah shrugged. "Then have Aims take care of him." The beefy butler could always be counted on to deal with an unwanted guest.

"As you wish, miss."

She waited until the door closed signaling the maid's retreat before beginning to play her favorite soft, haunting melody. Swaying in time to the piece, she lost herself in the passion and sadness it incited. After so little sleep the night before she needed something to soothe her restless mind. A smile curved her lips as she skipped her fingers across the keyboard, picking out each note with a sure feel. Though yet cool in the room, experience told her by afternoon it would be hot and sticky, unless of course the rain chose to spare them for a day. She sniffed. *Pity, it does not smell like rain.* She inhaled again, hoping she missed the damp smell forewarning a delightful storm. *No, everything still smells of dryness and dust.*

Someone knocked on the door, but she ignored it. A slight draft of heavy air brushed the back of her neck laid bare by her braid coiled on top of her head. Another servant no doubt, seeking her attention. They could wait. She had nothing but time these days.

"Miss? The lord, he refuses to leave. He says he's your guardian."

Guardian? She scowled when her fingers fumbled and played the wrong note, leaving a sharp echo in the room. "I have no guardian and certainly no need of one, Teresa." She picked up the tune where she left off. "Send him away."

Another draft tickled the back of her neck, confirming the maid left to follow her directive. Again she focused on the notes, losing herself in their purity. *Ah yes, softer now, like feathers brushing the air...*

Crash!

Delilah mashed the chord beneath her hands, her startled gasp covered by the mismatched moan of the piano. To compose herself, she took a deep breath and repositioned her hands. Seething with anger at the interruption, she rebuked, "Teresa, how many times have I requested to be left undisturbed during my morning practice? Honestly, if you cannot handle removing one simple man from my parlor, then I shall have to hire someone else who can."

"I am not a *simple* man, nor am I accustomed to being removed against my wishes."

Delilah froze at the unexpected baritone, laced with anger. *Good Lord, does the uncouth man think I will invite him for tea if he barges into my music room like a rampaging bull?* She resisted the urge to turn around and berate him, thus allowing him to see her weakness. "Please remove yourself from my music room."

Footsteps crossed the carpet, much lighter than she would have expected a man's to be. "I will not. I have been sent by the king and, as your better, demand you show me proper respect."

He stood right behind her, most probably staring at her, the unwelcome heat of his breath irritating the back of her neck. Anger radiated from his pores in a way that made her fingers curl on the piano keys. "*Respect?* You interrupt my morning in such a rude manner and yet demand respect?" She gave a hollow laugh to cover the nervousness his close proximity caused.

"I am Lord Frost, the Earl of Merryweather."

"So I have already been informed." She flexed her fingers before settling them back in their place on the keys.

The butler cleared his throat in the vicinity of the door. She grinned, the tension easing from her limbs. *Ah, Aims will take care of him.* "Aims, please see Lord *Frostbite* out, will you?"

The heat from the stranger's low growl brushed the back of her neck. "Of all the gall. Have you no sense of propriety?"

This overbearing man is getting very tiresome. Her fingers shook when she returned to the chorus of the song. He would leave if she ignored him, or when Aims retrieved a pistol and forced him out. Either way, sooner or later he would get tired of standing there, being snubbed.

"Stop!"

She disregarded his protest and switched to a dark and ominous tune, attempting to drown out his obnoxiousness.

"I said stop it!" A pair of large, warm hands covered hers. The chords faded as he held her fingers imprisoned against the smooth ivory.

She gasped. Her anger and fear began to make her lightheaded. "Release me this instant. Aims!"

The fingers on hers tightened. "Aims, if you move I shall break your mistress's fingers." The sinister threat was enough to elicit a yelp from herself and Aims.

"Now, see here, you cannot just go about threatening people in their own homes," she spat with false bravado.

Grunting, he released his grip. "By the king's own hand I have permission to speak with you on a matter of utmost importance." The rustle of paper proved his claim was probable.

She groaned. Perhaps if she allowed him have his say he would be more willing to leave when Aims showed him the door. "Very well. State your business and be quick about it."

The paper crinkled and his footsteps retreated to the settee. "Perhaps you should read the missive from the king yourself."

How was she to get around this one with any dignity left intact? "Aims can read it for me."

"You cannot read."

Delilah frowned at the statement. Of course she couldn't, not in the manner he expected; however, she was not about to tell him. Why didn't he just go away? She slid along the piano bench to the opposite end, griped the sturdy corner of the instrument and got to her feet. Turning, she directed a bright smile in his direction. "State your business, my lord, then be gone with you, for I have many things to do this day." Any hopes of his retreat faded at the creak of the chair and approach of his whispered tread on the carpet. Lowering her head she attempted to avoid his direct gaze.

"Is something amiss?"

She caught the edge of concern in his query. *He's going to see my short-coming.* "There is naught wrong but your refusal to come to the point, my lord." She bit her lip. He was standing there, staring at her; she could sense his demanding gaze. His scent tickled her nostrils. Frowning she tried to place the odd, yet familiar odor. *Minty and…fresh grass?* She shook her head to redirect her thoughts. *If I do not move away from him, he will discover my secret.* In her haste to flee she forgot about the edge of the bench beside her, and her knee caught the brunt of the impact. In desperation she struck out for something to grab hold of to retain her balance.

A firm hand steadied her. "You are *blind*."

Anger resurfaced at his shocked utterance. *Why must I face more humiliation at another man's hand?* "Yes, my lord, I am naught but a helpless invalid you have come accosting."

"I am sorry. I did not know."

His voice carried the oh-too-familiar trace of pity, and bile rose to the back of her throat. Delilah shoved him away and braced herself against the piano leg. "Just state your business and leave."

He stepped back, clearing his throat. "I have been appointed as your guardian by the king."

She scowled at him. "I have no need for a guardian. I am perfectly safe and content to stay as I am."

"You cannot mean that."

"Why? Because I am blind?" she snapped.

"No," he answered, too quick for it to not have crossed his mind. "You must want to make a match and get married—every young woman does, so I am told. You would make a lovely addition to any man's life."

"Are you proposing marriage to me, my lord?"

He coughed and then cleared his throat again.

She smirked. *I have put him on the spot now. Time to watch him tuck his tail between his legs and run. If I could see.*

"No, that is to say, the king has put me in charge of settling your father's affairs…and seeing you wed to a suitable gentleman."

He does not get it. She turned on him with undisguised fury. "And just whom do you suppose would want a blind wife?"

"I…well, I am sure there would be many a gentleman who would find you acceptable. Your father has left you a considerable dowry by even a duke's standards."

Her hands shook with the force of her contempt. "If you think to buy me a husband, my lord, then I suggest you leave now. I am no one's charity case." She stomped in the direction of the door, realizing too late she forget to count the steps in her distress. Her shoulder glanced off the door jamb when she turned too early to navigate the opening. When the butler came to her rescue she shook off his hands with a hiss. Face aflame and appendage throbbing, she hurried across the foyer and marched up the stairs to her bedchamber. Letting her anger get the better of her, she slammed the door.

Chapter Four

Tyrone stared at the empty doorway with a frown. Well, that could have gone better. *Why the devil didn't the king, or even the damned butler, warn me of the girl's affliction?* A lump settled in the pit of his stomach. He knew well the hopelessness of the blind. Did the king think his personal connection an asset in this situation? *I will not stand by helpless and watch another life wither and die on the vine.*

The servant in question cleared his throat. "I will show you out, my lord."

Tyrone fixed Aims with a hard stare. Did the butler think a mere woman would make him turn tail and run? "You most certainly will not. I have orders from the king, and I mean to perform them to the letter. Show me to the study so I may go over the estate ledger."

The butler gave him a dirty look and glanced at the stairs. "Miss Daysland will be most upset, my lord."

"Are you arguing with the king's command?"

"Nay." He shook his head. "However, I would not want to be the one to further prick Miss Daysland's ire."

Tyrone crossed his arms. "Further?"

The butler looked down at the carpet. "She is a might sensitive about her condition, my lord, and we have seen fit to protect her from others' cruel jests."

"We?" Tyrone raised an eyebrow.

A slight flush colored the servant's cheeks. "Yes, my lord, the servants and I have watched over her since she was a small child. The squire would not have it any other way."

"I see." Tyrone shook his head. "She is naught but a spoiled wench then, used to getting her own way."

"Nay!" The butler met Tyrone's stare. "She is a kind-hearted lass, not spoiled in the least. She has a hard road in life, and we seek to make it easier for her." He glanced at the stairs again. "Without her knowing, that is, for it stings her pride to be seen as weak."

"Prideful is she then? Too good to be married off to any man? Well, I shall see to the detail post haste." Tyrone stalked from the room and went in search of the study himself.

What kind of damnable situation did he get himself into? A house where the mistress had the servants wrapped around her little finger and coddling her every move was not what he bargained on. The sooner he straightened out the squire's affairs the sooner he could marry the wench off. Lord, he was already sorry for any man who must endure her barbed tongue. He might have used a little more tact considering the situation if she'd met with him instead of trying to send him away.

He found the study and stepped inside. The room looked like it was unused since well before the squire's death. Dust collected on every available surface, even the charred remains of the last fire. He crossed to the desk and wiped a hand across the grimy surface. With a sigh he brushed it off on his trousers and sat behind the desk. It wasn't hard to imagine what shape the squire's ledger would be in. With reluctance he opened it. Sporadic entries proved the former owner did not put much stock in keeping accurate records. Tyrone groaned. So much for wrapping up his business here quickly and being on his way. It would take weeks to sort out the estate and ride around to check each fact and figure himself with the local villagers. Plucking the book from the desk he headed for the storeroom. It seemed the logical place to start.

•••

Two hours later he dusted off his pants and frowned at the cook. "There are only fifty pounds of flour here."

The woman looked away, busying herself sweeping up the spillage from his inspection. "Yes, my lord."

Tyrone glowered at her. "According to the ledger, some fifty bushels were ground just a month ago. My calculations say there should be at least three thousand pounds."

She shrugged and kept sweeping.

"Where have the rest gone?"

"No idea, my lord. Perhaps your figures are wrong."

He pondered her as she poured the sweepings back into the sack at her feet. "What explanation do you have for the missing meat?"

The woman shrugged again, refusing to meet his gaze.

Something is amiss. Turning on his heel he exited the storeroom, making his way to the estate farm yard. Grimacing, he picked his way through the rotting; feces covered the great yard to the main barn, which leaned in a precarious state weathered by the elements. Everywhere Tyrone looked were signs of neglect, from the pealing white wash to the rusty pitchfork propped against the wall. He pushed open the door sagging on one remaining hinge. It flopped open to rest in drunken fashion against the wall. Perhaps the squire was not as rich as he was rumored to be. Blinking, Tyrone let his eyes adjust to the meager light before scanning the deserted aisle way. Why were there no workers toiling away? He peered over the side of a stall. Dust coated the empty box, the straw bedding molding as if unoccupied in ages. Perhaps the livestock were kept out on pasture unless needed. He strolled through the barn to the doors at the far end, pausing when a giggle broke the silence. Following the sound he crossed to a large foaling stall and looked inside.

A young man gyrated on top of a naked, buxom lass, their moans of ecstasy ringing through the hollow barn. He stood transfixed for a moment, both shocked and amused by their antics. Is this how the hired help conducted themselves? No wonder the accounts and storerooms were so disorganized and messy. He cleared his throat. "I say lad, such pursuits are more suited to a bedchamber, after the work is done."

The woman's eyes flew open. Her mouth formed a large "O" of surprise before she scrambled to cover herself. The young man fumbled with the buttons on his breeches and turned to face Tyrone. His face flushed a bright red, reminiscent of robin's breast. "I beg your pardon, sir. There was not much to be done today, so I thought to take the day off with my girl here." He glanced back at the woman with a grin.

Tyrone fixed him with a non-indulgent stare, letting the incorrect address slide for the moment. "You thought? Did you not ask permission of your employer?"

"He has been dead and gone well over a month, so there is no one to ask."

"I see. What about the mistress of the manor?"

The man shrugged and the woman slipped from the stall, hurrying down the aisle half clothed.

"Well." Tyrone stepped forward, towering over the man. "You are hereby relieved of your duties."

"By whose authority?" Arms crossed, he gave Tyrone a cocky grin.

Tyrone grasped him by the shirt front and jerked the scrawny fellow off his feet. "By me, Lord Frost, the Earl of Merryweather, and by the King of England."

The young man's faced turned snowy white, his eyes bulging in their sockets. Yanking his shirt from Tyrone's grasp, he tumbled to the floor and then leaped up and fled the barn.

Frowning, Tyrone allowed the man to go. *Well, good riddance to bad rubbish.* He marched to the doors and made his way into the middle courtyard. The state of the yard and its corresponding barn was no better, and if truth be told worse than the last. A quick tour of the dairy, sheep pens, and chicken coop revealed no workers, or livestock, and further disrepair. Tyrone headed back to the main house disgusted with the state of affairs.

Chapter Five

Delilah shuddered when the door to her music room opened, banging against the wall. "I may be blind, but I am far from deaf and would prefer you knock."

"Good to know."

She cringed at the earl's condescending tone. "Not *you* again. I thought you were taking stock of the place."

"I was."

"Well, I am amazed you have finished your perusal of my home in such timely fashion. I hope you are leaving now." She pivoted on the piano bench and stood.

"I have not finished and I am not leaving, so sorry to disappoint you."

His mockery grated on her nerves. "A pity. However, I think you must disappoint many a lady." She smirked.

"Hardly." He snorted. "'Tis a pity you have no sight. If did you would be treated to a view of my handsome and much sought after physical prowess, miss."

She pouted, wondering if he believed his own dribble or was just playing with her. It was apt to be the former if his attitude were any indication of his personality. "My, you are rather full of yourself. I can only assume you boast with false confidence."

He chuckled. "Ah, alas you will never know now, will you? It is a pity you cannot see for yourself."

Arms akimbo she pierced him with a sightless stare. "You think I cannot? There are many ways to see other than with one's eyes, Lord Frostbite."

"Frost," he corrected.

A smirk curled her lips. "One who has no sight learns to see with their ears, hands, and mind, my lord."

"Really? Then I dare you to try and describe me."

Incensed by his taunt, she crossed the room. When she detected his form she resisted the urge to slap him, instead extending her hand in search. Her fingers came into contact with his velvet waistcoat. Two buttons below her eye level and two above. *He is tall.* Not so uncommon, most people were taller than her. She ran her hand up his broad chest encased in fine linen to the lacy cravat at his throat. *He dresses well.* Her fingers sought their way past the material to his neck, following the thick muscles that merged with his strong, square jaw. *Perhaps he is kind of handsome.* His breath tickled her forehead as she traced the line of his jaw to his high cheekbones, and then across to his straight aristocratic nose. *Handsome and rugged if truth be told.* The scent of mint tinged his warm breath and she inhaled, savoring it as one of her favorite smells. Like her herb garden.

Frowning, she redirected her thoughts to her perusal of the gentleman before her. She skimmed over his full wide lips. *No facial hair.* His breath brushed her fingertips. The light sensation made her lick her lips, the overwhelming desire to kiss him causing her hand to shake. *Am I daft? Kissing him is the last thing I want or should do.* Biting her lip she continued her investigation, sliding her fingers up along the side of his head. She combed his sideburns before she found the tiny crow's feet and indentation of his eyes. *Early to mid-thirties I would say.* Short, spiky lashes stroked her fingers as he blinked. She rose on tiptoe to run her digits through his thick, wavy hair. *Most likely dark brown or black, since blond hair is usually finer and red, curlier.*

Dropping her hands she stepped back with a confident smile. "You are taller than average, well built. I would say dark hair, black maybe, and not unhandsome compared to most. You spend a lot of time outdoors by the feel of your skin, and the crow's feet by your eyes date you at perhaps two and thirty." She smiled at his sharp intake of breath.

"One and thirty, actually."

She shrugged. "Close enough."

"How did you learn to do that?"

A giggle escaped her lips at the wonder in his voice before she smothered it, remembering how much she disliked him. "I do not know. It is a skill I acquired at a very young age."

"So, you go around feeling people's faces?"

"No, not always. I can tell a lot about a person by the way they walk and talk as well."

"For instance?" The settee creaked as if he sat.

She crossed her arms. "I can tell you are used to being obeyed, have no sense of humor, and are sitting on my settee without being asked."

The settee creaked again and his voice was closer this time, like he leaned forward. "Perhaps you are playing tricks and are not blind, at least not completely."

Delilah snickered. "No such luck, my lord. Being blind is nothing to jest about. I take my…affliction…very seriously." Air whistled past her face. She scowled. He was not the first to wave his hand back in forth in front of her to see if she would blink. "Now, if your curiosity is satisfied would you mind removing yourself from my music room?" Again the settee creaked. She tilted her head. Did he settle in to stay?

He cleared his throat. "I came to speak with you about the storeroom and barns."

With a sigh she sat. It appeared he was in no hurry to leave her be. "What about them?"

"They are empty."

Empty? She pondered his words for a moment. "Impossible. Though harvest is not yet finished it has been a good year. Besides, there were plenty of stores left from the previous harvest."

Annoyance stiffened his tone. "I assure you, Miss Daysland, I checked each storeroom and barn myself. They are almost empty and there are no animals on the place."

As if on cue Delilah detected the light tattoo of hoof beats heralding Jester's presence on the veranda. She stood, crossed to the French doors, and flung them open. "I beg to differ, my lord. It looks to me as if there is indeed an animal on the place." The pony entered the room, brushing her skirts as he passed by.

"Good Lord! What is that?"

She laughed at his astonishment. "This is Jester, he is my guide and yes, an animal."

"You allow the creature free run of the house?"

The urge to shock him further was too great to resist. "Of course. He *is* housebroken."

"Housebroken?"

Delilah crossed to the piano bench and sat, knowing the pony would follow and stand beside the instrument. "He has been trained to soil outside, not in the house."

"Oh." The earl grunted.

He grew quiet, something she suspected he very seldom did, and she wondered what he was thinking. Perhaps he thought her noddy? That was better she supposed, then he would be less eager to wed her off to someone and leave her be. "If you will excuse me now, Lord Frostbite, I would like to return to my practice." She was surprised when his footsteps retreated out the door without him refuting her improper term of address. With a self-satisfied smirk she returned to playing.

• • •

Delilah headed outdoors to work in the herb garden after her practice, savoring every last fleeting ray of the sun's warmth before winter would suck the heat from it. A slight breeze, heavy and rich with the scent of rain, lifted the tentacles of hair escaping her braid from her damp neck. A shower would be just the thing the garden needed after she churned up the sun-baked soil around the few plants remaining. On her knees she searched for each plant with one hand and dug with great care around them with a small trowel. Perhaps tonight she would slip outside during the rain and immerse herself in its refreshing drops. She stabbed the dirt with a ruthless thrust of the trowel. *If Lord Frostbite is not around.* No doubt the starched shirt wouldn't approve of her escapade. What was the king thinking to send such a man to Westpoint? She was doing just fine on her own. There was no need for someone to watch over her like she was some kind of invalid. With a final jab she buried the trowel to the hilt and sat back on her heels. *Oh Papa, why did you have to leave me? Why did you take the mountain trail on such a stormy night?*

A heavy tread roused her from her contemplation. She swung around.

"Miss Daysland?"

The voice was familiar yet she couldn't place whom it belonged to. "Yes? Who are you and what are you doing in my garden?"

The man cleared his throat. "So sorry to disturb you. It is Augustus March. I have come to see how you fare these days."

Not him again. Did she not already chase the insolent whelp from her father's graveside once? "Baron March. I was not aware you would be calling on me today."

"I…well that is to say, I was in the vicinity and thought perhaps I should drop by to check on my dear friend's daughter." The nervous edge in his voice almost made her laugh.

"The vicinity? Since we are in the middle of nowhere in particular, I shall have to assume you exaggerate, sir." *Dear Lord! I better get him out of here before Lord Frostbite shows up and decides the baron is a match for my hand or before the baron himself goes out of his way to convince him of such.* "As you can see I am fine, sir, thank you. Now if you will excuse me, I would like to finish cleaning out the herb beds before it rains." Picking up the trowel she turned her back on him, resuming her activity.

The shuffling of his feet warned he was not quite ready to leave. "I was wondering if you, ah, have lent some time to considering my offer?"

She rolled her eyes and sighed. "You mean your preposterous and insensitive offer of marriage at my father's graveside, before his coffin was yet covered?"

He cleared his throat again. "I did say I was dreadfully sorry about that," he whined, grating on her nerves. "I was simply concerned for your welfare."

"Spare me your insincere drivel, March. All you are concerned about is my father's wealth, now mine by right." *The cad! How dense does he think I am?* Resisting the urge to turn around she groused, "I am blind, sir, not daft."

"See here, you judge me wrong."

All the whining in the world couldn't quite cover the uncanny edge in his voice. Clenching her teeth she jabbed the trowel into the ground. The sudden sharp scent of witch hazel gave evidence she broke off a stalk in her preoccupied state. Her instincts told her he couldn't be trusted. She rubbed at the back of her neck, where despite the heat the hairs raised in alarm. "You shall not have to fear for my well being any further, sir, for the king himself sent one of his loyal subjects to see to my welfare."

"He has?"

The higher octave of surprise in his inquiry made her smile. "Oh yes, a very well-to-do man. I suppose the king felt it was in my best interests to marry me off quickly, before the riffraff came knocking on my door." Though she said the words with sweetness she allowed a trace of malice escape to inform him of her sarcasm.

"Oh." A hint of anger clipped his reply. "In that case, I should go. All the best to you and your betrothed, Miss Daysland."

She stifled her giggle as his footsteps faded away. Guilt pricked her conscience and she brushed its accusations aside. *I did not lie exactly, merely left out a few minor details of the arrangement.* She turned back to her weeding. *What Lord Frostbite does not know will not hurt him or the baron either.* The sole problem left to solve was how to get rid of the Earl of Merryweather. He was not going to give in to her insistence she was fine on her own. Perhaps she could bribe him to leave her be? She bit her bottom lip. It would all depend on how loyal he was to the king. It was farfetched to think it would be an option the uptight man would consider, if there was even enough money to bribe him. Could she pretend to be engaged to someone? No, he was sure want to meet the man and settle her dowry. Her fingers landed on a tuft of fox glove. Perhaps she could poison him? She shook the uncharacteristic, sadistic thought from her head. Was she losing her mind? Murder was not an option, even if she could bring herself to do such a thing. *There must be a way to make him see reason…*

A drop of water splashed her nose and she tipped her face heavenward. The distant rumble of thunder and another drop splashing her cheek foretold the welcome storm. After yanking the last weed from the herb bed, she picked up the trowel and headed back inside whistling for Jester. By the time she reached the veranda the pony was close at hand, following her in to shelter from the storm.

After washing up she went to the library, the pony ambling along behind. She seated herself on one of the window seats with a book of poetry her father wrote for her. Most of them she knew by heart from reading them over and over. The poems gave her a sense of peace and closeness to her father that she was desperate for. Flipping to one of her favorites she made herself comfortable, tucking her feet up beside her and settling in to spend a stormy afternoon. With a sigh of contentment, Jester, too, made himself cozy, nuzzling her knee before he lay down, reminiscent of a dog asleep at his master's feet.

The door to the library clicked and footsteps padded across the carpet toward her.

"Did you bring me some tea, Teresa?"

The earl's rich baritone, still new, startled her. "No, I did not, however, I could send Teresa for some if you would like."

She shook her head. "No, it is quite all right." The ticking of the clock punctuated the silence.

At length the earl cleared his throat. "There is a horse asleep at your feet."

"A miniature horse, actually." She stifled a giggle wishing she could see the look on his face, sure it would match his incredulous tone. Turning her attention back to the poem, she attempted to dismiss his presence.

"What on earth are you doing?"

"Why I am reading, of course." The clock on the mantle ticked by the seconds while she waited for him to ask the expected question. *One…two…three.*

"I beg your pardon? How is that possible?"

She snickered. *A mere three seconds. His mind works fast.* "I can feel the words."

This time she couldn't help laughing at the astonishment in his voice. "No, I am not noddy in case that is what you are thinking."

"That is not what I was thinking."

"Of course not." She shrugged, wondering why she cared what he thought.

The earl chuckled. "Dear lord, is the animal snoring?"

She smiled, her mood sweetening a little. "He does it often."

"I see." He cleared his throat. "So are you some kind of witch who has eyes in her fingertips?"

His ridicule was nothing new to her; she heard it all before from others. "I am reading. I can feel the ink of each letter raised off the page."

"Ink soaks into parchment," he pointed out with a definite trace of disbelief.

"Most, but not the special sap ink my father makes...made." Delilah swallowed the lump rising in her throat at the thought of all the sacrifices her father made for her before his death. "The sap makes the ink thick and it sticks to the surface of the paper to form a raised letter."

"May I see?"

Reaching out she sought his warm hand. His strong fingers stroked hers in an intimate gesture that made her stomach tighten and her breath hitch. How did one slight touch render her smitten with him? She should be insulted by his boldness, yet in some small way she desired it, craved it. Why? Was it because it was new, uncharted ground?

Shaking off the sensation she placed his fingers over the title of the poem, *Ode to a Spring Robin*. "Close your eyes and feel the letters with your fingers." She assumed he obeyed when she traced his finger over the large raised O. "What character do you feel?"

He made a small sucking sound as if squeezing his bottom lip between his teeth. "An 'O'?"

"Very good. Are you peeking?"

"No."

The unflinching utterance of his words convinced her he spoke the truth. "Try the next one." She moved his finger to the second letter.

Again he made the small sucking noise before he answered. "A small 'o' and an 'l'?"

"No." She retraced the character with his finger. "The two are of the same letter."

"Ah, a 'd'."

She smiled. "Correct. Try the next one. It is more difficult than the other two."

He brushed her arm as he sat beside her and traced the character. The scent of mint tickled her nose. Why he always seemed to smell of her favorite herb, she couldn't fathom; nonetheless she liked it. She waited with patience as he moved his fingers back and forth along the letter.

In the end a sigh filled with frustration slipped from his lips, caressing her cheek. "You are right. This one is more difficult. I give up, what letter of the alphabet is it?"

"An 'e'."

He moved his hand. "You are right."

She giggled. "Of course I am."

"Will you read the poem to me?"

"Why?" She pursed her lips, unwilling to trust his intentions.

"Because you can and it fascinates me."

Against her better judgment she settled her fingers over the text, trying not to let his presence rattle her. Thunder shook the window panes at their back. Once the sound died away she began to read. "I shall never see a bird a lovely as thee, with breast of fire, inflaming my desire…" As she read Delilah tried to ignore his disturbingly male presence but could not help savoring his minty smell. For some reason his proximity made concentrating on the letters beneath her finger tips harder than ever before. She stammered over the last few lines of the poem and then flattened her hand against the page.

"Amazing. You astound me, Miss Daysland."

Delilah swallowed, both pleased and shy in the face of his praise. "Thank you."

"Are you a fan of Byron?"

She smiled. "I am. I am a fan of most literature, much to my father's dismay. I'm afraid I taxed much of his time re-writing all my requests so that I might read them for myself."

The earl chuckled. "That would account for his neglect of the account ledgers."

A sigh escaped her. "I have tried never to be a burden on anyone."

"Forgive me, I did not mean to imply you were a burden to your father. I am sure he loved you and took delight in the things you are interested in." A warm hand came to rest upon hers. "I admire your desire for independence."

"Do you?" She titled her head in surprise. By his former demeanor the earl did not seem the type to admire independence in a woman.

"Yes." He shifted beside her on the settee. "I knew someone… who suffered from your affliction. She did not have the spirit you possess and died like a flower which withered on a vine. It broke her family's heart to see such a beauty give up."

Her heart softened a little toward the earl. "I have simply tried to make the most of life, my lord, as it is. The problem is some refuse to see me only my affliction. After my disaster of a coming out ball my father and I thought it best to stay as we were."

"What happened at the ball?"

She closed the book in her lap with a snap. "Everyone whispered. I heard them. Not one young man asked me to dance. Many came forward to greet me but it was as though they only did so to satisfy their own morbid curiosity, not out of any desire to know me. It was humiliating and I swore to never subject myself to such a display again."

His warm hand sought her fingers and squeezed with gentle sympathy. "It is a shame many of the ton are so lacking in compassion and acceptance. It should not be that way."

Delilah analyzed the tone of his voice but could not find any trace of pity or ridicule. Clearing her throat she slipped her hand from his under the guise of setting the book aside. "I agree, however it matters not now for I am content in my life here."

"But you are all alone."

"I am not alone, I have Jester and the servants, besides, I fill my time with my pianoforte, the herb garden, and reading. I find my routine enjoyable."

"I will admit the pony is loyal, though not human companionship. As for the servants…"

Delilah changed the subject unwilling to admit her loneliness especially since her father's passing. "Could I press upon you to visit the book shop next time you are in the village? I would dearly like to hear something new besides these tired old poems I have read a thousand times. The village vicar comes by once a week to read to me in my father's stead, though he prefers to read from the holy book. I am hoping to cajole him into something a little more entertaining than the scriptures."

The chair creaked giving evidence the earl stood. "It would be my pleasure, Miss Daysland. I shall be sure to bring back something to peak your interest when I go this afternoon."

She listened to his footsteps retreat from the library. Perhaps the earl was not so bad. He liked poetry and Byron after all.

Chapter Six

Delilah tossed and turned, fighting the memories refusing to allow her to sleep. The nightmare on the cliff grew wearisome. The dream of the little girl with curly hair, frolicking with the colt around a fire came with frequency, too, since her father's death. She understood the returning nightmare, but why this one scene from her childhood surfaced again and again she couldn't say. Perhaps because it was one of her last sighted memories? With a sigh she sat up, swung her legs over the bed and searched for her slippers. She found them with ease and, clad in her night dress, slipped from the room.

Static filled the air when she made her way downstairs. It was impossible not to flinch at the almost deafening thunder shaking the window panes on the first floor. Goosebumps and the hair on the back of her neck rose. She loved storms; the crackle of charged air, the crashing thunder that sometimes shook the foundations, and the smell of wet earth being rejuvenated by the nourishing rain. This was the storm of all storms it seemed. Waves of thunder crashed almost on top of each other, the wind moaning and howling its anger upon the earthbound mortals quaking in fear.

Trailing her fingers along the walls, she made her way to the kitchen. The cook wouldn't mind her quest for a midnight snack. In fact, the woman made sure there was something left to nibble on from the evening's meal just for her. The servant's thoughtfulness warmed her.

Entering the kitchen Delilah groped her way to the table and then along it to the larder. There on the middle shelf, as always, sat a plate with a few cheese slices and a miniature loaf of rye bread. Beside it sat the customary cup of almond wine. With a grin she carried her spoils to the table and followed its edge back to the door. A scuffling reached her ears before a loud clap of thunder concealed it. She froze. After the rumble died down she listened. It was quiet, yet she couldn't shake the feeling someone was there. A shiver of apprehension made its way down her rigid spine. "Who is there?" A slight intake of breath caused her to turn in the direction of the door. "Who is there, I say?"

A subtle dampness and the musk of oiled leather reached her before pain exploded in her head. The plate and cup slipped from her fingers. The clatter of the china broke the silence. Her mind struggled to focus. Somehow she managed to scream, the echo ringing in her ears as she slid to the floor.

•••

"Miss Daysland? Can you hear me?"

The earl's question refused to register to her sluggish mind.

"Miss Daysland?"

She moaned. "My head."

"Lie still."

The high note of concern in his tone frightened her. Was she gravely injured? Raising a shaky hand she touched her head where it hurt most. Her fingers slipped through hair sticky and warm. *Am I bleeding?* "What happened?"

"I was hoping you could tell me. I was in the study when I heard a scream rivaling any banshee's. I followed the noise and found you lying here unconscious. You must have slipped and hit your head." He dabbed at her throbbing head with a cloth. "Where is your pony?"

She drew a sharp breath at his awkward attempt at first aid. "Jester sleeps outside at night, for I have no use of him after I retire. And, for your information, I did not slip. Someone hit me." She snatched the cloth from his fingers and shoved his hand away.

Disbelief tainted his words. "There was no one here except you. Why would someone hit you?"

"I am telling you, someone hit me." She tempered her anger, knowing mild-mannered reasoning was the way to win any situation. "I heard someone in front of me. When I called out they struck my head."

He helped her to her feet. "That is absurd. There is no one here, and I doubt one of your loyal house servants would have done such a dastardly deed. They are all, so far as I can see, ridiculously protective of you. You must have simply banged your head on a cupboard or something."

She wrenched her arm free from his grip. "I know someone was here and hit me."

"Fine, fine. Someone hit you, if you so insist." He patted her hand. "You need to go upstairs and rest."

His lackluster assurance made her grit her teeth, but because of her dizziness she accepted his lead upstairs. Someone did enter the room intending to hurt her. The question was who and why? How was she to protect herself from it happening again when she couldn't see her attacker?

Her maid met them at the door and drew Delilah into the bedchamber. Shooing away the earl she fussed, helping her mistress into bed and tucking the covers tight around her. "Oh dear. Why didn't you ring me if you needed something, miss? 'Tis not safe for you to be wandering the house alone in the dark. There are so many things you might hurt yourself on."

Delilah frowned. "I did not hurt myself. Someone hit me."

"Hit you?" A whoosh of air whistled from Teresa's lips. "None of us would do such a thing, miss."

"Well someone did." Delilah cringed when the maid dabbed the cut on her head.

"I can't believe it, miss. Perhaps we have a thief in the house." A note of alarm strained her words. "Shall I ask his lordship to order the house searched?"

Her new guardian's usurping authority made Delilah grit her teeth, yet she gave in to the servant. "Please do."

Doubts assailed her. Did she imagine the whole thing? Perhaps she knocked something off a shelf, which in turn struck her as the earl believed. Could she have imagined the presence? Could it have been the wind making her think she heard something she did not? No, her senses were too keen to make such a mistake. The thought came to her in a dizzying flash: perhaps it was the earl. Could he have tried to hurt her? She was always safe wandering the estate alone, until now…until he came.

Chapter Seven

Delilah decided to forgo her usual morning piano practice because her head was still achy from the evening before. Instead she wandered out to the garden, whistling for Jester. The pony was beside her within minutes. "Bench, Jester." Hand on his harness, she permitted him to guide her down the path to the stone bench beside the fountain. There was a slight nip to the air this morning, more to do with the coming fall than the storm the night before, she suspected. She sat on the cool stone, immersing herself in the birds' melodic calls to soothe her raw nerves. Not a single feather of a breeze ruffled the curls already escaping her tidy bun, a clear indication the afternoon would be muggy and unbearable. Taking a calming breath, she savored the rich earthy smell, her favorite after a rain. She absorbed the sounds of her pony munching grass a few feet away and the buzz of a honey bee as it sought nectar from the flowers. Those simple sounds always relaxed her. As was her practice she vented her thoughts to her guide. "I am at a loss for what to do, Jester. A search of the house found no sign of a trespasser. Someone tried to hurt me, but who?"

The pony snuffled and continued to graze.

"Why would someone want to harm me? Surely not one of the servants, for they have never been anything but protective and considerate." *The earl was the first to my side. Did he hit me? Is he after my money? Perhaps it is all just a ruse to make me think I am vulnerable, and therefore consent to his matchmaking under the guise of protecting me.* She brushed aside the unsettling thoughts.

Though each idea contained merit, she was unable to commit to any theory with so little evidence.

Footsteps approached. After careful consideration she determined them to be the earl's by the soft, sure tread.

"You should be resting."

Frowning, she folded her hands in her lap. "I am resting."

"Upstairs, I mean, lying down."

"One does not have to lie down to rest. Besides, I feel fine," she lied, trying to ignore the slight throbbing of her head. He snorted, giving her reason to believe the large lump on her temple was in all likelihood uglier than the gentle inspection of her fingers this morning led her to believe.

"Do you still think someone hit you?" His tone carried the slightest hint of mockery to it most people, except her, might have missed.

She shrugged. Perhaps it was best to let him think she discarded the idea for now.

He sat beside her on the bench. "Something strange is going on here. I think it is best if I find you a husband as soon as possible. For your protection, I mean."

"My protection?" She knew this was the excuse he would use. "You are making more of this than it is, my lord."

"Am I?"

With effort she made her response as firm as possible. "Yes."

He snorted again. "Are you not the one who is convinced someone intentionally did you harm last eve?"

"Are you not the one who is convinced my servants are stealing from me?" Cocking her head, she awaited his answer. His heavy sigh was enough to show her needle irritated him. *Checkmate.*

"Come on." His warm fingers gripped hers, tugging with gentle persistence. "I will show you the truth of my claim."

"Show me?" She gave a hollow laugh, snatching her hand away. "Have you forgotten I am blind?"

"Not at all. Come on." Again he took her hand in his warm one, pulling her to her feet. Settling it in the crook of his arm he led the way.

Having no other choice she followed. When they got to the house he turned toward the barns. With trepidation she dug in her heels. "Stop. I cannot go this way. I am not familiar with the path."

"Have you so little trust in me you think I will allow you to stumble and fall?" The quiver in his reply shamed her.

Could she trust him? Did she have a choice? Taking a deep breath, she followed his lead with disguised caution, stifling the urge to thrust out her hands and feel the way for herself. They walked for a few minutes in silence before the temperature decreased. As their footsteps took on a hollow echo she discerned they entered the barn. The smell of moldy hay and dust tickled her nose, confirming her suspicion. She sneezed.

"Bless you."

She was about to thank him when she realized there were no sounds of animals snuffling in their stalls or munching feed. "Where are the animals?"

"I asked myself the same thing." He paused to kick something out from under foot. The object rolled up against the wall with a hollow clunk. They continued on. "There is not an animal in any of the barns, and everything is covered in dust as if none have been here in a long time."

"I can smell that." She scowled, irritated he believed she needed his sighted observations.

"Oh, yes, I suppose you can."

They stepped out into the courtyard and she raised her face to the sun. The fresh air was welcome after the abandoned odor of the stable. After walking through all four barns she was satisfied he told the truth. Deep in thought, she allowed him to escort her back to the house. *Why are not at least a few stock in the barns?*

Could the earl be right about the servants stealing from me? A thought came to her and she decided to voice it. "Perhaps the stock is out to pasture."

"No, nor are there any un-harvested crops in the fields." He paused at the foot of the back steps. "What happened to your father?"

She puzzled his question. What did her father have to do with the missing livestock? "He rode out one day in a storm. The stable lad said he fell from his horse down into a steep ravine. By the time he was found it was too late." She shivered, trying not to think of the hours her poor father must have suffered, lying there in the midst of the storm, broken and bleeding, hoping for help to come. "Why?"

His hand covered hers in a comforting gesture. "Did it ever occur to you perhaps his death was no accident?"

Though the idea was voiced with soft inquiry, the words startled a gasp of shock from her. Was it safe to admit to him she wondered the same thing? No, it was better to keep the idea to herself; she wasn't sure she could trust the earl. "Who would want to do such a terrible thing and why?"

Fierce resolution stiffened his answer. "I do not know, but if it is the case I mean to find out."

Was he truly interested in what happened to her father or was he only trying to divert any suspicions she had as to his involvement in her attack the evening before? If he too found her father's death suspicious then had her gut feelings been right all along?

Chapter Eight

Delilah seated herself at the piano, resting her right hand on the familiar keys. She allowed her fingers skip along the keyboard and then back in a simple warm-up scale. She repeated the gesture with her left hand before striking a few major chords. Fingers ready, she began the intro to one of her favorite pieces, humming and swaying in tempo with the light-hearted melody. Soon she was lost in the world of the piano notes dancing behind her sightless eyes. Images from long ago mingled with the tune. The memory of color was a small joy in her dark world. A bird with a fiery red breast, sunny daffodils bending in the summer breeze, and Jester as a tawny color colt, wobbling toward her on laughably long legs. A six-year-old's vague, rusty memories were all she retained, but they were something at least. *How old would Jester be now? Sixteen? Yes, he turned sixteen this spring. He has many years yet. What will I do when he is gone?* She pushed the thought from her mind. It was morbid to think of such things now; she chastised herself, returning her attention to the last few bars of the music. When the final note faded away she smiled and dropped her hands to her lap.

"That was beautiful."

Startled, she pivoted on the bench to face the door. "How long have you been standing there, my lord?"

"Since the first few bars." Lord Frost's footsteps crossed the carpet. "You play very well."

"Thank you." Disgruntled at his encroachment into her solitude, she turned her back on him.

His normal stiff clip softened. "I did not mean to offend you by listening."

"You did no such thing."

"Then why are you angry?"

She settled her fingers back on the keys. "I am not angry."

He chuckled. "Annoyed then."

Shrugging, she played a few light chords. "What makes you think so?"

"Your face is a mirror to your thoughts, Miss Daysland. Your emotions are as transparent as glass."

With a grimace she thumped the chords harder than necessary. So he could read her thoughts from her expression? It seemed she must take more care to keep her expression neutral. How to accomplish this without being able to see to judge for herself was the issue. "You are intruding on my practice. It is beginning to be an exasperating habit, in my opinion."

He grunted. "Does my interruption bother you, or is it my presence in your home that is the root of your frustration?"

"Both."

"I see." He sighed as if it grieved him to be the cause of her bitter mood. "Well, rest assured as soon as I figure out where all the livestock and supplies have disappeared and see you happily wed, I will be out of your hair."

"Ha," she spat. "As I told you before, there is none who would want a blind wife."

"Oh, but there is. I have even arranged a small dinner party with a few potential suitors to prove it to you."

She slammed down the key guard and spun to face him. "You did what?"

"I arranged a dinner party tonight."

The smugness of his statement pricked her ire even further. "How dare you! This is my house. I did not authorize any such party."

The former stiffness returned to his response. "Do you forget I am now in charge here?"

Anger rushed through her veins and she sprang to her feet. "I confided in you. How dare you put me on public display like… like some sort of pathetic circus sideshow?"

"Sideshow?" The astonishment in his tone made her cringe. "I was merely trying to show you how desirable you are. Why do you see yourself as pathetic?"

Struggling to keep her tears of humiliation under control, she crossed her arms. "I do not see myself that way, my peers do. To them I am less than a woman. I have nothing to offer any man and to try to make me believe anyone sees me any different is cruel."

"Do you really believe no one could see past your affliction?" He grasped her hand, prying it from its grip on her arm. "You are so wrong to think that way."

Tears long held at bay streaked down her face, and when she would have wiped them away his fingers sought her cheek and did so for her. "It matters not what I believe. I have heard the whispered comments, the mocking voices, and pitying remarks. Others decided that I am not of value which is why I have made my own world here."

His voice was soft and soothing. "Your peers are the ones who are wrong. You are so much more than blind." His fingers lifted from her cheek leaving it cool in their wake. "I will make it my duty to show them what I perceive."

She pulled from his grip, uncomfortable with his uncharacteristic gentleness. "What is it you think you see?"

"A beautiful woman who amazes me daily not with the things she cannot do, but rather the astounding things she can. My sis—" He paused to clear his throat. "Most women struck with your affliction would sit alone in a dark room and will death to take them. Instead you have gone out and made the world conform to you, to dance at your fingertips and bow to your command through love and perseverance. Despite your lack of sight you are the most gifted piano player I have ever had the pleasure of hearing."

Her lower lip quivered and she tucked it between her teeth a moment to still it. "You lie. You think simply to flatter me into compliance with your noddy dinner party."

"I assure you, I do not seek to do anything of the sort and I *never* lie."

She lifted her chin in stubborn conviction. "Never?"

"Never."

The finality in his words made her want to believe him. Still, she experienced the truth for herself many times at a man's hands. Rejection haunted the months of her coming out until she refused to bare her soul to it anymore and retreated. Her heart was safer here in her home. Now he wanted to bring men into her sanctuary to spurn her. "Are you so eager to be done with the king's command you would toss me to the wolves?"

"Is that how you see courtship?" His heavy sigh hung between them for a moment. "I assure you it is the furthest thing from my mind. I seek to see you happy, wed, and looked after for the rest of your life, not at the mercy of thieving servants who profess to love you, yet are stealing everything of value out from under your very nose."

The anger in his speech startled her. Did he really care? It was a difficult ideal to believe, for the only man who in truth cared for her was her father. "There has to be another explanation. I can't believe servants who accept me for who I am and have cared for me all these years would do such a thing."

"I have been through your father's books and made careful examination of the storerooms, estate, and barns. As I said before, there is no livestock to be found and little supplies left."

She ignored the impatience in his explanation. "Surely there must be some cause you have neglected to consider. Perhaps you have not found the correct storerooms—"

"Why is it so hard for you to believe the servants would steal from you?"

She stood her ground. "They have always been loyal."

"Aye, while your father was alive to keep his eye on them. I found the stable boy fornicating in the straw just the other day. When I told him to return to his duties he had the gall to ask by whose authority I would command him. That kind of disrespect speaks volumes of the servants here."

Anger plucked at her emotions. How dare he say such things? Though he did say he never lied. No, she refused to believe such a shocking tale. Still, did she not see the truth for herself? Or rather hear and smell it? Damn her useless eyes! For the first time in many years she found herself helpless, and she did not like the feeling. "If you will excuse me, you have given me a headache." She rose, moved around the piano bench to the veranda doors and whistled for Jester.

"Do not think to use such an excuse to get out of the dinner party tonight."

At his warning she set her teeth and ground them together. "The thought never entered my head," she snipped. Hoof beats clattered across the veranda and the pony brushed her skirts. Trailing her fingers along his neck she let the harness slip into her hand and then clicked to the pony to walk on. She half expected the earl to follow, but her and Jester's footsteps were the only ones to reverberate against the stone.

A stroll in the garden would settle her thoughts. The path they took was familiar and in effort to give her mind something to toil over rather than the upcoming dinner party, she pulled the harness to the left, steering Jester onto the path to the stables. Despite the fact Jester was an equine, they never frequented the barns. Jester preferred to sleep on the veranda or beside the garden fence where he could hear her call should she need him. True to his protective nature, the pony's steps slowed to allow her to test each place she put her feet. Again the air cooled to alert her they were entering the barn. Her guide clip-clopped along, the sound echoing in the empty structure.

"Whoa, Jester," Delilah commanded.

The pony stopped.

She released the harness, struck out for the stall door, and leaned against it. "Where did all the animals go?" she asked, more to herself than Jester. Though she relieved half of the staff of their duties not long after her father's death, she gave them more than adequate compensation, rewarding the remaining ones with a small, yet well-received raise. From what Teresa told her the wage she paid each employee was well above the norm, so what reason did they have to steal from her? It did not make any sense.

Something rattled at the far end of the barn aisle.

Pivoting, she faced the direction the sound came from. "Is someone there?"

A slight rustle in the straw made her reach for Jester's harness.

"Hello?" Perhaps it was a rat out scavenging for bits of grain left from the horses who used to reside here. Footsteps approached from the opposite direction. She spun around wondering if two people might be in the stable with her.

"Miss Daysland?"

A sigh of relief slipped from her lips at the maid's call. "I am in the stable, Teresa."

The servant's footsteps crossed the wooden floor boards. "What are you doing in here, miss?"

"Nothing." Delilah reached for the harness and tugged it to cue her guide she wanted to go back to the house. "Jester and I were just taking a walk."

"Well come on back to the house. We have only a few short hours to get you ready for the earl's dinner party."

Despite the unwelcome thought, Delilah submitted to the maid's escort back to the house, the noises in the barn forgotten.

Chapter Nine

Delilah forced herself to sit still while the maid fussed with her hair.

"You look beautiful, miss."

"I shall have to take your word for it, I suppose." Though she tried to keep the vexation from her voice and brow, she did not succeed. Pressing fingers to her forehead she smoothed away the telltale wrinkles and sighed. The slight headache that nagged all morning still lingered in wait behind her temples. It threatened to become a full force skull pounding, which experience foretold would lay her low for a day at least.

A knock on the door announced the arrival of Lord Frost. Getting to her feet, she fixed a smile to her lips as the maid opened it. The slight brush of material upon material and minty scent alerted her to the earl's presence. "I am perfectly capable of walking down the stairs by myself, my lord."

"As is every lady; however, I thought to show my support and ease any nervousness you might have." His tone switched from teasing to admiring. "You look lovely in that mauve dress—it brings out the shine in your black hair and color of your eyes to perfection."

"So glad you approve, my lord, not that your approval or my outwardly loveliness will matter to anyone downstairs." She brushed past him out the door, both irritated she couldn't see for herself her appearance and annoyed his praise made her want to. She was content in her dark world, for the most part, until he showed up. Why all of a sudden she cared what she looked like was a mystery. Besides, her appearance was not going to attract any attention from the opposite sex. The earl's ridiculous little dinner party was going to be a horrendous flop. Descending the stairs, she stifled the sudden urge to return to her room and don the shapeless dress she used for her midnight escapes. The earl's footfalls close behind left little doubt he would refuse to go along with her charade.

A murmur of voices drifted down the hall from the large parlor. It irked her that the parlor she used as a music room because of its marvelous resonance would be the scene of her humiliation. Pausing, she took a deep breath and willed her shaky legs to move toward the sound. The breath caught in her chest and panic began to eat its way to her very core. *I cannot do this.* "I am sorry, I did not mean to make light of your kind compliment. I am not used to dressing for dinner or my appearance mattering. It is just...I cannot do this, I mean, strangers, in my music room. They will stare and whisper..." She gasped when the earl took her hand, his action catching her off guard.

He placed the palm of her hand on the arm of his velvet dinner jacket. "Relax. Take a deep breath. Every man in there will adore you."

"Every?" she breathed. Her throat constricted and her mouth went dry. "How many did you invite?"

"Only six."

Only six? Dear Lord, he might as well have invited ten, or twelve, or even twenty. One man at a time I can handle, but six? This will be a disaster.

Giving her a little tug he led her toward the voices. As they stepped into the room the conversation hushed. She lifted her chin, forcing a bright smile to her lips.

"Gentlemen, so glad you could all join me tonight. May I introduce our hostess, Miss Delilah Daysland. Miss Daysland, I would like to introduce Lord Deerfoot, Lord White, Sir Micheal

Rutherford, Sir Augustus March, Mister Charles Knight, and Mister Devon Carhurst."

Delilah stiffened at Baron March's introduction. How did the obnoxious man finagle an invite? With effort she kept her false smile in place, nodding as each one kissed the back of her hand in greeting. "Gentlemen, I am pleased to meet you." *I suppose there is no time like the present to put my plan in motion.* With deliberate carelessness she stumbled and tripped, knocking over the end table she knew held a crystal decanter of brandy. It toppled to the floor with a resounding crash. "Oh dear, so clumsy of me. Happens all the time I am afraid."

The room was so quiet she could hear the mantle clock tick before the earl cleared his throat. "I believe dinner awaits us." He took her arm in an iron grip, propelled her to the dining room, and seated her.

She remained silent as the courses were served and the conversation began to flow. Each guest it seemed went out of his way to include her, but her inability to distinguish to whom she was speaking and her overall frustration at being put on display kept her answers brief and curt.

"Miss Daysland, it was a tragedy to hear of your dear father's death."

Forcing a small smile to her lips, she turned her head in the direction of the speaker. "Thank you, Lord..." *Good God, who is it seated to my left?* Grasping at straws she tossed out a name. "Deerfoot."

The gentleman in question cleared his throat. "Sir Rutherford, Miss Daysland."

Her cheeks heated at her blunder. "So sorry, sir, please forgive my mistake."

Conversation stilled. The only sound for a few moments was the delicate clink of silverware against china. She shifted in her chair. *Will this torture never end?*

At last the earl spoke up. "Lord White, I hear you have made quite a name for yourself in the quest for alternative hothouse growing methods."

"Quite, I am afraid. You see I did not intend…"

Delilah tuned out the uninteresting conversation as the all too familiar twinge started in her temples. At least a headache would allow her to plead illness and retire to her bedchamber. No man here would want a clumsy and ill wife. Though she doubted the earl would let her slip away until at least the meal was dispatched and the men retired for cigars and port in the study.

"Miss Daysland?"

Her attention returned to the dinner conversation. "I beg your pardon?" A gentleman responded, which one she couldn't say.

"I was just saying no one has seen you in years. I wondered perhaps if you have been on a long tour of Europe?"

"No." She frowned in his general vicinity. "I am afraid seeing Europe's many sights would be quite lost on me, sir, do you not agree?"

"Ah, yes. I suppose so…"

She bit the inside of her lip. *My father would be very displeased at my rudeness by putting the poor man on the spot like that.* She was about to apologize but decided against it when she detected a slight groan from the head of the table where the earl sat. *Let him salvage the dinner conversation now.*

"Lord Deerfoot, you must tell Miss Daysland all about the new race course being designed. She is quite the horse enthusiast and has the most amazing pony I have ever seen. He is her guide." Despite her needling there was a definite ring of admiration in the earl's tone.

"A guide pony?" the gentleman to her right, whom she assumed was Lord Deerfoot, inquired. "I have never heard of such a thing."

"Neither had I. However, he is the most remarkable little creature. He escorts Miss Daysland safely all over the estate and wears a cleverly constructed harness for her to hold on to. Right, Miss Daysland?"

Checkmate, my lord. Well played. Perhaps this game will not be as easily won. Delilah resisted the urge to scratch the earl's eyes out for once again insisting she be the center of attention and pasted a bright smile to her lips. Left with no other choice, she launched into an explanation of Jester and his talents. At least she could speak on a topic she knew something about and was comfortable with.

•••

When the meal was over she rose with the intention of excusing herself, but as if sensing her plans the earl tucked her hand in the crook of his arm. "Gentlemen, I hope you do not mind if I dismiss the usual port and cigars in the library in exchange for some musical entertainment tonight. Miss Daysland is an extremely accomplished piano player. I think we can cajole her into playing us a lively tune or two."

Stifling her groan she allowed him to escort her to the music room. Apparently the earl was not about to give up yet. *I will show his lordship how unaccepting my peers can be.* Settling in behind the piano she purposely hit the wrong keys and then smiled. "So sorry, gentlemen, it is most difficult to play when one is blind." The earl cleared his throat in warning; she ignored him. Again she began the piece and played it in its entirety, sprinkling in as many off notes as she dared. When she finished an unenthusiastic smattering of applause was enough to tell her she won this round. "Thank you so much, gentlemen. I practice eight to ten hours a day, right, Lord Frost?" She almost giggled out loud at his huff of exasperation. Instead she affected a pretty pout and pivoted to face the men. "I am afraid I have little else to do, being blind, you see." She could sense the earl's stare and anger directed at her. Despite it she grinned. *You will think twice before you throw another dinner party in my honor.*

Her head began to pound in earnest and she rubbed her temples. "If you will excuse me gentlemen, I feel one of my many headaches coming on. I beg your leave to go lie down." When the earl did not refuse her retreat she smothered a smile and made her way upstairs to her bedchamber. *Checkmate again, my lord.*

Chapter Ten

Tyrone leaned back in the chair, staring at the barren study hearth. Little by little the squire's vast wealth was being siphoned off—how and by whom he did not know. It appeared worse less than the ledger led him to believe. With a snort he tossed the useless book back on the desk. How pathetic was a servant who professed to love and protect his blind mistress and then stole everything out from under her? It was lower than low in his opinion. He finished his drink and stood, crossing to the window to look out over the gardens.

The moon rode high in the evening sky, its hazy glow promising another stifling night with little relief from the ever present sticky beads of perspiration. Patches of light fell here and there, leaving the shrubs and bushes in partial mystery. Something short and bulky moved from the bushes into the path of a stray moonbeam. The bulk took on the form of the pony, trotting with purpose toward the kitchen door. Did the creature sleep where the food was prepared? *Good Lord, I hope not.*

The pony paused as if he knew he was being watched before continuing on to the herb garden gate. A billowy figure materialized from the shadows. The pony and the figure melded into one, turning away from the manor.

Who was about at this time of night? Tyrone glanced at the mantle clock, noting the hour was indeed well past one. Turning his attention back to the garden, he sought out the mysterious apparition, at last picking it out from the row of bushes by the back gate close to the woods. The objects before his eyes seemed to blend in with the gate and then vanish.

Turning away from the window, he sprinted out of the room and down the hall to the back door. He exited the house and jogged through the garden, slowing his pace when he neared the back gate. Pausing, he listened for any sound before lifting the latch to exit.

The woods stretched out before him at the edge of the lawn, cool and dark. Straining for a sound, he loped across the grass, at last catching the faint thud of the pony's feet on the pine needle carpeting of the forest floor. He turned in the direction of the sound, feeling his way with caution along the darkened path. He tripped, trying to make his way through the dark, and winced, fearing his clumsiness would alert his prey. For a moment he thought he lost them, until the slight thud again emerged from the normal night noises of crickets and frogs. In time, the rush of the little waterfall replaced all other sounds. The air cooled and took on a welcome, refreshing dampness. Keeping to the cover of the bushes lining the pool, he observed the figure separate from the pony. The covering of clouds obscured Tyrone's view. Long hair flowed loose down the woman's back as she stepped to the bank and slipped her dress over her head. She bent to sit on the edge, glancing over her shoulder, as if sensing him there and then waded into the water.

It appeared his wood nymph was back. Stepping forward he tugged off his breeches, shirt, and boots. This time he did not intend to let her go as easily. As quietly as possible he eased into the water. She took no notice of him as she floated toward the fall on her back, her pert breasts catching the moon's rays before once again slipping behind the clouds. Sinking under the water he swam in her direction, resurfacing an arm's reach away.

With a gasp she flipped over and tread water. Her face turned to him, her features indistinguishable in the dark. "Who is there?"

He smiled. "It is just I, sweet wood nymph, come to pay homage to your glorious beauty once again."

"*You.* Leave me be." Tilting her head as if listening she tread water with one hand, crossing the other over her breasts.

His smile fled as he recognized the familiar lilt. *Miss Daysland is my mysterious wood nymph.*

Intrigued he swam closer, reducing the distance between them. "Why? I have permission to wander this forest."

"I think not."

Reaching out he grasped the arm covering her breasts and yanked her to him.

A squeal of outrage laced with fear fled her lips. "Unhand me! What do you want with me?"

"I merely desire to pick up where we left off." Before she could protest his lips found hers. He covered them, licking the tiny droplets of water from their plump surfaces. She shivered, whimpering as he stroked his tongue along her bottom one, and then sighed. Seeing his opportunity he slipped his tongue between her lips to explore her inner recesses, pulling her in full against his nakedness as he did so. She stiffened and for a moment he thought she would fight him, but instead her arms encircled his neck, her fingers playing with the little curls at the nape. Growing bolder he deepened his kiss, moving his hand to play with the tight nub on her breast. This time she tore her lips from his with a startled gasp.

Flailing in the water, she splashed his face. "Release me this instant."

The tremble of her limbs and the high note of alarm in her demand compelled him to step back and release her. As he opened his mouth to apologize he lost his footing on the slick, rocky bottom. Down he went, under the water, fumbling to find purchase on the pool bottom. By the time he found firm footing, she reached the bank. After scrambling up it she tugged on her discarded dress.

"Miss Daysland, wait!" He waded to shore. "I am sorry, I did not mean to behave in such an inappropriate manner."

She leaped aboard the waiting pony and jabbed her bare feet into its sides. Her howl of outrage did nothing to appease his guilt as she galloped recklessly from the clearing.

"Damn it!" Snatching up his clothing and hopping on one foot, he attempted to shove the other into the leg of his trousers. He swore again as she rounded the curve in the path and disappeared from sight. Clutching his boots, he bolted after her.

A startling shriek added urgency to his stride. He rounded the bend in time to see the riderless pony slide to a halt and then carry on in the direction of the house. Fear clutched Tyrone's chest. Even in the dark he knew the shape lying across the path was Delilah. He reached her side out of breath and knelt down. *Please let her be all right.* He said a silent prayer as he rolled her face up. After brushing away the twigs and leaves stuck to her face, he put his ear to her mouth. To his relief she moaned, her sweet breath skimming his cheek. "Miss Daysland?"

Her eyelids fluttered and she opened her eyes.

He breathed a sigh of relief. "What happened? Are you all right?"

"I am fine…just knocked the wind…out of myself." She sat up and then shoved him away. "Why did you pull me from Jester's back? You could have seriously injured me."

He stared at her for a second, lost for words. "I did nothing of the sort. The pony spooked and dumped you."

"Nay! You pulled me off. I felt you grab the back of my dress." She scrambled to her feet.

"I did no such thing. I swear. The pony spooked."

"Liar!" she hissed. Turning her back on him, she stalked off down the path.

He hurried after her. "Look out." Grabbing her hand, he steered her around the trunk of a tree just before she would have walked into it. "I *never* lie, Miss Daysland."

With a snort she accepted his guidance but remained rigid and silent.

It was useless to defend himself against her claims. When her anger abated maybe then he could make her see reason. Resigned to her silence, Tyrone led her down the path back to the garden gate. Once there she wrenched her arm free from his grasp and marched up the steps. Stiff backed, she crossed the veranda and stomped into the house. The door banged behind her. He cringed at the sound. It seemed every conversation they entered into ended in a slamming door. Shaking his head, he turned back to the path to the woods to search for whatever spooked the pony. Perhaps he could prove his innocence.

Why did the woman insist he was out to hurt her? There was nothing for him to gain by her injury or death. It was not as if he needed her money. Guilt niggled at him. That was not precisely true. Wasn't he marrying Miss Deval for financial and political gain? Nonetheless, surely Miss Daysland knew he would never stoop to hurting someone for monetary reward. He groaned. No, how would she when her own servants seemed to be after her inheritance?

Jester materialized by the garden gate as if nothing was amiss, startling him. Tyrone opened it and let the pony in. The beast appeared no worse for wear, he noted before shutting the gate behind him and heading for the trail through the woods. An hour later he returned, none the wiser as to what caused the pony's flight.

Chapter Eleven

Delilah made her way downstairs later than usual the next morning. Caution stilled her steps as she entered the breakfast room, listening for any sign of the earl. When no noise drew her attention she made her way to the buffet. She groped for the lid on the first warming tray, lifted it off, and sniffed. The buttery aroma of scrambled eggs greeted her. Running her fingers along the edge, she located the spoon and slid a plate closer. After placing a spoonful of eggs on the plate, she replaced the lid and felt for the next tray. A deep inhale of its contents made her smile. *Ah, honeyed ham, one of my favorites.* She stabbed a couple slices and added them to her plate, along with a flaky croissant and a pat of creamy butter. Then she heard it, a soft sound most wouldn't have noticed: the scarcely detectable "shush" of material upon material, as if someone crossed their legs. Delilah spun around, dropping the lid with a metallic clang. The light scent of mint reached her.

"I did not hear you enter, my lord." She tried to keep her tone light but couldn't help the slight hint of outrage at his presence.

"I did not mean to startle you. I was reading the morning paper here all along." As if to prove his claim, the newspaper crinkled.

Snatching her plate from the side board she angled toward her chair, counting the steps to the edge of the table. She set the plate down, grimacing when its clink betrayed her mood. "Good manners dictate one would give notice they were here upon my entry."

A soft chuckle escaped him. "I thought you would have heard my presence. Besides, I enjoy watching how you take pleasure in the simplest sounds, smells, and textures of the world around you."

"I am glad to know my antics amuse you, my lord." Snubbing him, she sat and speared a piece of ham, popping it into her mouth and chewing with exaggerated attention. It appeared her attempt to avoid the earl was foiled for the time being, a fact that did not please her in the least. She jabbed another piece of ham on her fork and lifted it to her lips.

"I thought last night's dinner party went rather well, do you think?"

She frowned, dropping the fork with a clatter, her tidbit forgotten. "Rather well? I have never been more uncomfortable in my life. I will never forgive you for so callously putting me on display, like a pathetic, lame broodmare paraded about for inspection. Did I not tell you how it would go?"

"You cannot expect a man to offer for you when you sabotage yourself," he pointed out with a haughty air.

She clutched the lace tablecloth in her fist. "I do not *expect* or want any man to offer for me, as I have already told you. Is it so obscene to you?"

"It is not obscene to expect someone to desire you. You are smart, witty, beautiful, and remarkably self-sufficient. You seem the only one who thinks an offer is impossible. Makes me wonder if you use your blindness as an excuse not to marry." The harsh edge in his voice softened. "Are you afraid you might find someone who will love you?"

His words held an element of truth she was reluctant to admit to anyone, least of all him. "Why can you not leave me be?" she whispered, a tear slipping down her cheek. "Why must you persist in this? No good can come of it."

When his chair scraped across the floor she swiped the tear away, steeling herself for his denials and pleas. Instead his footfalls came around the table, his minty smell filling her nostrils. His warm, calloused hand enclosed hers where it rested, still squeezing the table cloth between her fingers. She jumped when his finger stroked her cheek with gentle intimacy.

"If only I could show you what I see. You are a woman like no other, proud, strong, and so deserving of a man who will cherish and make you happy."

Delilah was woefully tempted to fall into his arms and allow him to kiss her again. Her tongue slipped out to moisten her lower lip of its own accord and his finger followed its path. Struggling to find her voice she whispered, "Show me…" Tilting her face to him she waited, her heart pounding against her breast. Her eyes closed and for the tiniest moment she almost laughed at the irony of the lashes lying against her cheeks. Why close her eyes when she couldn't see? Then his breath tickled her lips. Damp and warm, they moved over hers, sensual and light. With a sigh of longing she opened for him, inviting him to play. He took her invitation with the slightest of groans, deepening his kiss. The thrill of the forbidden contact made her toes curl inside her satin slippers. His fingers slipped down to cup her jaw. With a sigh she slipped her arms along the plains of his velvet waistcoat to twine around the thick column of his neck. He tasted of eggs, salty ham and the familiar mint. Slipping his mouth from hers, he kissed the hollow, sensitive area behind her ear. She dipped her head to give him better access.

"I would marry you if I could," he whispered, the breath from his words brushing her damp skin atop his lip's caress. He pulled away with a tortured moan.

Her heart leaped into her throat at the thought. "Why not?"

His breathing was irregular and deep as he retreated to his chair. "I have already entered into a courtship with another."

The apologetic hint in his tone unleashed her wrath. Shoving her plate away, she leaped to her feet. "Bastard," she spat and fled. She made her way to veranda, exited the house, and whistled for Jester. He was at her side within moments. Lost in a turmoil of emotions, she allowed him to lead her where he chose. They went down the steps and crossed to Jester's favorite napping spot beneath the old apple tree.

When Jester laid down; Delilah settled herself beside him, resting her head against his neck. "What has come over me?" she mumbled. "I practically threw myself into his arms and he rejected me. I should have known he would. I do not know why I was angry at his reaction. Oh Jester, papa would be mortified by my display of wantonness."

• • •

Tyrone headed for the study but paused when he passed the window over-looking the back lawn. Beyond the window pane the sun cast a cheery feel across the landscape. Deciding it was far too nice a day outside to be stuck indoors he changed course to the veranda instead. As he shut the door behind him he spied Delilah curled up on the grass beside the dozing pony. Perhaps he should apologize and explain the situation to her. Maybe he could appeal to her practical nature and convince her marriage to some suitable gentleman was not the end of the world. With firm resolve he descended the steps and crossed the lawn. He was only a few feet away when he realized her lips were moving. He assumed she was talking to the pony and stopped to listen.

"I am in such turmoil. When my father was alive everything was comfortable and routine, now, with the earl here…well, one moment I find myself enjoying the company and other times… Oh! The man seems determined to drive me noddy. I cannot seem to make him see reason on this marriage idea. What is so wrong with wanting things to stay as they were? Why must I marry, just because I am a woman? It seems a silly rule, if you ask me." Delilah lay back against the pony.

"I suppose marriage would not be so bad, I mean if I could find a man who could see me and not my affliction. Perhaps someone who would allow me to follow my own pursuits, liked the same things I do, and would not drag me to one humiliating social function after another. Someone like my father."

She sat up. "The earl thinks I use my blindness as an excuse against marriage. Do you think I do, Jester?" The pony blew through his nostrils and Delilah bit her lip. "I think he may be right, though I would never admit it to him. Oh dear. I fear I frightened every man within reach away with my behavior last night. Maybe the earl was right and I should have given them a chance. Now what will I do? I suppose I owe his lordship an apology, though it serves him right for springing the whole situation on me that way."

She twinned her fingers in the pony's mane. "I liked his kisses, you know. I know I should not have; a well-bred lady does not go around kissing men in the woods, or the dining room for that matter. No one has ever kissed me before. Every girl wants to be kissed you know." The pony snorted as if refuting his mistress' claim. Delilah's lips curved into a small smile. "It's true. You can snort all you like, Jester, but what would you know of a girl's desires? You only desire to eat, sleep, and go for a wander in the woods now and then. Your life is simple and uncomplicated." Jester opened one eye and sighed before returning to his nap.

Tyrone stood, undecided whether to interrupt her musing by announcing his presence. Against his better judgment he stayed quiet and listened as she continued her one sided conversation.

"I am afraid as usual I have made a mess of things." She buried her head against the pony's neck. "I have no one to confide in but you, Jester, and you are not much help in matters of the heart I am afraid." Her shoulders shook and muffled sobs reached Tyrone's ears.

Maybe Delilah was not as prickly as she tried to appear. Did her fear and loneliness cause her to shield herself behind a sharp tongue? He couldn't really blame her for being bitter at the cards fate had dealt her. Her affliction left her unsure and vulnerable, and the loss of her father would have been a deep blow. The obvious solution would be to wed Delilah himself, but that was not possible. He could not honorably cry off his courtship of Miss Deval, even if Delilah would have him, besides, the king would surely frown on the arrangement. The king ordered Tyrone to see Delilah suitably wed, not to court her himself. And there was also the matter of his political aspirations. Miss Deval and the king were his stepping stones to a brilliant political career.

Tyrone turned away and crept back to the house, unwilling to let Delilah know he witnessed her private thoughts and tears. His ward's plight deeply troubled him and he felt compelled to ease her fears but was at a loss as to how to go about it.

When he entered the study his gaze fell on the books he purchased at the village shop. A book of poetry and a sea faring adventure caught his eye and he hoped they would provide a little entertainment for Miss Daysland. He glanced out the window where Delilah still rested curled up to the pony on the grass. Perhaps now might be a good time to read.

Tyrone scooped up the two books and hurried back outside. This time he took care to make his steps heavy and whistle a jaunty tune to be sure Delilah heard his approach. He noted her wipe the tears from her face with her sleeve under the guise of pushing a lock of hair from her cheek. "Miss Daysland?"

She cleared her throat. "Yes?"

"I found a couple books I thought you might enjoy while in the village."

A small smile graced her pink lips. "Thank you." She held out her hand.

Instead of giving them to her he seated himself across from her on the grass. "Would you like to hear some poetry or a swashbuckling tale of the dangerous sea?"

A soft giggle, like tiny bells slipped from her lips. "Oh, the sea tale please. I do love a good adventure, though my father said that type of book was not for the likes of a lady."

Tyrone could not help but chuckle at her unbridled enthusiasm. "I shall endeavor to skip the most un-lady-like parts then," he teased hoping to draw another delightful giggle from her.

Her lips formed a small pout though her eyes twinkled. "Do not dare. Those are the best parts you know."

He smiled. "As you wish." After settling back on his elbow he lay the book on the grass and opened it to the first chapter. "When I first saw the *Percephany* she was anchored in the English Harbor…"

Tyrone glanced at Delilah now and again as he read amused by her rapt attention to the tale. Her facial expressions betrayed her emotional involvement in every scene. During an especially tense one she worried her bottom lip between her teeth which he found charming. Before he realized it he was lost in her animated delight.

Chapter Twelve

Delilah smoothed the brush over Jester's coat, running the fingertips of her free hand along after to relish the satiny feel of the slicked hairs. Grooming the pony was a welcome respite from the conflicting thoughts swirling around in her mind since reading with the earl the day before. "Your winter fuzz is starting to come in, Jester. It will not be long before we shall frolic in the snow, I think." The pony sighed as if mourning the passing of summer. She smiled and ran the brush down his neck. "Do not be so sad. You love Candlemas and the hunt for the perfect Yule log." This time her sigh was the one of mourning. "It will not be the same without Papa."

"Your father would want you to be safe and wed by the time the winter storms fly, Miss Daysland."

Delilah grimaced and continued brushing. "What are you doing here, March?"

"Is that the way to greet a fawning suitor?"

This time she swung around at the baron's preposterous claim, brush in one hand and the other on her hip. "My what? Whatever gave you the idea I would welcome the likes of you as a suitor?"

"Lord Frost did accept my request just this morning in fact."

The smugness in his reply made her want to smack him. "Oh, he did, did he? Well, we shall see about that. No man will tell me whose favor to endure." Dropping the brush she made to stomp off to her father's study.

The baron stayed her with a hand on her arm. "Have you considered the idea his lordship might be behind the attacks on you of late?"

She froze, the idea making her blood run cold. The thought had crossed her mind but never taken root. "How do you know of them and what makes you think the earl is to blame?"

"He told me. Does it not seem strange you were in no danger until he showed up here?"

A chill crept up her spine at the sinister edge to his tone. He was right. Her life was simple and uneventful before the earl arrived. She touched her lips remembering his kiss. Danger arrived on the eve of the earl's appearance. So did desire …

"Accept my suit, Delilah, and I shall keep you safe."

Scowling at the baron's forward use of her given name, she drew herself up tall and returned to brushing her guide. "I have no intention of ever marrying."

"Yet marrying you off is the earl's sole goal. Perhaps I may suggest a compromise?"

Her hand on the brush stilled. Curiosity overcame her resolve to spurn his pleas. "What kind of compromise?"

"You accept my suit, publicly, and in exchange I will permit you to live out the rest of your days here with no strings attached."

Though appealing, the idea did not sit right with her. She turned to him, the brush forgotten in her hand. "What do you have to gain by such a deception?"

"It is simple. You will give me control of all your assets, in return I will allow everyone to think we are married, give you a monthly allowance, and you can return here after Lord Frost has gone. No one would be the wiser. You would be free of ever having to entertain a suitor again."

She mulled the idea over in her mind. What did she have to lose except a large amount of wealth she would never spend or need for her simple lifestyle? The stronger question was whether she trusted the baron to keep his end of the deal. "What if you should want to marry another one day? After all, you shall need an heir eventually."

"A petition for divorce is an option, though still very taboo. If we fail to ah, consummate the marriage, there will be little contest to annulling it."

The idea of lying with the baron made her stomach turn. Most likely he was as repulsed by her as she was by him. But would the earl fall for the ruse?

The baron cleared his throat. "Well?"

"All right. The marriage will be in name only. I shall return to live here as soon as the earl has gone to London." It would be easy to fool the earl and a simple solution to her problems. Unease settled in her stomach. Wouldn't it?

The baron took her hand and kissed the back of it. "It is settled then. I shall tell the earl you have consented to be my wife and urge him to apply for special license so we might be wed as soon as the banns are read."

Prying her fingers from his grip, she shook her head. "First you must draw up the agreement and specify the amount of allowance you will settle on me."

He was quiet for a moment. "All the better, I shall tell the earl I want your dowry to remain in your hands. It alone is more than enough to keep you for the rest of your days."

The little voice in her head warned her to stop and consider the arrangement with due care and attention but she silenced the cries. "All right. See it is so."

• • •

"There you are."

Delilah turned her head in the direction of the earl's advance. "I was taking in the last of the summer sunshine."

His footsteps ceased and the air cooled as his form blocked the sunlight from her upturned face. "I just spoke with Baron March. Is it true?"

She kept her voice calm and unconcerned. "Is what true?"

Exasperation clipped his speech. "Have you accepted his suit then?"

"Will it prevent you from throwing another insipid dinner party?"

"Most assuredly."

"Then yes, as a matter of fact, I did." Try as she might she couldn't force a sincere smile to her lips.

"I see."

Puzzled, she analyzed the strain in his voice. He did not seem very pleased. Is this not what he wanted? After all, he was assigned to see her wed.

Before she could draw any conclusions he continued. "The baron has asked a special license be procured, so you may wed in two weeks' time. Is this what you want?"

Her stomach twisted into knots, yet she forced her lips to form the words she must. "Yes. It is."

A minute passed until a bird's lone call broke the awkward silence. Did she miss his exit? She listened close. No, though very faint she could detect shallow breathing and the familiar minty scent of him. Why didn't he say something? "My lord?"

He cleared his throat. "Very well. I shall see to the details right away." The sharpness in his quiet statement gave her pause. He was not happy with her choice. This time his steps were heavy as they receded toward the house. Should she call him back and inquire why he was not pleased? She shook her head. What did she care? Soon she would be rid of him and her life would be as it was before. It was what she wanted since he barged into her music room she told herself.

It occurred to her that she failed to ask if he found the reason for the missing supplies and livestock yet. How was she to solve the mystery on her own? Perhaps the baron might assist her. On the other hand, if the baron took the bulk of her fortune, would it not be his problem to deal with? Why did things seem so complicated and…grim?

Chapter Thirteen

"Miss Daysland?"

Delilah sighed, her hands poised over the keys on the pianoforte. "I am practicing, Teresa."

"I am sorry to interrupt, miss, but Lord Frost sent me to summon you to the study."

Delilah thumped her fingers down in a discorded position on the keys, the horrible notes fitting her sour mood. "Whatever for?"

"No idea, miss."

It was time to lay down the rules of her house as they were to the earl. The constant interruption of her routine was getting on her nerves. Had she not done as he wanted and accepted a suit? What could he want with her now? She rubbed her temples and stood. *I should be happy to have found a way to remain at Westpoint, so why am I so cross? I got what I wanted. The earl will soon be gone from my door and I will be left in peace. Alone. Perhaps alone was not exactly what I wanted…*

"Miss, shall I tell him you are indisposed?"

"No, Teresa, there is no need." Delilah marched from the room, her back ramrod straight, running her fingers along the wall to guide her way. As she neared the study the baron's voice carried from within. She paused a few steps from the door.

"Six weeks, Frost? That seems a rather long courtship for two people who have known each other since childhood. I was thinking more along the lines of a few days at most."

"Dare you question the king's law? It will be two weeks at least before the banns are read anyway."

The baron grunted. "Fine, I shall wait two weeks to have the marriage performed."

"What is your hurry, March?"

"The woman has accepted my suit and it seems a waste of time to play at courtship," the baron whined.

"Courtship is not play."

"I…you know what I mean. It smacks of a way for you to avoid the inevitable, Frost. You are not harboring feelings for Miss Daysland, are you?"

"No, do not be absurd."

Delilah clenched her fists. The earl's answer was far too quick, as if he couldn't be smitten with one of her ilk.

"I would just like you to show some affection for the girl, March. Make her feel as if you hold her in your esteem at the very least. You do care for her?"

"Of course I do. Would I offer marriage if I did not think highly of her? Why, she is my dearest childhood friend."

Dearest childhood friend? The total amount of times we have even conversed with each other I can count on the fingers of one hand. Clearing her throat, she stepped into the room. Two chairs scraped across the floor. She couldn't help but note the irony of them rising every time she entered a room. What was the point when she couldn't see the gesture anyway? "My lord, I am fast getting tired of having my practice interrupted by your whims. Unless there is something urgent requiring my attention I prefer to be left undisturbed."

"Rest assured I deem your courtship something requiring urgent attention, Miss Daysland. Is that not right, March?"

"Well, yes, it is, I suppose."

Delilah crossed her arms and scowled in the direction of the baron. "You do not sound at all convinced of this. Regardless, I see no point in it."

"Well, I…"

The earl interrupted. "Makes no matter, the king wishes a suitable courtship take place. I will give you two weeks to do so and appease his majesty, not a day less."

It was all she could do to keep from groaning out loud. It was bad enough to marry the man but to suffer his companionship for two weeks beforehand? It did not sound as if the earl was willing to budge on the matter though, so she forced a smile to her lips. "Very well. How shall we go about it?"

The tension in the room was as thick as pea soup. A chair creaked and then the earl spoke up. "It is a lovely day outside; might I suggest you two get to know each other better during a short horseback ride? I can call upon the groom to have a mount ready for you in the time it takes you to change into riding attire."

Despite her reluctance she nodded. "All right, I shall change and be back down shortly."

• • •

Delilah frowned when the baron placed her hands on a saddle at eye level. "This is not Jester."

"My spirited gelding cannot keep pace with one as slow as your guide beast. I thought you would not mind riding the mare here. I was assured by the groom she is a very tame and gentle creature." Without waiting for her to accept, the baron cupped her foot in his hands and hoisted her aboard into a sidesaddle.

Once atop the animal Delilah arranged her riding skirt as best as she could. The groomsman passed her the reins as the baron settled in his own saddle beside her with a creak of well-used leather. His mount pranced, its feet drumming a nervous bugle call on the courtyard cobblestones. The baron's horse sidestepped into the mare, who threw up her head and shifted aside. Delilah grasped a handful of mane, afraid she might fall from the animal if it bolted. Much to her relief however, the animal moved ahead at a sedate walk.

"Are you comfortable, Miss Daysland?"

Tight-lipped she nodded. She was very uncomfortable on the unknown animal, with him, but she was not about to let him know, to show any weakness.

They rode in silence for a while until they crossed from the clip clop of the drive to the softer swish of the grassy fields. The scent of ripe apples, grass, and walnut trees wafted on the air. She inhaled a deep breath, appreciating what her senses relayed of the ride.

"Beautiful day, is it not, Miss Daysland?"

"I suppose." She turned her head to listen for the groomsman. From the faint sound of his mount's tread she gauged him to be many yards behind. "At least the earl did not see fit to accompany us."

"Yes, quite. Though I fear his insistence on a long courtship is going to grow quite wearisome."

As much as she desired to be wooed and courted by a man, she couldn't agree more with Baron March. It was better to just get the whole sham over with. "As long as he does not insist on an engagement ball. I loathe crowds." She sighed. "The whole idea of marriage is tiresome. I would give anything to avoid it."

"You cannot back out now, my dear. I would not like to be cuckolded and made to look a fool."

Something about his tone did not sit well with Delilah, yet she couldn't put a finger on it. Perhaps she was imagining something sinister to his reply. Maybe the idea of someone trying to harm her was getting to her, feeding her paranoia.

The horses turned a corner. *Whack!* Before Delilah could wonder at the sound her mount bolted. Taken off guard, Delilah clutched the mare's mane in effort to keep her balance and lost her stirrups, thanks to her unfamiliarity with a sidesaddle. With a shriek she clung to the horse's neck to keep from falling. The reins were jerked from her hands. The mare stumbled and Delilah lost her precarious grip. She cringed in the brief moment she was suspended in nothingness, awaiting her body's collision with the ground. Instead she was yanked backward by an unseen grip. Without standing on ceremony someone slung her across a horse's sweaty shoulders.

"Are you all right, Miss Daysland?" the baron inquired, his voice calm despite her close call.

The horse came to a halt. The pounding of blood in her ears eased. Taking a shaky breath, she slid to the ground, her rubbery legs making it necessary to lean against the animal. "I think so. What happened?"

Hooves thundered toward them and gravel sprayed against her skirts. "I caught your mare, Miss Daysland. Appears someone hit her with a hunting arrow," the groom panted. "I saw the fiend riding off at a gallop but could not close the gap to purse him on my slower mount."

"Dear Lord! Who would do such a heinous thing?" the baron cried. "It is a good thing I was with you, my dear, else something terrible might have happened. Why, I saved you from a terrible fate."

Delilah was about to point out the incident would never have happened if she was not riding an unfamiliar mount but decided it better not to look ungrateful for the baron's assistance. "Yes, it was good you were here."

"Help Miss Daysland back on, John, and be quick about it."

"Perhaps I should not ride the mare back if she is injured." At this point Delilah would rather walk back to the manor than chance another incident.

"No, no, the mare will be fine. It is a minor wound. John will lead her to be sure there is no other chance of an accident on the way home."

Still shaking, Delilah submitted and the groom hoisted her back into the saddle. They started off again at a slow pace for home. Despite the groom's hold on the now sedate mare, Delilah gripped the saddle with both hands.

"The sooner you marry me, it appears, the better. I do not think this was an accident, Miss Daysland."

The thought had crossed Delilah's mind, too, though she remained reluctant to voice it. "You do not?"

"No. Lord Frost was the one who suggested a ride today to get us out of the manor. It also seems curious he should want to take so much time having me court you instead of just seeing the marriage done and returning to London, do you not think?"

She bit her lip. *I did seem a strange coincidence, and the courtship was a bit too drawn out for one so eager to return to London.* As the baron pointed out earlier, nothing was amiss until the earl arrived. Except perhaps for the thefts, although those could have been done since his coming, too. Her mind churned with the possibilities of his deceit and self-proclaimed innocence. There was naught she could do but stick to her normal routine and keep her wits about her until she wed the baron.

• • •

Delilah sensed him there when she entered the dining room. She allowed the footman to guide her to her seat without a word and place the linen napkin across her lap. Wine gurgled into the glass to the right of her plate before a bowl was placed before her. A smile curled her lips at the scent. *Potato soup with tiny bits of salty bacon, thick cream, and wild onions. One of my favorites.* Lord Frost interrupted her pleasure.

"Did you have an enjoyable ride with the baron today?"

She froze with her spoon halfway to her mouth. It appeared he did not know of the accident earlier in the day, or was pretending not to. Should she call his bluff, if in fact it was one? Undecided she answered. "I did not enjoy it, as a matter of fact."

"Why not?" His silverware clinked against the edge of a bowl and then a short puff of air whistled through his lips.

"I do not like riding any horse other than Jester, for starters." She blew on her own scoop of soup before savoring it.

"For starters? What else about the afternoon met with your disapproval? Was the baron forward or not solicitous of your needs?"

She set her spoon down. "On the contrary, Augustus was most attentive. In fact, he saved me from a horrible fall."

His spoon clattered to the table. "What fall? What happened?"

"I was hoping you could tell me, my lord." Her fingers twisted the napkin in her lap into a knot. Would he admit he injured her horse? That was doubtful, but he might quit trying to cause her distress if he knew she and the baron were onto his schemes.

"What are you talking about?"

With all the courage she could muster she explained. "Someone shot my mount with an arrow. The groom found the evidence. Augustus kept me from harm by scooping me off the horse when it bolted."

"And you think *I* shot the animal?" He couldn't have sounded more surprised if she accused him of killing his own child.

Doubt niggled at her mind. Maybe she was wrong. Or perhaps he was just a good actor. "Well, the baron was with me at the time, so it could not have been him."

He snorted. "And the fact I was *not* there makes me your prime suspect?"

He did have a point. She shrugged.

"Bloody hell! Are you serious? I wondered why the king sent me out here to see you wed. It is obvious now. He sent me here to determine whether you are completely noddy."

Her bottled anger uncorked, clawing its way to the surface. "Someone is trying to hurt me and you dare call me noddy? My life was not in peril until you showed up!" She cringed when his fist slammed into the table top, the vibration radiating with his own indignation.

"By all that is holy, I swear you are the stubbornest woman I have ever met. I try to tell you your servants are stealing from you, yet you refute the idea. Now someone, by your own admission, is trying to harm you, yet I am the villain?"

Scrambling to her feet she tossed her napkin, not caring if it landed on the table or the floor. "Now I am stubborn as well as noddy? Are there any other character flaws you would like to add? Since you see so many disparaging traits, it is a wonder you think to pawn me off on any man!"

His chair scraped across the floor. "Perhaps it would be best to speed up the nuptials for your safety."

He stomped from the room and she winced as the front door slammed behind him, smothering an ungentlemanly profanity.

Delilah returned to her seat and stirred her soup absently. Was she being stubborn? Perhaps she should not have accused him of treachery, after all she didn't have any firm evidence of such on his behalf, and most of the time he seemed solicitous of her needs. Her mind wandered back to reading on the lawn. She enjoyed the rousing sea tale and the rumble of his deep voice as he read to her. A smile tweaked the corners of her lips. He even changed his voice to fit each character in the book, something her father never did. It made immersing herself in the tale that much easier.

She shook the pleasant memory from her mind. The earl would be returning to London and she would be married to the baron in short order. There was no point in getting used to the earl's companionship. The sooner she wed the better. The earl did not care for her; after all he did not bother to ask after her welfare or even that of the injured horse. Convincing her of her servants' traitorous intents and marrying her off was all he cared about.

Chapter Fourteen

Delilah waved away her maid. "Enough of this, do whatever is acceptable and leave me be."

Teresa heaved a sigh. "But Miss Daysland, you want everything to be perfect for the grand day. There are so many things to be done and mere days to complete the list."

"Please." A groan escaped her lips. Delilah fumbled for the cup of tea on the table beside her. "Teresa, you have been with me since I can remember, so may I confide in you?"

"Of course, miss, I would never betray your confidence."

She smiled, knowing the truth of the maid's words. There was no one more loyal than Teresa. "This marriage of mine is naught but an agreement between the baron and myself to further our own agendas."

The maid giggled. "Isn't that the way of most marriages, miss?"

Delilah grimaced. "No, no, not like that exactly. Once the vows have been read I will return here to live as I did before. The marriage will be in name only, ensuring my continued way of life and the baron the funds to refurbish his estate."

"I see, miss. Lord Frost has already found appointments for much of the staff. Is the baron to hire new servants?"

"No, and Lord Frost is not to know of the arrangement with the baron. I want you to pick half a dozen house servants who are most loyal to me and arrange for them to stay back after everyone leaves. I will return a day or two after the nuptials are complete and then everything will be as before." She took a sip of her tea and smiled. "At last, things will be as they were, quiet and predictable."

"As you wish, miss."

She noted the maid's exit, well pleased with herself. *Take that, Lord Frostbite. I have bested you at your own game.* The grin on her lips slipped as she made her way to the veranda doors. Somehow the hard fought victory seemed petty now. Why did she feel so guilty for deceiving the earl? It wasn't as if her deceit would hurt anyone…Opening the doors she stood and savored the mid-afternoon breeze. The light cadence of hooves proved Jester was there, as always, waiting for her.

"Good afternoon, Jester. Shall we go for a walk?"

The pony nickered soft and low, brushing against her skirts.

"I was just thinking the same thing."

Delilah spun around at the sound of the earl's voice. "You startled me, my lord."

"I am sorry, it was not my intention. I thought you would have heard me approach."

"That's nearly an impossible feat, for a man you walk like a cat on the prowl." With a sigh she smoothed the wrinkles of annoyance from her brow with her fingertips. "Forgive me for being snappish—I am not myself today it would seem. Must be this confounded heat."

His hand closed over hers and he shifted it to rest on the soft fabric of his sleeve. "It is understandable given the weather and all the excitement of your upcoming nuptials."

Her stomach coiled at the thought of the dreaded day she kept at bay in her sub consciousness. "Perhaps."

"Miss Daysland, I…"

"Yes?" Delilah forced her breathing to remain steady.

"I wondered if there was anything you need, for the nuptials I mean."

In effort to ignore her guilty conscience she forced a stiff smile to her lips. "No, there is nothing, my lord, thank you for asking."

"Oh."

Was his response one of relief or disappointment? She couldn't discern. They continued down the path in unnerving silence for a while.

Coming to an abrupt halt the earl rotated to take both her hands in his. "You will not hesitate to come to me if you should need me…I mean, need anything?"

"Of course, my lord." His breath tickled her forehead. For a moment she wondered why his breath always smelled so sweet. Did he chew mint leaves? Perhaps it was some kind of soap he used. She sniffed before she could help herself. No, there was a mild vanilla scent of soap to him, beneath the herb.

He chuckled. "Do you enjoy my scent?"

Heat flooded her face and she shrugged from his light grip. "I just wondered why you always smell of mint."

"I drink it seeped into a tea."

"Oh." She puzzled his answer for a moment. "I would have thought you would drink something stronger, my lord."

"Stronger? No, I dislike most spirits and liquor. Mint is good for the digestion I hear. Why is it you always smell delightfully of citrus?"

Pleasure at his notice curved her lips. "I love oranges. I eat one every day and have the juice infused in the special soap I use for my hair. It keeps my locks clean and easier to untangle."

"I shall remember that," he murmured.

Would he? Silence stretched between them and Delilah fidgeted with the ribbon on her sleeve. "Is there something else, my lord?"

"I just wondered if perhaps you would care to read for a while? It is so nice a day out…"

Since Delilah could think of no suitable excuse and she was eager to hear the rest of the story she nodded. Besides, it seemed safe enough to admit to herself that she rather enjoyed sitting with him. As they seated themselves on a bench by the path she pondered her conflicting emotions. *He is not the enemy anymore.*

By accepting the baron's false suit I vanquished the earl from foe to friend, have I not? Still, if it was not for him I would not have had to even consider the idea of marriage. She groaned internally. *Either he is a friend or a foe, he cannot be both. Maybe I really am noddy.*

"Now, let's see, where did we leave off last time?"

Casting her thoughts aside she redirected her attention to the story. "We were at the part where the pirate captain was about to make the hero walk the plank into the shark filled waters below." A small shiver of excitement stole up Delilah's spine.

"Ah, right, here we are. A most exciting part to be sure. John stepped to the end of the plank, the captain's sword point resting between his shoulder blades and looked down at the churning water…"

Delilah lost herself in the tale, the earl's smooth voice adding to her enjoyment.

• • •

The earl closed the book with a slight snap. "Shall we leave off there for today?"

"I suppose, though I am dying to know how John is going to escape from the collapsed tomb. He must save his love, Maria, for if he does not it will be a most disappointing tale."

Lord Frost chuckled. "Ah, so you do have a romantic streak, Miss Daysland."

"Of course, every woman desires romance."

His voice softened. "Do you desire romantic gestures from the baron, Delilah?"

Delilah bit her lip. "No. I mean, perhaps under different circumstances. There is nothing romantic about being forced to marry, my lord."

A hint of regret colored his reply. "I am sorry this match is not the one every lady dreams of. It was not my intention to force you into anything you did not desire. Marriage is a necessity for you under the circumstances."

"In the king's eyes only." She struggled to keep her tears of frustration at bay. "It is simply not fair that I do not have a say in the matter. My father did not seek to see me wed, why should the king care?"

Silence stretched between them until it was broken by the earl's heavy sigh. "It is the king's duty to see to the welfare of his subjects, and mine to do as he requests."

Delilah crossed her arms. "Why, because you are his loyal subject?"

"Yes, no, it is more complicated than that."

"I fail to see how."

"It is a political matter."

"My welfare is a political matter?" Delilah snorted. "I assure you, my lord, there can be no possible political reason to force me into marriage. My father was a simple country squire and poet, not a political figure."

The earl shifted beside her on the bench. "The politics are between the king and I, and have naught to do with your father. I have designs on becoming the next leader of the Whig party and as such need the backing of the king to seek such a high appointment. He has offered his support in exchange for my help in this matter."

"Oh." Delilah dropped her hands to her lap. "So, I am naught but a political agenda. No one is concerned about what I want or need."

"That is not true, Delilah. I care about what you want and need. I know you want some romantic notion of love but there is not time for months or years of searching for a true love that may never be found. After all, most men and women live happily in their marriages without love at all, that is the way of it."

"As you pointed out, my lord, I am not like most women."

"Indeed you are not." The earl stood and squeezed her hand. "If you will excuse me, I have some pressing business matters to attend."

The dried leaves crunched beneath his feet as he moved in the direction of the house.

Delilah leaned back on the bench. Why did that have to be the way of it?

Chapter Fifteen

Delilah rolled over the morning of her wedding and groaned. Hours of strange dreams made her toss and turn until the wee hours, leaving her tired and out of sorts. Flopping onto her back, she assessed the situation. Since the incident on the horse there were no other unusual occurrences, for which she was grateful. Still, the strain of expecting one wore her nerves raw.

Perhaps she was too rash in accepting the baron's suit. Maybe she could still back out. She frowned as the downstairs clock struck ten, its forlorn chimes echoing throughout the great house. The wedding guests would be here in mere hours. With a sigh she rang for Teresa. There was no turning back now. It wouldn't be so bad. After a few days at the baron's to accomplish the ruse, she could return to her former life.

The door opened with a click. "You must hurry and dress, Miss Daysland," Teresa chirped, far too merry for Delilah's resigned mood. "His lordship did say to let you sleep in this morning, but I'll not be responsible for you being late."

Was the earl trying to sabotage the wedding? Delilah almost wished he would. How romantic would it be if he called a halt to the proceedings and announced his everlasting love just like in some of the romantic poems her father wrote? She frowned. *Good Lord, I am as noddy as everyone else believes. As if it would ever happen.* "Let us get on with this." Swinging her legs over the side of the bed she got up and counted the steps to the dressing table. With little enthusiasm she waited while Teresa fastened her corset in place and tugged the laces. "Not so tight, Teresa, I should like to be able to breathe."

The maid giggled. "Yes, miss."

When she finished Delilah sat so the maid could fix her hair.

"Shall I pin your hair with the seashell combs your mother left you?"

Delilah shrugged. "Do as you please."

It didn't take long. With a sigh Teresa gave it one last pat, her tone well pleased with herself. "Perfect. Now which dress would you prefer to wear today?"

"What difference should it make to me? This day is designed to get my life back, the cut and color of my gown will not change it." When the maid sighed Delilah relented. "You decide what will flatter me most, Teresa."

"Hmm…I should think the deep violet muslin, for it matches your eyes so beautifully."

Delilah tried to recall the exact shade of her eyes, but the color eluded her memory. "A good choice, Teresa." Standing, she held up her arms to be clothed with the delicate gown. "I feel like I am being cheated, like I'm cheating myself."

Teresa's gentle hands guided Delilah to turn around and then she began to do up the tiny row of buttons along the back of the gown. "How so, miss?"

"One's wedding day should be filled with excitement and anticipation. I cannot help but wish I was marrying some handsome young man who spouts poetry to my loveliness and makes my heart flutter. It sounds silly I know."

"It does not sound silly at all. The baron is not unhandsome, if you'll permit me saying, miss."

"Perhaps, but this is hardly the day of my dreams. If my father were still here…" Delilah squared her shoulders. "Listen to me pining on about silly dreams. I agreed to the arrangement because it is practical and accomplishes my goal." When Teresa fastened the last button Delilah turned around and favored her with a weak smile. "It is almost time."

•••

The clock downstairs didn't finish striking twelve when the knock Delilah was dreading came. She turned to face it as the maid hurried to open the door. Goosebumps rose along her arms from the slight draft as it opened.

The earl cleared his throat. "You look lovely, Miss Daysland."

"I shall have to take your word for it," she snapped. "I am sorry, my lord, thank you for the compliment. I am nervous and did not mean to be short."

His footsteps whispered across the carpet and then ceased before her. "That is perfectly understandable. Perhaps on such a momentous occasion we can dispense with the formality? Call me Tyrone." Warm fingers closed over hers and then he placed a wide flat box on her palm. "I brought you a wedding gift."

She ran her fingers over the textured surface. "What is it?"

"Open it and find out."

Curious, she fingered the clasp and lifted the lid. Following the line of the box, she slid her hand down to rest on something smooth and cold, tracing the object in a circle with her fingertips. It was a necklace she realized, with tiny teardrop stones dangling at regular intervals along its chain. "Thank you, Tyrone. I am sure it is lovely."

"Here, I will put it on you."

She pivoted so he could slide the cool gems around her neck and couldn't help shivering when his rough fingers brushed her nape as he fumbled with the clasp.

"They match your eyes, you know."

"Violet?"

"More dark like your eyes when you are angry." He finished with the clasp and placed his hands on her shoulders, turning her back to face the door.

Her heart fluttered in her chest as his hands remained lightly on her shoulders. She should be angry at his comment, but instead a sense of breathless anticipation tightened her chest. Attraction to him was foolhardy. He was the enemy. Wasn't he?

"I never lie."

The echo of a slamming door broke the moment and he stepped away. "Come, the guests await you in the chapel." He tucked her hand in the crook of his arm and escorted her downstairs.

Her chest grew tighter as she was overtaken by a moment of sheer panic. The closer they got to the estate's chapel, the louder the guests' voices became. Her palms grew moist with sweat. Little by little her distress increased. The struggle for air became more difficult as the panic attack intensified.

"Delilah?"

The concern in Tyrone's voice gave her something to cling to, to focus on in order to stay afloat in the tidal wave of fear engulfing her. *What if I have made a mistake? What if Augustus does not live up to his word? All these people…watching…staring…witnessing my fate.* Her fingers clawed his arm.

"Delilah? Are you all right?"

"I need to sit." Her knees buckled and she sagged against him. Tyrone's strong arm encircled her. "Right here? Now?"

"Yes," she gasped, her head beginning to spin.

He lowered her to the grass and pressed her head between her knees. She struggled to take slow, deep breaths. Unmindful of her delicate dress scrunched in her clammy hands, she willed her mind to relax.

"Is there something I can do, some way I can help?"

Delilah shook her head. "No." *Those hated crowds of people. Always watching, whispering…waiting for me to make a fool of myself.* As her chest began to tighten again she forced the thoughts from her head. Squeezing her eyes shut she concentrated on taking deep breaths, exhaling slow and steady until the spinning sensation stopped. *I can do this. All I have to do is walk down the aisle, repeat the simple vows, and it will all be over.*

A familiar nicker gave her hope. "Jester." At the soft clip clop of his approach she held out her hand until his leg brushed it. With a grateful smile she pulled herself to her feet using his harness. "Jester will take me the rest of the way."

"Jester cannot give you away."

She snickered at his disgruntlement. "Yes he can. Jester, chapel." The pony shuffled forward. As she stepped into the chapel the rumble of voices hushed. Forcing the smile to remain on her lips, she continued on to the front of the room. *This is just a formality. In a few days my life will go back to the way it was. Forever.* Tyrone's footsteps fell into step behind her.

The preacher's voice startled her from her inner thoughts and Jester came to a halt. "We are gathered here today…"

• • •

Delilah paused on the threshold of the ballroom. Crystal clinked over top the laughter and soft music playing. Her light-headedness returned when she realized there must be close to a hundred guests in attendance to celebrate her supposed joyful union. She tightened her grip on her new husband's arm but he strolled on, oblivious to her alarm. *Is everyone staring at me? Oh, how I wish this night were over.* Augustus deposited her in a chair and left to procure a glass of champagne on her behalf.

Fighting a sense of abandonment, she perched on the chair toying with the ruffles on her skirt. Why did there have to be a celebration ball anyway? No one here knew her, or in all likelihood cared who she was; besides, their marriage was a sham to foil Tyrone's plans. The orchestra began to play a light, fanciful waltz. She tried to lose herself in the forbidden melody, her fingers taking up position on an imaginary keyboard of their own accord. Playing as part of the orchestra would be much preferable to sitting here as the object of every gossip's attention.

"I have brought you refreshment."

Stilling her fingers she sought the glass Augustus held. A cool crystal goblet was pressed into her hand. Wrapping both around the delicate vessel, she raised it to her lips and sipped the contents, more for something to do than out of thirst. The tangy champagne bubbles teased her taste buds before sliding down her throat.

Augustus cleared his throat. "I suppose to complete the ruse of an adoring couple, we should dance."

Delilah almost choked at the idea and lowered the glass in haste. "To a waltz? I am surprised you allow such an inappropriate dance."

"I hear it is all the rage in France." Augustus sniffed. "And I make the effort to keep up with all the current trends."

No doubt it accounts for his need for money. She sighed. Why should she care what he did with her father's blunt once she returned home with her dowry? "If we must dance then let us get it over with." Truth be told she loved to dance, though the prospect was far from thrilling with one of the Augustus' ilk. Tyrone, she surmised, was apt to be a skilled dancer. She rose and held out her hand. Biting her lip she chastised herself for allowing her thoughts to wander in such an unacceptable path. Tyrone didn't want her any more than any other man. Delilah tried to concentrate on copying her husband's steps rather than her present situation. *One, two, three. One, two, three.* The overpowering stench of his cologne made her eyes water. His arms were like iron bars, imprisoning her against his bony chest. She fought the urge to revolt and flee.

"Excuse me, may I cut in?"

Relief flooded her limbs at Tyrone's request.

Augustus stiffened beneath her hand.

As if sensing his displeasure, Tyrone added, "I would have this dance with my charge before I return to Westpoint to pack."

Her partner released her. "By all means, Lord Frost. You must of course have the honor before you leave."

"Very considerate of you, sir. Miss Daysland—I beg your pardon, Lady March, will you do me the honor?"

Left with little choice in a room crowded with onlookers, she tipped her head in an acquiescent nod. "Of course, my lord." His sleeve slipped beneath her fingertips, warm and soft. He rested his hand at the juncture of her waist, his other cupping her fingers in a gentle grip. Together they picked up the strains of the fanciful waltz, he leading and her gliding along with more grace at Tyrone's direction.

"Are you well pleased with the baron, Delilah?"

"As pleased as one who is forced to wed can be, my lord."

"Hmm. You seemed to be in a hurry to attend your nuptials for one so reluctant to marry."

In response to his observation her steps became unsure and she faltered. "You were the one in a hurry to marry me off and return to London."

"I only sought to do the right thing by you, nothing more." His gruff answer didn't quite cover the remorse in his words.

Tipping her nose with an arrogant sniff, she rebuffed him. "And who are you to decide what is the right thing? I was content to go on as I was before you." If it wouldn't have drawn undue attention she would have left him standing in the middle of the floor, though in truth she was at a loss as to the way back to her chair.

He sighed as if dealing with a naughty child. "And allow you go on fooling yourself into believing all was well? Once those blasted servants of yours drained every asset from beneath your nose, what would you have done?"

She bowed her head in defeat. There was nothing she could do in fact. But her total loss at what to do with the situation was not something she cared to admit to him or anyone else. Fumbling for anything to satisfy him, she lifted her chin and scowled. "I would have fired the lot of them and hired ones whom I could trust to be loyal." His snort of disbelief didn't help bolster her flagging self-esteem.

"It is hard to instill loyalty and trust in servants when they know they have the undeniable advantage, my dear." His observation was neither mocking nor sympathetic.

Tears welled up despite her resolve to face him with distance, and she blinked them away lest he see. "How dare you! I existed just fine in my own world, until you came along. You pretended I was desirable with your teasing lips, and then dashed my confidence with rejection." She wrenched from his grasp.

When she would have struck out on her own through the crush of warm bodies he stayed her with his hand. "Forgive me, Delilah. I had no intention of promising you anything with a few misplaced kisses. It was unfair of me. I regret misleading you."

"I was a game, nothing but an amusement to you. You are no better than any other man I have met, my lord." Jerking her arm from his she fled through the varied textured maze of people. Somehow she found herself in a quiet corridor, the sounds of the ballroom faint but still present. Soft footsteps approached.

"My lady? The earl bid me to see to your welfare."

Delilah sniffed and dabbed her eyes with a delicate lace handkerchief from her reticule. "Who are you?"

The girl's voice softened. "Just a maid, my lady. May I see you above stairs to your bedchamber?"

"Thank you. I have endured enough humiliation this night."

• • •

Delilah stumbled, banging her shin against a chair in the bedchamber. Clenching her teeth she rubbed the bruised limb. If she must stay at the baron's for a day or so it would be best to have the maid remove most of the furniture. Hands outstretched, she made her way past another chair, end table, and dressing screen to the window. She followed the grainy textured wall to the corner and then made her way along the next until her hip bumped a larger object. Leaning forward she investigated it. A soft bedspread smoothed beneath her fingertips. *At last.* She perched on the edge and then climbed between the covers.

It was strange to be in a room not her own. She rolled over on the lumpy mattress. Between the unfamiliar surroundings and uncomfortable cushioning, it was doubtful she would sleep much this night. It would have been easier to have the baron stay at Westpoint, and she wondered why neither of them thought of it. Yawning, she rolled over onto her side and listened to the peculiar noises around her. Footsteps passed by the door. Laughter carried from the entrance way, a guest departing in all likelihood, and a door closed. Outside the window the wind moaned and howled, rattling branches against the windowpane. A lone cow bellowed, its forlorn call lending an eerie air to the place. *I hope Jester is safe and snug in the baron's stable.* Somewhere downstairs a clock chimed. "Bong…bong." *Two past midnight.* She yawned again. Though her body was weary, her mind churned with restless energy. Too bad she couldn't brave a trip downstairs to the kitchen for a bite to eat.

The click of the door latch made her sit up. At the soft squeak of the hinges and the creak of a loose floor board, she tilted her head toward the door. "Who is there?"

The swish of a cautious tread and the scent of liquor made her recoil against the headboard. Clutching the covers to her chest she inquired again, "Who is there?"

"'Tis jus me, wife, come t' take my rights by marriage." The bed dipped under the baron's weight.

Was the man drunk? "We had an agreement, Augustus."

He snatched the covers from her grip with an evil chortle. "Did you really believe I would s-tick t' s-such a ridic…ridiculous agreement," he slurred. "I'll 'ave no reason for you t' take the property mine by marriage away."

Panic rose in her chest and she tried to slide from the bed only to find herself imprisoned between his arms braced on either side of her torso. "You are drunk, sir."

"Of course I am. Why else w-would I s-sleep with such a pathetic creature as you?"

Her mind raced for a way out of the situation. "I thought you possessed some honor at least."

He laughed. "You daft wench. When I t-tire of your wares it'll be a s-swift tumble down the stairs for you. My plan t' get you t' accept my s-suit worked. 'Twas too easy t' get you t' believe the earl meant you harm."

Terror fueled her courage. She braced her feet against his chest as his liquor-saturated breath came closer. With all her strength she shoved. Augustus grunted, and then tumbled off the bed, landing with a loud crash. Something clattered on the bedside table before coming to rest on the floor with a dull clunk. On her hands and knees she crawled to the opposite side of the bed. Augustus moaned. *It was him all along. How could I have been so gullible?* Listening for his pursuit, she scrambled from the bed and darted in the direction she thought the door should be. The same bruised shin caught the chair, toppling her to the floor. She staggered to her feet to the sound of her nightdress tearing. It dawned on her Augustus was silent. Was he passed out from too much drink or had she inadvertently killed him? Suppressing the urge to find out, she groped her way to the door, one ear tuned for his approach.

Luck was with her when her hand closed around the smooth knob. It twisted with ease beneath her hand and she crept into the hallway. Biting her lip, she tried to remember which way the stairs were. A little more than a dozen steps to the right, she concluded, perhaps two without someone's sure steps to guide her. She placed the palm of her right hand against the wall and shuffled forward as fast as she dared. Before she thought it possible, her hand slipped from the wall into emptiness. Teetering on the edge of the top step, she flailed for the railing, heaving a sigh of relief when her hand closed around its sturdy wooden arm. Step by step she descended the carpeted steps until her feet reached the hallway below. All was quiet, for which she was glad. If someone happened along, how would she explain what happened to her husband? Surely she would be held at fault for any injury or death of the man she wed. Panic resurfaced when she realized she didn't know which way to go.

Taking a deep breath, she pushed her fear aside. *Think, Delilah, think.* A vague recollection of walking forward and then turning left came to her. Arms outstretched, she turned right and walked forward. After a few moments she bumped into a door jam. She eased her way around it and kept walking until her palms came in contact with a solid wooden surface, and she slid her hand down it until she found the knob to open the door. A gust of wind whipped her hair about her head as she stepped outside. Not bothering to close the door behind, she made her way down the steps to the drive before pausing to consider which direction to go. How was she to find her way home? A whinny carried above the wind. Pivoting to the left she followed the sound until she walked into a rail fence. It stood to reason she would be black and blue by the time she made her way home, if she managed to get there at all.

"Jester?" A welcoming nicker made her sigh with relief. "Thank God I found you, my friend." Crawling between the rails she ran her palms along his side, searching for the harness. "The fiend left you out in such horrid weather, too," she crooned. The pony nuzzled her arm as her fingers closed on the hand strap. She patted him. "Now all we have to do is find the gate." She urged him on, trailing one hand along the rough top rail, unmindful of the splinters that pierced her tender flesh. On and on they trudged parallel to the enclosure fence. When she began to think she somehow missed the gate, her hand snagged the latch. "Whoa, Jester."

The pony halted, waiting with his usual patience as she fumbled with the braided rope loop. Eventually it popped loose and the gate creaked open. After leading Jester through, Delilah scrambled aboard and urged him forward with her heels. All she could do was hope he could find his way home in the midst of the growing storm.

The wind howled, flapping her tattered nightdress and unbound hair around her. Delilah shivered, her teeth chattering when an icy gust cut through the flimsy material. True to his character Jester plodded on unaffected. The moan of the rising wind drowned out the sound of the pony's hooves. A couple drops of water against her wind-chapped cheeks were the only warning before the downpour began. Frigid rain pelted her mercilessly, turning her nightdress into a soggy second skin. The chill was unbearable. She let go of the harness to lean forward and wrap her arms around Jester's neck, pressing her body to him to savor the little warmth his furry coat could give.

How far was it from the baron's to her own estate? On the road it took almost an hour by coach going at a smart clip. She grimaced as brush scraped her leg, snagging her nightdress. Going cross country as it appeared they were should be quicker, provided Jester was heading in the right direction. The groom led him over after the ceremony, but would Jester recognize the route to take? The seeds of doubt began to grow in her weary mind. *We are going much slower and Jester's legs are a lot shorter than the carriage horses… What if we get lost? Anything could happen to me out here alone… Was there a better way to handle Augustus? I cannot go back…*

A lone wolf howled nearby. Apprehension tightened her grip around the pony's neck as his steps faltered. His head swung in the direction of the daunting sound. Did he see the creature lurking in the bushes? Was it watching and waiting for its chance to pounce? *Noise. I need to make noise to scare it away.* She opened her mouth to holler at the beast but then thought better of it. She didn't want to alert the wrong creatures of her presence here, alone in the dark with no protection.

Do not think about the cold. Think about getting home, to my room, to my warm bed. She coughed into Jester's wet fur. *I am still cold.* A sound in rhythm with the wind caught her attention. "Bang…bang…bang." The noise grew louder until it was right in front of them. The rain ceased as Jester clip clopped across a wooden floor. The smell of fresh hay, dust, and straw tickled her nostrils making her sneeze. The sound echoed. *Jester must have brought me to an empty barn.*

With difficulty she eased her cold, stiff limbs from Jester's back and leaned against him, shivering. The pony shuffled ahead, leading her into a deep pile of soft straw. With a violent shake, he sent droplets of water flying in all directions, further soaking her. "Jester!" With a sigh she copied his primitive movement for lack of a towel, attempting to rid herself of her own excess moisture. The pony snuffled in the straw, pawed once, and then settled down for the night. Delilah followed suite and covered herself with straw for a blanket. Curling up beside her pony in the dry, makeshift bed comforted her. Despite the banging, or perhaps because of its steady rhythm in the storm, her eyes became heavy. She drifted into an exhausted slumber afraid of what tomorrow might bring.

Chapter Sixteen

Tyrone heaved an exasperated groan, swinging his legs over the side of the bed and glancing at the timepiece on the table. It was well past two in the morning, yet he couldn't sleep. Delilah's sudden change of heart regarding the baron's proposal, and marriage in general, still didn't sit well with him. Something wasn't right, though nothing sinister had happened since Delilah agreed to the baron's courtship. Everything was as it should be…or was it? The livestock, crops, and supplies were still missing. In light of his ward's recent marriage there was nothing more for him to do here, yet he hesitated to leave. Why? Was it because of his desire to never leave an untied end or fear he failed in his duties? Perhaps it was more. He did have feelings for Delilah Daysland. Why didn't he act on those feelings? He shook his head and lurched to his feet. *Act on what?* The tenderness he felt for her was based on admiration of what she could do and accomplish, not on love for her…wasn't it? Though his heart screamed the truth, he refused to permit the idea to settle in his mind. It didn't matter anyhow, for she was a married woman now. Her new husband would see to her welfare and finances. She and the theft of her property was no longer his concern.

After glancing out the window at the rain beating against the pane, he headed downstairs to the study. He'd missed something, some vital part of information somewhere that would clear up the matter of Delilah's missing stock and supplies. The question was, what? His footsteps echoed as he crossed the tile foyer, reminding him of the emptiness of the house. Most of the servants left not long after the wedding festivities to take up or find positions elsewhere. Only a handful of servants were in attendance to see to the upkeep of the great house. His mind wandered back to the night he found Delilah sprawled on the floor. She looked so frail and helpless lying there with blood oozing from a gash on her scalp. Did someone hit her as she claimed? If so, could it be the same person responsible for the thefts? It made no sense. Why would someone want to hurt her? He shook his head and seated himself behind the study desk, fairly sure murder was not the intention. Who would gain from murdering an heiress other than someone who stood to inherit in her absence? There was no one in line to the squire's fortune but Delilah. Still, someone wanted to scare her. The question was who and why?

After lighting the lamp he flipped through the file he compiled on Delilah and the servants. The sole claim to his former ward's fortune would be through marriage. *Marriage.* Her union with the baron. Nothing specific troubled him about the man, which made it all the more strange the alliance should bother him. He frowned. His feelings for Delilah made him suspicious of the man, nothing more. Rummaging through the desk, he pulled out the squire's old ledger containing more personal notes than financial recordings. Something about the baron mentioned within its pages nudged his memory, but just what it was he couldn't recall.

Tyrone went through the book page by page from the beginning, scanning the entries until he found the one he was seeking.

Met the new baron. Boy is a remarkable resemblance to his parentage. Wonder if the former baroness has confided the truth to her son? He seems very taken with Delilah, which causes concern.

Tyrone leaned back in the chair and pondered the entry. What truth? Why would the squire be concerned with his daughter catching the young baron's eye? He skimmed the entries until he came to the day of the squire's death.

The young man is getting bolder with his questions. Surely he knows why I turned down his request. It is time to put an end to this.

He closed the ledger. Put an end to what? Well, if Tyrone wanted to know a family secret, then he would need to turn to someone indebted to the household. A devoted servant. He jerked the bell pull to summon the butler, who was still in residence. While he waited he flipped through the ledger for any further reference to the baron.

It was many minutes later before a sleepy eyed Aims appeared. The butler yawned, rubbing a hand through his tousled gray hair. "You rang, my lord?"

Tyrone gestured to the chair across the desk. "Have a seat, Aims."

The butler blinked and then took a seat. "Is there something you need at such a late hour, my lord?"

"Yes, as a matter of fact there is. I need information. It seems I have missed something crucial in my hunt for the lecher bleeding your former mistress dry. What have you heard among the employees lately?"

Aims crossed his arms, setting his lips in a tight line. "As you well know, my lord, a good servant does not gossip."

Tyrone waved an impatient hand. "Yes, yes, I understand, yet it is a matter of utmost importance. You want to see Miss Daysland safe, do you not?"

"Of course, my lord."

"Then tell me what you know of the baron."

The man cleared his throat. "The baron, my lord?"

Tyrone pushed the ledger toward Aims and opened it to the last reference to the baron. "Explain this entry to me."

Aims took the book and read the page, his brows bunching. When he was done he set it down on the desk. "I have no idea what you want from me, my lord."

"I want you to find out from the baron's servants who his sire is and what request the squire would have turned down."

• • •

Delilah moaned and snuggled closer to the furry mass beside her. Her whole body shook with cold in the dampness of the barn, yet her head was burning and heavy. When footsteps approached her resting place she tried to force her stiff body to move, but failed.

"What the…Mum, Pater, come quick! There's a girl sleepin' in the barn!"

The pony scrambled to his feet as Delilah reached for the harness. She lurched to her feet and staggered over the lumpy straw away from the strange voice.

"Bloody hell, 'tis a girl!"

She swung toward the second voice, sleepy, disoriented, and afraid. "Please forgive me. I did not mean to trespass. I only sought shelter from the storm last night."

"Who are ye and why were ye traveling out on such a night?"

"I am Delilah Daysland. I was trying to return to my home, Westpoint Manor, when I got lost in the storm."

Delilah flinched at a woman's sharp intake of breath and whisper, "She tells the truth. See her eyes? She's the squire's daughter all right." For once perhaps her affliction might help her out of trouble, for surely they would help a blind woman find her home.

"Matt, John, see to Miss Daysland's pony while I take 'er to the house for a bite to eat and a cup of tea." A small work-roughened hand clasped hers and drew her forward. "Just come with me, miss, I'll see ye put to rights, I will." The woman patted Delilah's hand. "Why ye did not knock on the door, miss, is beyond me."

Grimacing at the woman's lack of grasp of the obvious, Delilah found herself propelled from the barn, mud squelching beneath her shoes. She coughed, the simple action making her chest hurt and her head throb. Moaning she raised a hand to her temple.

"Oh dear, I fear you've caught yerself a ditty of a cold, miss. A good hot cup of tea 'll help." A door opened and she was drawn into the warmth of a house. The smell of fresh, yeasty bread filled her nostrils, making her stomach growl loud enough she was sure the woman heard it. "Ye jus' sit yerself down here by the fire. I'll get the tea heatin' and some biscuits."

Delilah was settled on a hard chair by a crackling fire and a hot cup of strong tea pressed into her hands. "Thank you, Mrs.?"

"Call me Mary. Tell me, Miss Daysland, why were ye headin' back to Westpoint when I hear tell ye married Baron March yesterday?"

Taking a sip of the tea, Delilah struggled to find an explanation that didn't sound silly in light of the situation. In the end she sighed, set the cup on the table, and decided to go with the truth, at least in part. "I was offended when my new husband came to my bed foxed."

"Oh dear, disparaging to be sure. Even so, was it wise to flee by yerself in the middle of a storm?" Mary tut-tutted.

Voices announced the men entering the room so Delilah bite back her reply. There was no sense in telling the entire sordid tale. The easiest thing to do was send someone for the earl to come fetch her home. The door opened and two sets of footsteps approached. "Please kind sir, I ask you go to Westpoint and inform Lord Frost I am here so he may come posthaste and escort me home." A fit of coughing doubled her over. When she regained her composure the three were whispering among themselves in a corner.

"…baron."

"No…"

"…reward for her return."

"Merryweather…"

The swish of shirts and a gentle hand on her shoulder heralded the woman. "Here, miss, let me put ye to bed. Ye can rest until the earl is brought round to fetch ye."

The hairs on the back of Delilah's neck prickled. Could she trust these people? She wanted to believe she could, but the little voice in her head shouted something was wrong. "No, just point me in the direction of the main road and Jester will see me home."

Against her will she was taken to a bed and forced to sit. "Oh dear no. What kind of people would we be to let the squire's daughter wander the roads alone and unprotected?" With gentle prodding she was encouraged to lie down on the thick straw-filled tick. The woman washed her cold, muddy feet with warm water and tucked her into a thick downy quilt. "Rest now."

Despite her unease Delilah drifted in and out of a restless doze. Each time she awoke she listened for any sign of the earl, but the only sound was Mary moving about the cottage. Huddled in the cocoon of warm blankets she pondered the situation. *The men have been gone a long time. Did Tyrone already return to London? Perhaps I did not sleep very long…* Yawning, she closed her heavy eyelids. Tyrone would come for her soon. He would know what to do.

Chapter Seventeen

Tyrone exited the house, shutting and locking the door behind him. The last of the servants wandered down the road in the direction of town as he climbed into the waiting coach and four. He glanced out the window as the conveyance pulled away. Why did he feel the urge to stay? He was not the type to take to country life. Back in London his large townhouse and favorite clubs awaited him. Country life was too simple and quiet for the likes of a notorious bachelor like himself. A slight smile curved his lips when he thought of his mistress ensconced in her townhouse awaiting his attentions. He tried to picture the last time he saw her, but the only image coming to mind was Delilah's laughing face. With a grunt he shook her from his mind. They passed the forlorn looking group of servants and picked up speed. He had done what the king commanded and saw the wench married. Guilt thinned his lips. *Maybe not happy, but at least complacent with her lot in life.*

The carriage rolled through a puddle from the previous night's storm, the resulting muddy spray drenching the windows and obscuring his view. Without warning the coach slowed. He braced himself for the unexpected stop. One of the horses whinnied, answered by a softer nicker. When the coach's movement stopped Tyrone eased from his seat and pushed open the door. Jester stood on the side of the road, muddy and wet, his copper-brown coat matted with burrs.

"What the devil?" Tyrone stepped from the carriage and looked both ways down the road. There was not a coach or person in sight. "How did you come to be out here by yourself?"

The pony shook his head, splattering bits of muck onto Tyrone's trousers and waistcoat. He grasped the pony's harness as the coachman climbed down from his perch atop the driver's seat. "Secure Jester to the back of the carriage. We will return him to the baron's on the way to London."

They resumed their journey at a slower pace to accommodate the pony's shorter stride. What was the pony doing out here on his own, so far from his new home? Did the animal escape from his enclosure and head for his former home, like a lost dog or homing pigeon? No matter. He would see the animal back to Delilah's side and have a chance to be sure she was content with her position at the baron's.

His heart constricted at the thought she might be as unhappy as he was at the moment. Did he make a terrible mistake allowing her accept the baron's suit? He didn't fit in her quiet, controlled world any more than she would fit into his busy London one. Besides, she didn't want to marry him or any other man. He shook his head. She did marry though, because he left her no choice. Did he rush her into a marriage filled with misery just because he longed to return to his own empty life? It was possible; nevertheless, there was naught he could do about the situation now.

Settling back against the plush cushions he contemplated his own life. He would be expected to offer for his current intended's hand upon returning to London. The girl would make a brilliant political match and a suitable wife from among the debutantes circulating the many ballrooms this past season. He frowned trying to remember Miss Deval's face yet failed to picture the lass he'd spent so much time wooing. His thoughts wandered back to Delilah, curled beside him on the sofa, guiding her slender fingers along the words of a poem. Those strange, haunting violet eyes lay her soul open to his heart like a book to an information hungry reader. The sweet melodies she played still rang in his ears when his head touched the pillow each night. He loved every slight touch, word, and movement she made. The reality of his blunder sunk in. He forced her into the arms of another to protect his connection with a woman of higher standing.

He was roused from his regrets when the carriage turned onto the path to the baron's manor on the bare hilltop. The estate appeared to be flourishing; however, a closer inspection drew attention to the little bits of neglect and disrepair here and there. A sagging hinge, a barren field, an empty paddock where livestock should graze gave hint to the need for further funds. Delilah's dowry and estate holdings would give the baron the capital to expand and solidify his fortune, ensuring her well-being for many years to come. True, it seemed the baron was a fortune hunter, but could Tyrone blame the young man for marrying the income he needed? Wasn't he guilty wooing his London debutante for political gain? Ambition was something to revere not frown upon.

The carriage rolled to a stop in the turnaround in front of the main steps. Without waiting he exited before his groom could set the step for him. Marching to the door he nodded to a footman lounging on the bottom step, and then peered closer. The young man looked familiar to him. He scowled, realizing it was the lad he banished from the stables a few weeks prior. Still practicing his slacker ways it appeared. Before he could lift his hand to knock a sour-faced butler opened the door.

"Please tell Miss Daysland—I mean the baroness, Lord Frost has come to ask after her and return her companion, Jester," Tyrone said at the butler's inquiring look.

"I am afraid the baroness is indisposed at the moment, my lord, but your groom may take the pony around back to the stables. Leave him with the barn master." The butler shut the door in his face with a sharp click.

Tyrone loitered there for a moment, taken aback by the servant's rudeness. Delilah probably was indisposed this morning due to the excitement of her nuptials the afternoon before; however, the butler's attitude was quite inexcusable. Annoyed, he turned on his heel and stalked to his coachman, who waited with the pony in hand. Taking Jester's lead he headed around back of the manor to the barns to find the stable master himself. He found the man grooming a tall, gray gelding.

"I have come to return Jester. He was on the road headed for Westpoint Manor."

The groom put down his brush and frowned. "He must be quite the escape artist, my lord, for this morning I did find the gate unlatched and the creature gone." He glanced about and then stepped closer, lowering his voice. "I fear something is amiss, my lord, for there were tracks in the mud by the gate."

"Tracks?"

The groom nodded. "Tracks made by someone with small, bare feet. The baron and a couple men left shortly after daybreak. I did think it strange on the morn after his wedding and with his head bandaged too."

A bad feeling welled up in the pit of Tyrone's stomach. Did something terrible happen to Delilah? He handed the pony's lead to the groom. "Put Jester in a secure stall while I ask after the baroness at the manor." Turning on his heel he headed back to the house.

"My lord?"

Pausing he cast an inquiring look over his shoulder. "Yes?"

The groom glanced at the manor. "I hate to ask, but could you keep what I said between us? I would not like to incur the baron's wrath. All the same, I worry for the lady and should not like to think I may unwittingly hide some information of value, if something devilish is at foot."

"Rest assured I will keep our conversation secret. Thank you for speaking your mind." Tyrone nodded and hurried to the house. He pounded on the doors, noting the lazy stable boy was no longer hovering on the steps.

The butler opened the door within moments, scowling when he spied Tyrone standing there. "May I be of service, *again*, my lord?"

Tyrone drew himself up tall and fixed the servant with a no-nonsense stare. "I wish to speak with the baroness immediately. It is a matter of utmost importance."

"As I said, the lady in question is still asleep and asked not to be disturbed for any reason."

The butler made to slam the door in his face, but Tyrone wedged his foot against the jam. "As Miss Daysland's guardian, I insist on seeing her. I suggest you summon a maid to wake her."

"Perhaps you should wait in the parlor until the baron returns, my lord." The man looked over his shoulder as if hoping the baron would appear.

"Miss Daysland is not here, is she? Where is she?"

The butler swallowed. "I don't know, my lord. There was a commotion last night and upon investigation, his lordship was found on the floor of her bedchamber, bleeding and unconscious. Once revived, the baron was in a state and swore to bring her back."

Alarm surged through Tyrone. His chest tightened and his heart lurched. "Were they accosted in their marriage bed, and the lady kidnapped?"

"I think not, my lord, for the baron seemed more shocked and angered than concerned for the lady's welfare."

Tyrone ran down the stairs and back to the stable to summon the groom. "Saddle a couple of horses and turn Jester loose."

"Yes, my lord." The stable master disappeared into the recesses of the barn to do as he was bid while Tyrone paced the muddy yard. Barefoot prints meant Delilah left in such haste she didn't have time to even don her slippers. What happened to make her flee in such panic? Riding out in a storm on Jester was foolhardy. In her distress did she meet with an accident, or foul play attempting to make her way back to Westpoint Manor?

Within moments he and the stable master were mounted. Tyrone slipped the lead off the pony and then followed as Jester trotted from the stable yard and headed across the fields. Would the pony take the same route he had in the storm? He prayed they would find Delilah safe and no worse for wear somewhere along the way.

Chapter Eighteen

Delilah rolled over when the door opened. Footsteps of more than one person crossed to the bed.

"Aye, 'ere she is. Take 'er quickly and be gone 'afore the baron comes lookin' fer 'er then."

Without warning she was lifted up, blankets and all, and slung over a broad shoulder. Her breath caught in her heavy chest and then released in a fit of uncontrolled coughing. By the time she could inhale again she was settled in a wagon box. The conveyance rumbled into motion. How could she have doubted the farmer's kindness? He arranged for her to be returned to Westpoint Manor after all. She must remember to send the family a lamb in thanks for their service.

The wagon rolled on, bumping and bouncing over ruts and rocks for what seemed like hours. She began to worry all was not right. Perhaps it was taking so long to get to the manor because they were going slow. She strained to pick up the hoof beats over the harness jingle. The rhythmic clip clop told her they were going at a steady trot. Her inner voice told her they should have reached Westpoint long ago. Despite the rocking she managed to pull herself into a sitting position against the wooden box of the wagon. "Good sirs, have we crossed onto Westpoint land yet?"

"Nay, my lady. Soon now, soon," came the gruff reply.

He was lying, she was sure of it. "Surely we should have arrived by now. Have you taken the wrong turn?"

"Nay, my lady. We have taken the long way out of concern for your comfort. Rest assured we shall be at our destination in due time." There was a quiet murmur of voices and then someone settled beside her in the wagon box. The smell of herbs and wine tickled her nose.

"Here, you must be thirsty. Drink this."

A skin was held to her lips. Her dry throat welcomed the sweet elderberry wine and she drank her fill, wrinkling her nose at the pulpy dregs in the last couple mouthfuls. When she finished the skin was removed. "To whom do I owe my thanks, sir?"

"Jal, my lady, and the other is my cousin, Ker."

"Very uncommon names."

"Not among my people."

Delilah frowned trying to place the thick, accented speech. "Your dialect is familiar to me. Where are you from?"

"I'm from the land, my lady, from everywhere any man can call home."

She caught her breath. "You are a gypsy?"

"Many call us that."

"Forgive me my rudeness, sir, for I have heard many a wild tale of such people."

He chortled. "I have no doubt. Many of which are true, some of which I'm sure are purely imagination."

"My father once allowed your people to camp on Westpoint land and entertain the townsfolk, at my mother's insistence."

"And now?"

Sorrow griped her at the mention of her mother. "My father refused to allow them there after my mother's death. In truth she begged to have them stay. I sensed my father did not approve of them, nor they of him."

"Your mother must thave been a fun-loving lady, if you've no mind me saying."

"She was." Delilah sighed. "I am told I have her looks. She used to call me her little gypsy doll."

The man's tone warmed. "I can see why, for you look like a gypsy for sure."

Delilah giggled and then sobered when she became aware of other voices and the smoky musk of a campfire. "Where are we?"

"We have arrived at my camp," he said, moving away from her when the wagon lurched to a stop.

"Your camp? You are supposed to be returning me to Westpoint Manor." She struggled when someone picked her up.

"Be still," the gruff voice from earlier admonished. "You are safe here."

She ceased her weak efforts. "But, why have you brought me here?"

"Deagan wished it so."

"Deagan? Who is he?"

"He is our voivode, or chief as you call him." The man paused, and the rustle of canvas and creak of a wagon step alerted her to another presence.

"You've found her. Has the bastard hurt her?"

Delilah turned her head toward the deep voice and the man who held her set her on her feet. "She has caught a chill, though I can't vouch for her treatment at the baron's hands."

She steadied herself against Jal. "Are you the one they call Deagan?"

"Yes, it has been many years since I've seen you, Delilah. You've grown into a most impressive young woman."

Curiosity made her forget her demands to be taken to Westpoint. "How is it you know me?"

"Come, we'll have a meal by the fire. I shall tell you all you forgot, or have not been told these long years, of you, the one you call mother, the squire, and Kata."

A warm, calloused hand grasped hers in a gentle grip and led her to the heat of the campfire. She was pressed to sit on a sturdy bench and someone handed her a warm wooden bowl. Delilah sniffed the inviting scent of rich vegetable stew and warm rye bread, her stomach gurgling in appreciation. After running a finger along the edge of the bowl for the spoon, she scooped up some of the stew, blew on it, and then savored the spicy taste as Deagan began to talk.

"I first met Isabella, the one you call your mother, the year before you were born. We were camped at this very spot when she and the squire slipped into our camp one night. Oh, she was a beautiful woman and a suburb dancer. None but a true gypsy heart could dance as free as she did. I was taken by her delicate golden beauty straight off."

Delilah caught her breath in wonder. She always thought she took after the dark-haired woman who came in her dreams. "My mother was blond? You have made a mistake, for the woman I remember was dark like me."

"I have made no mistake. The woman you remember was my sister Kata, your mother who served as your nursemaid for many years."

"A lie!"

"No, listen and all will become clear." The fire shifted, crackling as if he stirred it with a stick. "After the dancing wound down that first night she sat beside me and told me of her shattered dreams. Two years she was married to the squire and though he visited her bed each night, she didn't have a child to show for it. She asked me to cast a spell or give her some sort of fertility potion to change the situation."

Delilah leaned forward teaming with curiosity, her meal forgotten. "And did you?"

He chuckled. "Ah, my child, there are many things a gypsy can do, but conceiving a child is not magic, simply the act of love. Kata and the squire made love beneath a gypsy moon and you were conceived. It seemed the perfect solution for your mother to claim you as her own, since the squire could not marry my sister and could give you the life you should have. Eventually we moved on, but I never forgot her. The next time we happened by this way was almost a year later. One night Isabella and Kata slipped into our camp and brought you with them."

Delilah interrupted the tale right there. "It is not true. I am my mother's daughter."

"Nay, that is what you have been told and assumed was true. I begged Kata to return to her gypsy roots, yet she refused. She still loved the squire you see, and did not regret doing what she did to keep his love. I did not have the heart to take you away from her, so I made her promise to bring you to see me each time I happened by."

She leaped from her seat in denial. "Nay! You are a gypsy and therefore nothing but a trickster. Why should I believe your tale?"

He took her hand in his. "I loved Kata, still I let you be, for your destiny was the life of a titled princess, not a penniless wanderer."

Anger at their betrayal pricked her words. "I am no princess, but the unwanted daughter of a squire. My affliction is a curse for my illegitimate birth, and my punishment a life worth less than yours."

"No. You have been gifted with a sight beyond your eyes. It is not a gypsy curse, it is a special gift." He smoothed her locks from her cheek with a tender caress. "You were your mother's greatest joy and it nearly broke her heart when you went blind. Like you, she thought it her evil deed that caused the sickness, and she came to me for a spell to reverse your fortune. But we have no such powers. We have nothing more than a few healing potions, nothing to help in a case like yours." His voice took on a deep sadness. "All I could do was gift you with a wise guide and a talisman of protection to help you through life."

"Jester?"

"Yes, I could only hope he would see you through the dangers coming your way. Then Isabella died. Kata and the rest of the gypsies were banished from the squire's land."

Delilah sank down on the bench in shock, and for some strange reason a sense of well-being. If the tale was to be believed, she was free from any decree to marry the baron. Even though her sightless eyes didn't deter him, her less than noble heritage would. What was to stop her from following the gypsies?

"Take me with you." It was obvious her request took Deagan by surprise by the moments of silence ticking by.

At long last he cleared his throat. "You have a life, and I promised your mother I would not take you from it."

"Then why did you bring me here?"

His sigh hung heavy in the air between them. "I am selfish, I suppose. I wanted to know you and for you to know the truth about your heritage before I die."

"Do I not get a choice in my own life? Am I so disabled I cannot make the decision whom to marry and where to live?"

"Ah, my little jewel, you have the true gypsy spirit. What about Baron March?"

Repulsion filled her at the mention of the man's name and she tried to hide it, yet she suspected her uncle would see her true feelings. "He was a choice between the lesser of two evils, or so I thought."

"I suspected as much when I heard. You are right, however; the marriage cannot be."

Startled she lifted a brow. "How would you know? Have you met the baron?"

"He has dealt a few crooked blows to our people before. But no, I have not met him myself. I do know where he came from and his blood must not mix with yours. I feel your heart, my little jewel, and have seen your plight in Delinka's crystal ball. I had only to meet you and discern your heart to make my decision."

"I do not understand."

"Come, I will introduce you to Delinka and she will explain it to you, for she has the power to see things in the orb." Taking her hand he led her away from the heat of the fire. They walked a few short feet before he placed her hand on a smooth wooden rail and helped her climb two steps. "This is Delinka's wagon, come inside and sit."

Delilah allowed him to lead her through a narrow door and then took a seat on a low wooden stool. Her hands came to rest upon a table before her covered in a rough fabric.

A deep, feminine voice greeted her from across the table. "Greetings lost one. I am Delinka, drabardi of our tribe."

She jumped when cool, wrinkled fingers grasped hers in a light grip. "Drabardi?"

"Teller of the past, present, and future."

Delilah squirmed in her chair, unsure why the person behind the kind voice made her uneasy. "I do not know you."

"I have seen you many times, Delilah, in my dreams and in the fog swirling in the crystal ball."

"I do not understand."

"I know. Here, let me show you." The fingers moved her hand to rest upon a smooth, cold, rounded surface and then covered hers to keep it there.

Delilah gasped when the surface began to warm as if heated by a flame. "I am blind and cannot see what you seek to show me."

"Shh, you've no need for your eyes; open your mind to see."

A strange sensation spread from her hand upward. The tingling raised the tiny hairs on her arm and her head became foggy. A picture of a little dark-haired girl playing with a tawny colt swam before her mind's eye. *No, not playing, dancing together around a large flickering fire.* Her long, curly locks flowed around her to the beat of a drum and the singsong of a violin. A beautiful golden-haired woman danced with the child and the colt, laughing and twirling to the music. *It's her. My mother. The one I called mother, anyway.* A smaller, dark woman smiled from the shadows where she sat cross-legged on a colorful blanket clapping. *Kata, the nursemaid. My real mother.*

The image faded and before Delilah could withdraw her hand another took its place. This time she saw the fair woman lying still on a bed. A man sat beside her, clutching her hands in his. She knew without being told this was her father. The dark-haired woman hovered in the background. The man turned, anger and grief hardening his stare. He pointed to the door and then pushed Kata from the room.

Again the image faded, this time replaced by one of the baron arguing with her father on a stormy cliff top. She gasped, recognizing the nightmare that came to her each evening. The rain poured down drowning their words, distorting her sight. Without warning the baron leaped forward, tackling the squire about the knees. He went down and the two rolled over and over, until a blow left her father prone. He reached up as if pleading. The baron stumbled to his feet, lifted his fist to the sky in defiance and then kicked the squire over the edge of the cliff. Delilah couldn't help the cry of horror escaping her lips, echoing in the confines of the wagon. The image blurred as if the rain became harder, and then cleared to show two figures dancing around the flames of a roaring fire. A woman with flowing black hair, loose about her shoulders and violet eyes, half closed in pleasure, and a tall, clean shaven man. She knew in an instant it was her and the earl. They danced with wild abandon, caressing each other in a way that was sensual and provocative. The cold fingers lifted her hand from the surface of the crystal ball, causing the images to come to an abrupt halt.

"Wait," she cried out.

"That is enough, little jewel, for you are unused to seeing."

Delilah clutched her still tingling hand to her chest. "Why? How is this possible? Is it some sort of gypsy trick?"

"Drink this." Delinka pressed a wooden tankard into her hands. She raised it to her lips and drank the warm mulled elderberry wine. When she finished, the drabardi took the cup away and led Delilah to a low, narrow cot. "Sleep now, let your mind rest, and all will be clear when you wake."

The idea of sleep overtaking the confusion in her mind didn't seem possible. Nevertheless, she slipped beneath the rough wool blanket and drifted off into an exhausted slumber almost before her head hit the pillow.

Chapter Nineteen

Tyrone rode the baron's horse, following the pony's odd track. Jester kept going in the same direction, jogging along as if he knew the way. There was not much else to do but continue following the pony. Eventually they came to a barn an hour ride from Westpoint land. A young man looked up and paused where he pitched straw from a stall into an unhitched wagon by the door.

"You there," Tyrone addressed the fellow. "Have you seen a blind woman with this pony or on foot last eve or this morn?"

The young fellow glanced at the pony and the stable master before shifting his sleepy gaze back to Tyrone. "No, my lord. I'd remember seeing such a sight fer sure." He swatted at Jester when the pony made to push past him into the barn.

"Are you sure?" Tyrone dismounted, handed his reins to his companion, and followed Jester to the doorway of the rough lumber building. He peered inside. It looked like every other barn, littered with straw and smelling of manure.

"Quite sure, my lord." The young man shooed away the pony and turned back to forking dirty straw.

Tyrone stepped away. "If you should come across Miss Daysland, send word to Westpoint immediately."

The boy nodded and continued with his chores.

Tyrone remounted his horse and directed it to the main road. "Come, Jester."

The pony hesitated, but then trotted ahead until he came to the cottage. With a shake of his head and a defiant nicker he stopped at the door. At the sound it swung open, a middle-aged woman framed in the doorway. Her eyes grew round at the sight greeting her, a frail hand going to the shawl cast about her thin shoulders.

"Good day, mistress." Tyrone tipped his hat. "I am searching for a missing woman. Have you by any chance seen a blind woman in these parts today?"

Her eyes darted to the young man, now leaning on his pitch fork scowling, before swinging back to the pony. "No, my lord. I'm jus' a washer woman, see. I wouldn't know of any noble woman wandering the forest in a storm."

Tyrone pondered her for a moment and then looked to the sky. He didn't mention Miss Daysland was out in the storm. "The weather is fine this morning, mistress." When she blanched and looked at her feet, prickles of wariness rode his neck. Something was not right, he could feel it.

A thin, tight lipped man rode into the yard on a sorry nag, leading a sturdy workhorse. His eyes narrowed before he stepped from the swaybacked mount and snapped his fingers to the lad. "Can I be of service, my lord?" he asked, handing the reins of his horse and the work animal's lead to the boy.

"I have come in search of a young woman who is missing." Tyrone took note of the red ribbon entwined in the mane of the feather-footed draft horse. The ribbon was the trade mark of a gypsy bred animal.

"I've not seen any such girl, my lord. I've been gone these past days to purchase a new plow horse." The man shrugged.

"A fine specimen to be sure. Where did you purchase such a sturdy beast?"

The man darted a look at the woman. "At the market in Wyatt Town east of 'ere, my lord."

"Really? The beast has the look of fine gypsy stock."

"Could be." The man shrugged again. "There were some traders there. I've no qualms buying from the gypsies, long as I don't get cheated out of my coin."

Tyrone leaned forward. "Did he cost you a goodly sum?"

"Enough. 'Twas a good harvest this year and time to retire Samson there." He jerked his head toward the shaggy, brown mount. The animal, little more than bones and skin now, wandered in the rickety corral beside the barn.

"Indeed." Tyrone tipped his hat and called to the pony, "Jester, come."

The pony whinnied again and shook his head. The woman shrank back from the door and flapped her shawl to encourage the animal from her doorstep.

Tyrone rode forward, casting a curious glance inside the one room hovel. Nothing inside seemed out of the ordinary, he noted, leaning down and clipping a lead on the disobedient pony. "I bid you good day. If you come across the miss in question, please send word to Westpoint. There will be a handsome reward for her safe return." He rode off down the narrow, weed-filled lane, with the pony and stable master.

The stable master leaned forward in his saddle to peer at the ground. "Fresh wagon wheel ruts with the tracks of a large-footed horse between them. Someone else besides us also visited the farmer since the night's rains."

Had the baron been here? Tyrone studied the tracks. It was possible, yet he didn't think the baron would come looking for Delilah in a farm wagon. A saddle horse, too, it appeared had followed the wagon.

He glanced over his shoulder before they rounded the bend. The farmer was standing there, watching him. Did the man steal the workhorse? It was possible, he supposed, however sure-fingered gypsies would be more apt to pilfer an animal. It was more likely the horse was of gypsy stock since it did display ribbons of the wanderers brand in its mane. He turned to the stable master. "Have you heard of any roving bands of gypsies in this part of late?"

"Not around Wyatt, my lord, though they do pass through this way each planting and harvest I hear tell."

When they reached the main road the wagon tracks turned right. On a hunch Tyrone followed them to the junction of a field. The tracks crossed the open grass and entered the forest beyond. It couldn't hurt to see just who visited the farmer this morning.

The coolness of the shaded forest path was an inviting shelter against the early heat of the sun. The groom reined in his horse and pointed at the tracks in the soft dirt. "Look here, my lord. There are two sets of wagon tracks, one coming out of the wood and one going back in, followed by a single horse. A top of them, as if at a later time, are the tracks of a single horse, this time leading a heavier one behind. It is clear the farmer lied. The workhorse was not purchased at Wyatt, but most likely at the gypsy camp itself. Why did the farmer lie?"

Tyrone's gut told him it was something to do with Delilah.

In time the trail led to an open clearing where it appeared a number of wagons had been circled around the smoldering remains of a campfire. The gypsies were here as little as two hours ago, he was sure.

The groom looked to the sky. "It is getting late, my lord. Perhaps we should go back to the baron's to see if he has yet to return. Mayhap he has found her, or can shed some light upon the situation."

Tyrone nodded. He could follow the gypsy tracks all day, but what was the point if they didn't have Delilah? He wasn't even sure they saw her at all. The stable master did have a point. They were better off returning to the baron's to seek information. He pivoted his horse and returned the way they came.

Chapter Twenty

Delilah rolled over on the narrow cot, accustoming herself to the sounds and movement of the wagon. Could she believe the visions from the crystal ball? If they were true, Augustus was a murderer. Now that she was married to him, it stood to reason he would do her harm if he discovered she knew the truth, though he already attempted to, either deliberately or otherwise, in his drunken state. Tyrone was back in London, and no longer in charge of her well-being either, so who else could she turn for help? No one would believe her. They already thought she was noddy. On the other hand, Augustus wouldn't find her here. She would be safe with the gypsies.

The gentle sway and jingle jangle of the horse's harness lulled her into a sense of peace. Or was it the answers she found in the crystal ball? No matter, she was a gypsy. Her place was the earth, sun, and the stars above. She wouldn't be shunned by these people, her people, unlike the nobility that looked upon her with pity. She was safe here for the moment, until she could figure out how to foil the baron's plans.

The wagon slowed, turning in a wide arc before coming to a halt. She sat up and swung her feet to the floor as the door opened.

"Ah, my niece, you are awake." Deagan's voice carried a hint of a smile to it.

She smiled back. "I feel refreshed. Different somehow."

"The visions will do that to you. Here, Delinka has asked me to give you some clean clothing. When you are changed we will talk."

A bundle of soft cloth was pressed into her hands. When the door shut with a click and her uncle's footsteps retreated down the steps Delilah hurried to change. When she was dressed in the clean garments she followed the edge of the bed to the wall and then the door. She opened the door and hesitated.

"Let me help you," Deagan's dry, leathery hand grasped hers and guided her down the narrow steps to the ground. A light breeze tickled her cheek, the cool dampness of the air giving tell it was evening. Crickets chirped and people talked and laughed in hushed tones, as if afraid to disturb the creatures of the night. A nearby owl hooted as Deagan led her to a wide stump to sit. She arranged her skirt and paid attention to the sounds of the people setting up camp, unharnessing horses, and striking the flint to start a fire.

"Tonight we will rest, for tomorrow people will come from miles around to trade, buy potions from us, and be entertained."

Delilah sighed with wonder. "How I wish I could see the festivities."

"Tonight you shall feel it."

As if on cue a drum began to beat, accompanied by a tambourine and the soft whine of a violin. The music began slow and sensual, increasing in tempo until Delilah couldn't resist tapping her foot to the rhythm. "I wish my pianoforte was here."

Deagan clasped her hand and drew her to her feet. "Nay, my little jewel, feel the music in your veins and let your body play the way your fingers once did." Spinning her around, he put his hands on her hips in a most unsettling way, and despite her protests moved them to sway to the music. His breath tickled her cheeks when he whispered in her ear, "Feel the music, allow your body and soul finally be free, my little jewel."

Delilah relaxed and moved to the music. The beat invoked a flurry of movement, and when Deagan's hands slipped away she lost herself in the visions her mind conjured. Bright skirts, flowing blouses, and unbound hair swirled across her mind's memories. Yes, this she saw before and could remember. Abandoning all pretenses, she pulled her hair from its remaining pins, unmindful of where they scattered, and lost herself in the music, twirling and gyrating as free will took her.

The heat from the fire warmed her flesh, the snapping and popping of the sparks igniting her passion. With reckless abandon, she threw back her head, raised her hands to the heavens, and twirled around and around. A fever took hold of her body as the skirts of her gypsy dress flapped and waved in the heat of the fire. Never would she view music, dancing, or even her own body in the same light as before. She danced until her breathing came in labored gasps and then made her way to the stump just outside the circle of warmth, glad for the coolness of the night bathing her heated flesh.

"You did well, Delilah."

She couldn't contain her smile. "It felt wonderful, uncle."

He patted her hand in understanding. "You will fulfill your destiny soon, under the waxing moon."

"My destiny?"

"Ah, yes, my little jewel. You see, each one of us dies and comes back in another form, but keeps ties to that familiar to them during their last life."

"Are you referring to this thing called reincarnation?"

"Yes, some call it that. Each one of us is re-birthed many times during our soul's journey. Did you never wonder about your connection to Jester and the mark you both bear?"

Try as she might Delilah couldn't recall a mark. "I am afraid I do not understand."

"Have you never wondered about the stone around your neck?"

She touched the stone, now warm from the heat of her body. "What about it?"

His fingers brushed hers and fumbled with the stone lying between her breasts. "I have removed the lock of Jester's hair, now feel it."

Returning her fingers to the stone she rubbed it between her thumb and forefinger. A deep groove she never knew was there before made a ridge under her thumb. Brows bunched in concentration, she traced the lines until she thought she could make out the pattern. "A quarter moon?"

"Yes. It is the same mark Jester carries on his head and the same as the birthmark on your hip."

Pursing her lips she tried to recall Jester the last time she saw him many years before. A vague remembrance of a white crescent came to mind. Yes, it did look like a moon. "What does it mean?"

"Ah, Delilah, you have so much to learn about who you truly are." His sigh was heavy. "He bears the mark of the quarter moon, the phase to which you were both born. He was created to be your guide, protector, and anchor to this world. He is also a part of your past."

"I do not understand."

"The moon is your talisman. Jester and you were mates in your last lives."

Confusion and disbelief made her wary of his words. "I do not believe in such nonsense."

"Never say you do not believe in fate, for fate is what brought you here to me."

Delilah snorted. "If Jester and I were mates in our last life, then why have I come back as a human and he an animal?"

"It is not for us to understand but rather to accept. I believe he came back in his animal form to atone for his sins in the past life."

"Then my blindness is a punishment for some sin I, too, committed in a former life?"

"No. Your blindness is a gift, not a punishment. Jester was given to you as a guide to protect you until you could fulfill your destiny as a drabardi and marry the son of the great Romo baro. Delinka showed this to me just this morning in her crystal ball. I knew it was true when you asked to come with us."

"Who is this Romo baro?"

"The Romo baro is the leader of all the gypsies. You are destined to be the greatest drabardi of all time. The one who will guide our people into a time of power and freedom."

What was he saying? Was she supposed to be some kind of witch? "I am afraid you are too late, uncle, for I am already married to Baron March."

"That is no marriage. It was not done under the harvest moon and no bride price was paid to me. Besides, it is a sacrilege and can never be."

Delilah stood, her hands shaking with anger. "I have no wish to marry or become something of your fantasies."

"Are you still pure?"

Heat flushed her cheeks. "I…yes, but it makes no difference."

"It does; one must be pure to marry under the harvest moon, for when the moon waxes comes a time of great fertility. The harvest moon will be upon us in five days. After which you will be who you were recreated to be. You will carry the future great leader of the gypsy people in your womb."

The man is noddier than a wet goose. Does he truly think I am some gypsy form of Mary, a vessel to birth the great gypsy messiah? It is impossible. I am a blind woman of illegitimate birth, nothing more. Nothing less.

Chapter Twenty-One

"I want answers!" Tyrone elbowed past the startled butler into the baron's study.

Augustus looked up from his paperwork with a scowl. "I say, Lord Frost, a very undignified way you have to come calling on another gentleman."

"Spare me the pomp and ceremony. Where is she?"

The baron paled and then blinked. "Who is it you are referring to, sir?"

Tyrone fixed him with a withering stare. "You know damned well whom I am referring to. Where is Miss Daysland?"

Baron March's gaze slid away from Tyrone's. "If you are speaking of the baroness, she is right here where she belongs, of course."

"A lie. I came this morning to return Jester to her and she was nowhere to be found, nor were you. Care to explain?" Tyrone leaned across the desk itching to throttle the man.

"A minor misunderstanding I assure you, Frost. My lady wife is back above stairs safe and sound where she belongs. Why I only just returned home from begging her forgiveness after a small faux pas this morning." He poured a glass of brandy from the decanter at his elbow and offered it to Tyrone, who refused with a shake of his head.

"What kind of insult did you give her?"

"Ah, I simply refused to allow the smelly beast…uh, pony, of hers admittance to the house. I cannot have the creature soiling my expensive Turkish rugs now, can I?" The baron downed the glass of spirits himself.

Tyrone grunted. "The animal is housebroken."

The baron waved a hand. "Yes, yes, so the lady did explain after I went and apologized on bended knee. A rather touchy girl it appears, and I shall be most careful not to wound her pride again."

"What happened to your head?" Tyrone sat and gestured to the thick white bandage encircling the baron's head.

"Oh that." Augustus touched the wrapping with a cautious finger. "I admit to getting a little foxed last eve, sir, you know how it is. All the excitement over the wedding. Tripped over my own feet like a clumsy ox and banged my head on the corner of the Chippendale table over there."

Tyrone followed his motion, glancing at the table by the door. A plausible story he supposed, yet one which didn't sit right with him in the least. "Send for her so I may inquire after her satisfaction over her new marriage and inform her of Jester's return."

The baron fidgeted with his limp neck cloth. "I am afraid she is resting at present. All the excitement of our nuptials and the um…lack of sleep last night." He winked.

Tyrone grimaced at the man's poor taste in his reference to the marriage bed. "Indeed. Well, tell her I have returned Jester and am anxious to remove to London this day." He stood to go but paused. "Oh, be sure to keep a sharp eye on your livestock; gypsies are afoot again. I found evidence of their camp in Westpoint woods this afternoon. It seems the farmer down in the hollow purchased a new workhorse of gypsy stock, though he refused to say the truth about where he purchased it."

"Dually noted, Frost, thank you and be assured I will keep my new lady wife close at hand for her protection."

"See that you do." Tyrone nodded and saw himself out. He was in no hurry to return to London. Maybe he should avail himself of some gypsy hospitality. Some spirits and a bonny vixen in his bed for a night might help him forget he allowed Delilah Daysland to slip through his fingers. He shook his head to rid himself of the thought and returned to the baron's stables. After commanding his coachman to continue on to London alone, he checked once more on Jester. The pony paced and kicked at his stall door. The animal's restlessness concerned him, until it occurred to him Jester was not used to being confined. With a final pat he mounted his borrowed horse and headed for the town of Wyatt to find lodging for the night. Tomorrow he would return to London, gypsies forgotten, and resume his boring, predictable life. It was time he asked Miss Deval for her hand.

• • •

Augustus rang for the butler as soon as he spied Lord Frost riding down the driveway. By the time the sour faced man appeared, March had already formed a plan. "Benton, take that wretched pony from my stables at once. Go find the farmer in the hollow and pay him to deliver the beast to the gypsies for whatever they will pay for it. He is always willing to do a discreet favor. Be sure to be skimpy on pay for I'll not share more than a pittance of the profit."

The butler nodded and left.

"A mess. A terrible mess it all is," Augustus mumbled, pouring himself a glass of spirits. "Blasted gypsy wench. She will cost me everything rightfully mine with her antics. I will squeeze the life from her neck before the week is out."

Chapter Twenty-Two

Delilah touched the smooth orb with caution.

"Go on, my child. You have the gift of sight."

Warmth spread through her fingertips. "I am afraid, Delinka, afraid of what I will see."

"The truth cannot hurt you."

Tiny pinpricks of light danced before her sightless eyes until they converged to form a picture of a man, astride a horse, leading a pony. Her instincts told her it was Tyrone with Jester. *He is searching for me.* The image blurred and a farmer leading Jester replaced it. The man watched the ground as if following tracks. *Who has Jester and where is he taking him?* Thick forest closed in on the man and pony until they faded from view. Out of the dim a new scene took shape. A man smoking a pipe lay naked on a cot, great clouds of filmy white circling his head, making it impossible to see his face. A dark-haired woman leaned forward and kissed him. The smoke dissipated and Tyrone favored her with a lazy grin. An overwhelming sense of abandonment filled Delilah. *He loves another.* He was not for her, nor her for him. Her place was here. She let her fingers slip from the orb. *I am home.*

"Have you seen enough for now, chosen one?"

With firm resolve she nodded. "Yes, Delinka. What else are you to show me today?"

"There is much for you to process. First you will learn to see without the crystal ball." Rough, wrinkled hands took Delilah's and dropped a number of small articles in her palm.

Delilah rolled the smooth objects between her fingers, puzzling them. *Nine beans?* "What do I do with beans?"

"Have you a coin?"

She fished in her pocket and pulled out a shilling.

"Good, put it in your hand with the beans. Shake them gently and then let them fall as they will on the table."

Delilah closed her fingers around the objects, shook her fist, and dropped them to the table in a series of clicks.

"Ah, very interesting."

"What is it?" Delilah leaned forward, wishing she could see what the drabardi could.

"Your path is not as simple as Deagan thinks it is."

"What do you mean?"

"I see a curved line and four beans in a square."

"What does it mean?"

Delinka took a deep breath, letting the air hiss from her lips. "It means your path connects with one of a man. The curve means there is a problem with the path Deagan believes you are to take."

A man. Tyrone or Augustus? Perhaps both. Delilah sighed. "As I told my uncle, I am already married to the baron by the earl's, or rather the king's, command."

"Not to be. Deagan is wrong. You belong to this other man. Your paths were chosen when you were reincarnated."

"No!" Delilah shook her head. "I will not go back to the baron, he is ill."

"It is not the baron I've seen in my crystal ball, but a tall, dark-haired man. He is searching for you. He is the one with whom you belong."

Delilah held the tears welling up in check. "Lord Frost wants to do his duty to the king, nothing more. He does not want me."

The seer grunted. "Things are not always as they appear."

"Maybe not, but to one who is blind they are usually as they sound."

Delinka sighed. "Delilah, you must free yourself of all your bitterness if you seek to see your true potential."

Pressing her lips together, Delilah refrained from telling the elder woman just what she thought of this potential. Warm fingers curled over hers.

"Come, today I will begin to teach you the secrets of our magic."

Delilah rose and followed the drabardi from the wagon with a hand on the shorter woman's shoulder. "Do our people really possess magical powers?"

The woman chuckled. "Of a sort we do, for we know the magic of the land and mysteries of the water that help us tread this world. Others could harness the powers as we have but are too limited of sight to see it."

The idea of a blind woman being able to see better than one with perfect vision amused Delilah. They walked for a few short minutes before the woman stopped and knocked on what she assumed by the sound was another vardos, as the gypsies called their wagon homes. The door opened with a creak. The heavy musk of flowers, herbs, and other musty plants drifted from within, and she wrinkled her nose at their pungent odor.

"Is this her?" a man with a gruff voice inquired.

"Yes, this is Delilah."

"Huh." The step creaked. "She does not look like anyone special. I pictured someone more mysterious of stature, not a simple blind girl."

Before Delilah could defend herself the old woman hissed, "That is because you do not possess the gift of sight, Belcher. We all have talents, just stick to yours and teach her the healing things she needs to know."

"Do not chastise me, old woman, or I'll put a hex on your head."

The drabardi snorted. "As if you could. Get on with your teachings for we are running out of time before the harvest moon."

She removed Delilah's hand from her shoulder and placed it on a smooth wooden rail. "Belcher will take care with you, or he'll answer to Deagan and Galer."

Delilah smiled, liking the woman despite her rough demeanor. "Who is Galer?"

"He is your betrothed."

She stood there stunned as a whisper of fabric and the tinkle of bracelets heralded the drabardi's retreat. "My betrothed?"

"I see the old woman did not tell you everything. How like her." The man grunted. "Well, come in. I have much to teach you in little time it appears." The door creaked and the wooden rail under her hand quivered. Without much enthusiasm, she made her way up the steps.

It was stuffy in the little wagon, almost too warm. The room lingered with dozens of different smells to tease her senses. Her hip bummed against a table, and she reached for a corresponding stool when Belcher commanded her to sit. "What is it you are to teach me?" she asked, seating herself and resting her hands on the rough tablecloth.

"Our people are mostly lautaris and drabardis, or as others call them, musicians and seers. However, I am a chivihani."

"What is that?"

"According to the rest of the world, a witch."

She fought to keep from showing any alarm. "You cast spells and hexes then?"

He laughed, the sound malevolent and heavy in the closeness of the room. "When need be. Mostly however, I am an herbalist. I have studied the land and its plants. There is nothing I cannot cure with Mother Nature's supplies. Well…almost nothing."

She removed her hands from the table and clenched her fingers in her lap, lest he see them shake. "Why must I learn these things from you?"

"You and your betrothed will be the great Romo baros of our clans. To be a great leader one must know all of our ways."

Exasperation rose unbidden in her. Once again, someone was deciding the path of her life for her. Nothing changed. "What if I do not want to be this Romo baro's wife?"

He snorted. "As if you have a choice."

"I thought a gypsy's life was free and simple."

"Nothing is truly free, except nature itself. Now pay attention, for you have much to learn. We will start with teas. There are many teas for different ailments such as coltsfoot, red clover, dandelion, and liquorice root…"

Delilah sniffed the plants and herbs he held under her nose and concentrated on learning as much as she could, since it appeared she was left little choice in the matter.

• • •

"Oh, Uncle Deagan, the material is of the finest quality my fingers have ever felt." Delilah smoothed the cool silk beneath her hands. She smiled, trying to imagine the color and cut of the splendid gypsy sash she now wore pinned with a crescent moon-shaped broach. The scoop necked peasant blouse was light against her skin and the flared cotton skirt soft against her naked legs. It was freeing and comfortable, much like the simple servant's dress she wore the nights she slipped from Westpoint manor.

Her uncle chuckled. "It pales in comparison to your beauty, my dear."

Delilah rose on her tiptoes to press a kiss upon his whiskered cheek. "Thank you. I shall truly feel a gypsy now."

"Nothing makes me happier than to hear you say that." He patted her hand. "Come now, the festivities will begin soon, and I want you to render every London buck senseless with your dancing. In those violet and pink hues I'm sure there will be no man who can resist you."

With a soft giggle she accompanied him outside to the raised platform he built just for her. The pianoforte he'd traded his wealth of silver and gold for would be the stage for her musical numbers and dances popular with all the men who happened into their camp, in search of an evening of entertainment and trade. A sense of peace filled her as she pulled down the veil to conceal her face and settled her fingers on the keys. Never could she remember feeling so free, happy, and alive. Perhaps she was the gypsy future.

Chapter Twenty-Three

"Trust me, Tyrone. There are far more lively entertainments to be had tonight at the festival than you have ever seen in any London club."

"I am not interested in such pursuits, Perry, and I promised to call upon Miss Deval this evening."

Perry shook his head, tutt-tutting his friend's lack of interest. "You are getting far too serious over that filly, Ty. If you are not careful, you will find yourself trussed up and delivered to the altar like a Yule log at Candlemas, my friend."

Tyrone shrugged. "Perhaps it is time I settled down. Mayhap it will keep the king from sending me out on any more fool's errands."

"Are you still pining away over the blind recluse you married off?" Perry shook his head. "She is happily wed and out of your hair. Forget about her with a comely lass under the stars tonight. I assure you it will be an experience you will never forget." Perry leaned closer. "Those wenches can do the most wondrous things you can imagine with their bodies."

"I am sure they can, but I am to call on Miss Deval, as I said." Tyrone waved him away. "It is time I press her for a nuptial date. She has been leading me on for the last year. I will insist she accept my suit, if she will have me. Though damned if I can understand her parents insisting she make up her own mind."

"What is not to like, my dear boy?" Perry slapped him on the back. "The little chit's parents will be overjoyed at the prospect of their daughter marrying into the Merryweather name, even without a fortune. I dare say you are going to be a very popular man in the political field before long and what woman would not want that kind of prestige? I say ignore the chit's wants and go directly to her parents like any normal beau would do."

"Yes, yes, so I have been told." Tyrone grimaced and then downed the last mouthful of sherry in his glass. "I suppose I better be going; no time like the present."

"You do not sound very thrilled about the prospect, for a man going down on bended knee and proposing to the woman of his dreams."

"Is there such a thing?"

Perry raised an eyebrow. "A woman of dreams? I am told there is. Why are you entertaining the idea of marrying the woman if you do not want her?"

Tyrone sighed and pushed his glass across the table. "Do not get me wrong, Miss Deval is pretty and schooled in the arts as any well-bred lady should be, but..."

"But?" Perry signaled for the waiter to refill both their glasses.

"She just does not...I suppose I am fond of her. I am just not in love with her, you see." Tyrone sipped a second glass of sherry a passing serving wench set before him, trying to stall the inevitable.

Perry snorted. "Love is for mistresses my friend. Show me a man in love with his wife and I will show you a heap of misery underneath it all. If Miss Deval is a true lady, she will kindly turn a blind eye to any affairs you have. It is the best of both worlds: a lady to grace your parlor and a willing whore to warm your bed."

"I suppose you are right." Tyrone finished his drink and got to his feet. "Perhaps I will join you after I press my suit tonight. Maybe a night of revelry will be just the celebration I need to bolster my courage before I talk to Lord Deval on the morrow."

"Atta boy." Perry stood and slapped his friend's back again. "I am on my way then. Go past the park to the green down the main road and you will find the caravan." Tipping his hat at a jaunty angle, he grinned and strolled out of the gentleman's club, whistling a bawdy tune.

Tyrone shook his head, dropped a couple coins on the table for the drinks, and then headed for Lord Petagrin's ball, where he was sure to meet up with the young Miss Deval.

• • •

Milling couples crowded the ballroom. Laughter tinkled with the clink of crystal and the light strains of an orchestra. Tyrone lifted a glass of golden champagne off a passing serving man's tray and pushed his way through the heated bodies. A glimpse of shimmering black hair caught his eye through the swirling crush of bodies and he turned in that direction. Miss Simone Deval was surrounded by an impressive array of London's young swains. In the flickering candlelight her hazel eyes looked almost violet as she simpered and smiled at those vying for her attention. As Tyrone paused to watch, he was struck by the sudden realization his continued fascination with the young miss might have more to do with her startling resemblance to Miss Delilah Daysland than with her own charms. He studied her. Perhaps it was the opposite and his former charge looked so much like Miss Deval he was attracted to her. No, Miss Deval's abundant breasts, aristocratic nose, and limpid glances were unlike Delilah's subtle curves and witty persona. How could he have been so blind? What was he doing here? Oh hell and damnation! Why not marry the chit? So she was a substitute for Delilah; what did it matter when the one he loved was married to another?

Screwing his courage to the sticking point, he made his way to Miss Deval's side. "Good evening, my dear."

Her gaze slid away from the gallant young buck spewing prose to her loveliness. When it settled on him he was struck by the cattiness in her gaze, so unlike Delilah's honest stare. "Why, good eve, Lord Frost, how delightful to see you here." She turned to the tall man beside her. "Have you met Lord White?"

Tyrone nodded to the young man beside her. "Nice to see you again."

"Lord Frost," the young man returned. "I trust there are no hard feelings between us."

"No, should there be?" Tyrone lifted a brow, puzzled.

Miss Deval laid a possessive hand on the young man's arm. "Oh dear. You have not heard the news?"

Lord White cleared his throat. "Terribly inconvenient, Frost. Perhaps a private conversation on the veranda is in order, old chap."

Old chap? Tyrone fought to keep his expression neutral. *The fellow is a few years younger than I, but really…* "Anything you care to say to me can be said where I stand, White."

"Well, I would prefer any ah…confrontation and challenges to a duel be kept—" he glanced around the room with a slight smile, "confidential, as it were."

"For God's sake, White, what is it you think will so incense me to such violence?" Tyrone glowered at the man, his ire already pricked.

Miss Deval placed her hand on his sleeve and favored him with a coy smile. "What Lord White is trying so tactfully to tell you, my lord, is I have agreed to a match between he and I."

Tyrone blinked. Instead of anger or disappointment at such news, he was unaffected. In fact it was if an unseen weight was lifted from his shoulders. "Well, I suppose congratulations are in order then." He bowed. "May you be happy as the Duchess of Berkley, Miss Deval." With a shake of his head he turned on his heel and marched through the crowd.

Chapter Twenty-Four

Tyrone followed the path to the gypsy camp. He should be angry at Miss Deval's betrayal. At the very least he should have wanted to fight for her. Now her fortune was out of his grasp, and he found he couldn't care less although it seemed he would have to start the long process of finding another wealthy heiress to woo. He grimaced. He didn't want another wealthy, well bred, boring woman. He wanted Delilah. It was too late now, he'd thrown away his chance…or did she? No matter. It was not as if he could go back and change what was done. Music floated on the light breeze as he dismounted and tied his horse to the rope picket strung between the trees as a courtesy to the evening's guests. Tucking the sack of coins into the inside pocket of his fox coat where it would be harder for sticky fingers to lift, he followed the sounds of revelry. Rounding the bushes he paused, surveying the scene of wild abandon before him. Men of all classes lounged with gypsy women, many engrossed in various stages of lovemaking right there on the grass. Others danced in the moonlight or found other delights among the brightly painted caravans holding potions and elixirs of all kinds. His attention swung to a raised platform where a veiled figure played a pianoforte, shrouded in mist and smoke. The haunting passage carried a familiar tune, with an unquestionable gypsy flare that made him want to tap his toes.

A buxom beauty sidled up to him and ran her fingers in a coy gesture down his shirt front. "Come looking for some entertainment this eve, my lord?"

Perhaps a diversion was needed to rid his mind of Delilah and Miss Deval. He nodded. "How much will it cost me?"

She smiled. "It depends on what you desire. A dance would cost you little, but an evening would be most enjoyable for the both of us, I assure you."

"Perhaps we should start with a dance then, to help me decide."

"I am Nadia." She lowered her gaze and held out her hand. When he pulled a coin from his pocket and placed it in her open palm she stepped back. After testing it with her teeth she grinned and tucked it into the pouch hanging around her neck on a silver chain. "Sit down on the pillow, my lord, and make yourself comfortable."

Tyrone lowered himself to a small pile of cushions and reclined, propping on one elbow to enjoy the show. His gaze fixed on the gypsy as she began to sway in time to the music. Her lithe limbs waved and stroked the air in a rhythm all her own as she undulated in a most provocative way. To any other man her dance would have been enticing enough to warrant a paid evening under the full moon, but not for Tyrone. Though he found the practiced movements entertaining, his manhood stood down. By the time her dance was done Nadia was clothed in a beaded half chemise of sorts, showing off her sensual naval and silk drawers jingling with tiny silver bells sewn to the fringes.

With catlike movements she crossed to where he sat and lowered herself beside him. "Are you well pleased, my lord, with the dance?"

"I am well pleased."

She grinned and then lowered her hand to cup his manhood through his breeches. Her brows bunched and a tiny pout formed on her lips. "You do not seem well pleased. Perhaps your man-root needs a more physical kind of stimulation?"

He shrugged, permitting her fingers to stroke and squeeze him. "Maybe."

She narrowed her eyes with a sly smile. "For another coin I can make your manhood sit up and take notice of my charms, I'm sure."

He regarded her through half-closed lids. "Hmm, in a more private place with some comforts I suppose."

A musical giggle slipped from her lips. "As you wish, my lord. Come." Rising to her feet she tugged his hand until he rose and followed her to her wagon.

Ducking through the low door he glanced back at the platform. The gypsy musicians still played minus the mysterious figure on the pianoforte. Giving it no further thought, he closed the door and prepared to enjoy his purchased entertainment.

•••

Tyrone lay back against the pillows, flipping the brightly colored blanket over his groin as Nadia rolled from the platform serving as a bed. He raked his gaze down her naked buttocks, as she stepped to the table to light the reed of opium between her lips. His limp member remained unaffected as she turned and strolled back to the bed. Why didn't Nadia have the powers to make his appendage dance to her gypsy tune? He should be attracted to her, she was beautiful and willing, yet he had no interest in bedding her, something that had never happened to him before. His conscience told him Delilah was the root of his disinterest but he brushed it aside. He came here to rid himself of her memory not wallow in regret. He glanced at Nadia as she drew on the opium and frowned. After they smoked the dream stick he doubted she would be much pleased with his even more flaccid tool. He took the stick from her moist lips and put it to his own. The sweetness of her lip balm still lingered as he took a deep drag and blew the smoke in a lazy ring about his head.

After a few puffs she took back the reed, kissed him, and drew on it with a smile. "You should have your fortune told while you are here, my lord. Perhaps it will put you in a better frame of mind."

He gave her a lazy smile and took back the reed. "I do not believe in such frivolities. Besides, I am sure it would cost me, and I detest wasting more coin this night. "

Her brows bunched in displeasure. "Let it be my gift to you for a most enjoyable night to come."

The drug eased the tension in his body, leaving him little will to oppose her whims. "As you wish, seductress."

After turning down the lantern to make him more comfortable, she wrapped herself in a long shawl and stepped from the caravan.

Tyrone lay back and stared up at the water-stained roof, watching the rings of smoke rise and then dissipate. He wondered how Delilah was these days. Did she think of him? Was she happy with the baron? Perhaps she was with child by now. His lip curled on one side at the thought of a tiny, dark-haired cherub with violet eyes. He closed his eyes with a sigh as the drug made his lids heavy and his limbs limp. A light breeze caused his skin to prickle as the door opened and closed. *Ah, the fortune teller is here.* Not bothering to speak or open his eyes, he held out his hand. After a moment cool, wrinkled fingers took his in a gentle grip. A light expelling of air was the sole sound as the woman placed his hand on a smooth orb. After a few minutes of silence, the fingers holding his tensed.

A loud gasp made him chuckle. "Have you found some incredibly heinous accident about t' befall me in your crystal ball, oh great seer?"

"No, my lord."

"Get on with it then, I'm waiting for my fortune t' be told." He grimaced at the slur in his voice, the opium pipe not unlike the effects of liquor.

"As you wish, my lord."

Yes. As I wish.

She sighed, making him smile. "You are searching for someone. A woman."

He shook his head. "I was. I thought she skipped out on her marriage but found she returned to the arrangement of her own accord."

"You have yet to solve the mystery you started."

"So?" He shrugged. "There is no need, the woman in question is no longer in danger."

"You are wrong."

Grunting he opened his eyes and stared at the woman. "She is where she belongs."

The old gypsy stared into the crystal ball beneath his hand. "No. She is close."

With a snort he sat up. "Wrong, she is in the countryside. You will have to do much better if you expect me to fall for your tricks." Swinging his legs over the side of the platform unabashed by his nakedness, he yanked on his trousers and boots. "Good eve, madame." Shrugging into his shirt he left. *Heathen, tricksters the lot of them.* He stomped through the camp. Why was he angry? Was it the effects of the pipe? He suspected it more to do with Delilah and the ridiculous sense of misplaced guilt nagging him. She was married and there was naught he could do about it.

"Ty! I hoped I might find you here."

Tyrone stumbled and looked up to find Perry getting ready to mount his horse. "I was just leaving."

"Good, we shall ride together."

"Suits me fine, Perry. I've need for an escort home."

Perry peered at Tyrone and chuckled. "Ah, a little bliss you indulged in, eh?"

"Yeah." Tryone grinned and then frowned as a shaggy brown pony who looked like Jester wandered past. "Bloody hell. I must be high as a three layer cake, for now I'm seein' blasted ponies."

Perry laughed. "Come on, let's go."

Tyrone climbed aboard his horse taking one last look at the encampment, but the pony was nowhere to be seen. Next time he visited the camp he wouldn't indulge in the smoke, he promised himself as he rode away.

Chapter Twenty-Five

"Damn the bitch!" Augustus slammed his fist on the desk. "Three long weeks and there is still no sign of her. Where could she be hiding, Benson? She will ruin it all, all I tell you."

The butler poured another glass of port and pushed the glass across the desk to his employer's hand. "I've no idea, sir. It is as if she just vanished like one of those no good gypsies."

Augustus spat a wad of tobacco into the hearth and then took a deep swig from the glass. "It is all their faults, damned infernal vagabonds. The squire is nothing but a man-whore—but for him I would gain all that should be mine by birthright."

The butler didn't bother to point out the idiocy of his complaint, for the former squire was both the means and the end to the baron's claim to the vast fortune at Delilah Daysland's fingertips. "There is naught between here and Westpoint except two farms and the woods, unless she went the other way without the pony."

"We have looked everywhere," Augustus fumed. "People are starting to talk about her absence."

"No more than before I am sure, since she was a hermit of sorts before your marriage."

Augustus scowled at the butler. "For my purpose she must be dead, or at least imprisoned here, not missing."

"How hard can it be to find a blind wench?"

"Not hard, you would think, especially without the blasted pony." Augustus gulped down the rest of the port and rolled the glass between his stubby fingers. "I have already raped the

Westpoint storerooms, fields, and stables, but without the wench I cannot lay claim to a penny of the estate's coin or land."

Benson shook his head. "She wouldn't have run had you not gotten foxed and tried to force yourself on her."

"And I suppose your idea of honoring the bargain and leaving her to fend for herself at Westpoint would have been better?"

The butler shrugged. "I've no qualms about relieving my needs between a blind wench's thighs for the right coin. Even so, getting her in her cups would have made it easier and her none the wiser."

"Think you I want her bastard to claim what is rightfully mine?"

"That is the pot calling the kettle black, if you ask me." The man grinned.

Fury threatened to escape the baron's controlled demeanor. "The accident of my birth was just that, an accident. Allowing the likes of you to defile my own deliberately would be idiotic, to say the least."

"Not as bad as siring your own inbred bastard."

This time Augustus lost control. "Shut your gob, you daft bastard, before someone hears! Besides, I have no intention of letting her live long enough to give birth to any gypsy spawn. A neat trip down the stairs would have rid me of any guilt after dousing my lust with her. How did it all go so wrong?" he whined more to himself than anyone else.

The butler shrugged. "Perhaps you should offer up a reward for her safe return?"

"Bah! And waste more money on the wench? I already spent a ridiculous amount feeding all those useless villagers at my sham of a wedding celebration."

"Careful, those who you insult are the ones doing your dirty work for you."

Picking up the half empty glass, Augustus flung it at the butler. "Get away with you! You are doing naught but annoying me with your prattle." He grunted with satisfaction when the butler skulked out the study door and closed it behind.

It shouldn't be this complicated. Killing his father was the result of anger, disgust, and determination to get what was his by right. Augustus should have been able to claim the estate, but the old whore monger refused to acknowledge him for fear it would cost his precious gypsy spawn a suitor. No woman, even one as pathetic as her, deserved his money and land. He needed to find the wench before she ruined everything, but where was she?

Running a hand through his hair, he growled. He needed sleep, but even in rest his deeds haunted him. Storms and blood were the things of his nightmares, often concluded with visions of a demon pony whose human eyes pierced him with accusation. Was he so far gone in dementia a simpleminded beast took on a supernatural essence? No, he was sane, sane enough anyway. Maybe it was some gypsy curse heaped on his head for the death of his sire. He shook his head and poured another drink. Now he was being absurd.

A log rolled from the pile aflame in the hearth, sending a shower of sparks and uncanny apparitions to dance about the room. For the briefest second he thought he saw the pony's eyes flickering in the coals. It alarmed him enough that he sloshed the liquor he was pouring over his hand. It wouldn't due to waste his means of a dreamless sleep. *To hell with the glass.* Turning from the fire he raised the bottle to his lips and proceeded to drink himself into oblivion.

Chapter Twenty-Six

"My lord, there's a maid here to see you."

Tyrone looked up from the paperwork he was trying to concentrate on and ran a hand through his hair in exasperation. The butler shifted his weight and gave him an apologetic grimace. "A maid? Tell her I am not hiring and send her on her way." He rubbed his eyes, regretting the night spent with the gypsy girl and her "magic" pipe.

"She's not here for a job, my lord. The woman insists on speaking to you about Miss Daysland...I mean the baroness."

"Very well, send her in." Tyrone tidied his papers and set them back in the file on the desk.

A young lady was shown into the room and the butler closed the door behind her with a soft click.

Tyrone frowned. "You are Teresa, are you not?"

"Yes, my lord." The maid curtsied with her eyes fixed on the floor.

He leaned back in his chair. "What can I do for you?"

She glanced up, an uneasy expression crossing her face. "I wouldn't have bothered you, but I have nowhere else to turn."

With a sigh he leaned forward and propped his elbows on top of the desk. "What kind of trouble are you in, Teresa?"

Her eyes widened. "Oh no, my lord. 'Tis not what you think. 'Tis not me in trouble, but Miss Daysland. At least I think she is in trouble, though I can't say for sure and Miss Daysland bade me promise not to tell. I would not even think to betray her confidence either, my lord, except under the most dire of circumstances. Not very becoming in an employee—"

He held up a hand to put an end to her rapid commentary. "Slow down and get to the point, please."

She cleared her throat and took a deep breath. "Well, Miss Daysland thought to fool you, not to be dishonest you understand, but to protect herself."

He nodded, growing more and more annoyed by the moment with his own inability to understand what she was referring to. Impatient, he waved her on.

The woman's hands fluttered, washing each one with the other in distress. "She made a deal with the baron where she would have a marriage in appearance and return to Westpoint the day following her nuptials. You see, the baron has need of her inheritance and didn't really want to marry her, either. You know how it is with nobles, my lord."

He rolled his eyes. "Yes, yes, get to the point. Why is it you believe Miss Daysland is in trouble?"

"Well, it has been weeks now and Miss Daysland has not returned to Westpoint. I sent a note to inquire of her plans with no response, and then went to the baron's myself to ask after her, but was turned away by the butler who said my mistress was too busy to see me. 'Tis not like her to turn me away, my lord, not like her at all."

"I see." A bad feeling welled up in the pit of Tyrone's stomach. In truth Delilah was very close to the household servant, and the idea she would snub one of her favorite maids was disconcerting. "Rest assured I shall inquire after the baroness."

The maid wrung her hands. "I should not like it to be known I betrayed my mistress, my lord."

"I will keep your visit in the strictest confidence."

She nodded and then hurried from the room with a shaky smile.

Tyrone pondered the situation as the door closed behind her. *I knew it. Delilah agreed to the marriage too readily after all the fuss about having to give up her freedom.* Opening the desk drawer he rummaged for the file on Westpoint. Was Delilah back at the baron's as he claimed, or did something happen to her the night of the storm? If she wasn't there, then where was she, and why would the baron lie about it? The matter of the missing property still remained and the strange note in the squire's log about the baron and Delilah. He scanned the papers and then rang for the butler.

The man poked his head around the corner of the door within moments.

"Tell my valet to pack and send for my coach. I am returning to Westpoint on business," Tyrone instructed.

• • •

Tyrone leaned forward and peered out the window at the baron's manor as his coach rounded the bend. Though at first glance the estate appeared more prosperous than before, there were still subtle signs of disrepair. Shakes loosened from the recent storm littered the ground around the barn. Whitewash peeled on the ornamental gazebo, perched amid the overgrown roses in the circle of the carriage turnabout. He jumped down from his conveyance and marched to the door. It opened after he pounded on it twice.

The pasty faced butler peered at him. "May I help you, my lord?"

"Yes, I would speak with the baron immediately."

"I am afraid it is not possible, my lord, but I shall tell him you came 'round."

Tyrone glowered at the man. "Is the baron here?"

The butler tossed a hasty look over his shoulder. "He asked not to be disturbed, my lord."

"Disturb him."

"But—" The man jumped back when Tyrone stepped forward.

"Now." With the flat of his hand Tyrone shoved the door open and entered the baron's foyer. "March!"

The servant trailed in his wake as Tyrone stomped down the hall in search of the baron's study. "See here—"

"Stubble it! I will speak with the baron now, and God help him if he should give me the wrong answers to the questions I have to ask." He located the study and flung open the door.

The baron looked up from his spot behind a desk cluttered with papers. "Frost? What brings you here?"

Tyrone crossed to the desk, leaned forward and placed both palms on it to look the baron in the eye. "Where is my ward?"

The baron blanched. "I beg your pardon? Are you referring to my *wife*, Frost?"

"She is exactly who I am referring to, March." The baron was afraid. The tension in the air, the sweat beading on his brow, and the nervous tick of his right eye all gave testimony to guilt and deceit.

"She is resting right now. Do you have a message I may pass on to her, on your behalf?"

"No. I will speak with her now."

The man paled even more, his complexion taking on a ghost-like hue. "It is not possible."

Tyrone grabbed him by his shirt front. "Why not?"

"She's gone," Augustus squeaked, his eyes growing huge when Tyrone twisted the shirt tight around his fist.

"Where?"

Augustus shook his head. "I have no idea, been searching for her for weeks."

"Why?" Tyrone released the baron's shirt and thrust him back in his chair. "What did you do to make her run and hide?"

"Nothing." The baron rubbed his neck where a red mark remained from the shirt's pressure. "We had an agreement. She was to return to Westpoint Manor the day after our nuptials."

"She did not arrive there according to her maid, who came to you when she became concerned. Why did you lie and tell the servant her mistress was here?"

"Well, I did not want the whole land to know I misplaced my wife. I've no notion to be a laughingstock because the girl flew the coop and is playing games."

Tyrone's anger got the better of him and he slammed his fist against the desk, turning a stony stare on the baron. "Did it ever occur to you Delilah might be in grave danger? That she is not playing a game? You have wasted weeks nursing your own imagined wounds and left a blind woman out there, all alone, to whatever horrors might befall her! If anything has happened to her, rest assured, I will hunt you down and hang your scrawny body from the cliffs for the vultures to pick!" With a growl he stormed from the room and back to his waiting coach. Delilah was out there somewhere. Alone.

• • •

The night at the gypsy camp nagged Tyrone's mind as he trotted along the road from Winningham to the neighboring village of Four Corners. Was there any truth to the old woman's prophecy? She claimed Delilah was nearby. Where would he find the gypsies now? In exasperation he thumped his fist against his leg. His gelding skittered to one side in protest. Without thinking, he tightened the reins and patted the animal. He'd spent the last week looking for Delilah without a single sign of her to be seen. How could she have just disappeared without a trace like a gypsy? *Like a gypsy...* His mind returned to the fortune teller's prophecy.

Who better to ask than the nomads themselves? Perhaps in their journey they came across a blind woman and a fuzzy guide pony.

At a crossroad he turned his mount east to the place the gypsies camped a mere week ago. Would they follow the road to the next town, or keep to the fields where they could poach livestock to feed themselves? Urging his horse on, he cantered down the wheel-rutted trail.

The sun was dipping below the horizon when he came to the outskirts of Four Corners. He rode down the dusty street of the little village in search of the local tavern. If gypsies were about, someone there would know. A narrow band of light shone across his path, the disjointed sounds of peasant music filling the air. He reined in his horse and dismounted, tying the trusty animal to a hitching post beyond the fringe of light. Wisdom warned him to check the pistol at his hip before arranging his great coat to cover it. One never knew what could befall him in a small town tavern.

He stepped into the establishment and scanned the dim room through the haze of smoke. Voices hushed when the handful of merchants and townsmen inside turned to stare. With a curt nod Tyrone made his way to the bar and ordered a tankard of ale. The patrons resumed their merrymaking and he turned to the tavern keeper as the man set a foaming tankard of amber liquid in front of him. "It is not busy in here tonight, I see."

The man nodded, the ends of his thick mustache bobbing where they curled toward his nostrils. "Thanks t' them crooked gypsies camped out by the brook. Thieving varmints! I had t' drop the price of me ale jus' t' be sure I have customers. Gettin' so a man can't make an honest livin' these days."

Tyrone nodded in pretend sympathy. "Yes, a scourge to be sure. The gypsies are down by the creek, you say?"

The tavern owner nodded before moving off to pour another round for a group of men plying cards at a far table. Tyrone finished his ale, tossed a couple coins on the counter, a tad more than the cost of the drink, and left. Mounting his horse, he turned it in the direction of the bridge leading out of town. He crossed over it, almost missing the little used trail off to the right on the other side. Wagon tracks marred the grass following a path that wound around a grove of oak trees along the creek. The smoke from the campfires reached him before the wild music floating on the cooling night air. The customary rope picket was strung across a row of walnut and oaks, waiting for visitors to secure their horses.

A smile stirred his lips when he spied a young gypsy boy sneaking between the handful of mounts tied there, searching any saddle bags for loot he could abscond with. No one could say the vagabonds didn't earn their reputations as cheats and thieves. When the boy spied him, he leaned up against a tree as if he were staring at the stars.

Tyrone dismounted and crooked a finger. "Water and secure my horse, boy, and there will be a shilling in it for you when I return."

A greedy smile spread across the boy's face as he hurried forward and took the reins to Tyrone's horse. "Yes, mi' lord."

With a glance over his shoulder to be sure the boy was doing as he bid, Tyrone stepped through the grove of trees and into the gypsy encampment. A violin wailed through the night, accompanied by the jingle of a tambourine and the soft tones of a pianoforte. The painted wagons were circled around a large fire pit wherein blazed crackling flames, bathing the clearing in a soft golden glow. A few gypsies in colorful costumes lounged around it, waiting for customers he supposed. As he stepped into the circle of light his attention was drawn to the group of musicians who huddled beyond in the shadows of the trees. The veiled woman he recalled from his last visit was again perched on the pianoforte bench, swaying in time to the notes dancing from beneath her fingertips.

Turning away he sought the elder woman who granted his fortune the last time, but didn't see her among the reclining vagabonds.

A young woman sauntered up, pressed herself against him, and stroked the lapels of his coat. "Have you come for an evening's entertainment, my lord?"

He disengaged her fingers and held her aloof. "No, I have come to see the fortune teller."

She smiled. "Delinka is busy. Perhaps you would like your fortune told by fresh eyes, yes?"

He frowned. "I would prefer the same seer I saw last."

"I understand, my lord, but perhaps try this one, and if you are not happy you may see Delinka tomorrow eve for no charge."

One seer was as good as another he supposed, as long as he was tempted to believe in such things. "Fine, lead me to this new seeing one."

She affected a pretty pout. "First you must have a drink and a dance with me until she is ready for you."

Without bothering to ask why the fortune teller needed to be ready for him, he followed the girl to the fire. As the song faded she handed him a skin of wine. He lifted it to his lips and drank his fill of the potent concoction as a new song began, this time without a pianoforte accompaniment. Instead of dancing with the gypsy, he flipped her a shilling to perform for him in the light of the fire and sat on the grass. The song seemed to go on and on. His eyes grew heavy and his limbs relaxed. The effects of the drink, he concluded when the song ended.

"Did you enjoy my dance, my lord?"

He got to his feet. "Very much, but all the same I am ready to meet this new seer of yours now."

Disappointment creased her features, but she led him away from the fire toward one of the wagons.

• • •

Delilah seated herself behind the small table and sought the orb of glass, her eyes into the past, present, and future. It warmed and tingled as it did each time she touched it. Before it could show her something of herself, she dropped her hands to the silky tablecloth to rest on either side of it. Tonight would be the first night she would see the future for a paying customer. The idea both thrilled and terrified her. She was careful to ensure the wagon remained shrouded in darkness, with only a meager candle illuminating the room. Her blindness was not something she was prepared for her customers to see, not yet anyway. What if something terrible showed itself to her? What if she detected nothing at all of the person? When the door to the wagon opened with a squeak and cool draft, she took a deep breath to still her nerves. She was grateful for the veil concealing her face as someone sat down across from her. A fresh minty scent mixed with horse sweat tickled her nose making her sneeze.

The stool across from her creaked under her guest's weight. "Bless you."

She froze, hands pressed to the table top. *It cannot be. What is he doing here?* Should she run? No, it was improbable she would escape because he sat between her and the door. Her only hope was to try and disguise her voice to fool him until she could get rid of him. She licked her lips and held out her hands. His warm fingers slid across her smooth palms. A sense of foreboding filled her as she placed his digits on the crystal ball. *Why did the orb not show him coming? A warning would have been nice. Will he seek to have me returned to Augustus if he discovers my identity?* Tingling spread into her hands and she was distracted by a cloudy image overtaking her thoughts.

Tyrone loitered in a crowded ballroom, talking to a beautiful woman. She turned away and held out her hand to another, younger man who tarried by her side. His face tightened with anger before he stalked away. *Tyrone's suit was rejected.* She wasn't sure whether to be pleased or saddened by the outcome. He was free to marry her now, if he wanted to. She bit her lip. *I am not free.*

"You are quiet. What do you see?"

"Shh," she whispered. The scene faded and formed a picture of him mounted on a horse, searching the ground as he rode, as if looking for something. *Me. He is searching for me.* Hope flamed to life in her breast.

A soft nicker broke the tension. Delilah groaned. Why did the pony pick now, of all times, to wait at the wagon door for her? She was never ready to head back to the dancing fire before the lute sounded. He knew the new routine by now.

"Where did you get this animal?"

Panic surged through her and she clutched the cloth draping the table. If she answered him her identity in the darkened room would be given away. If she remained silent would he leave?

"I demand to know how you came by this pony, madame."

A chill crawled down her spine at his lethal tone. *I am trapped.* There was no way to get past him and slip out the door. Uncle Deagan coming to her rescue would be her single hope to keep the earl from dragging her back to the baron. She groped for the flint, struck it, and then patted the table until her fingers touched the rim of the second candle holder. A tiny sizzle, a flicker of warmth, and the mild sweet smell of the beeswax candle filled the room. She removed her veil. "He is mine, my lord."

The stool scraped and then clattered to the floor as the wagon rocked. The idea of Tyrone now towering over her, gave her pause. She fell silent under the force of his rapid questions.

"Delilah? What are you doing here? What kind of game are you playing? I have been scouring the country for you."

"I have been here, with my family, the whole time." She swallowed and forced a smile to her lips. "Jester, fetch Uncle Deagan."

"Uncle Deagan?"

She nodded and listened for the soft tread to confirm the pony left on his errand before answering. "My Uncle Deagan's command brought me here."

"I thought you have no family? Why would your uncle bring you to live among the gypsies?"

"Sit down, my lord." Delilah waited until the stool creaked under his weight before continuing. "I am guilty of deceiving you but not for the reasons you think. I thought Augustus would help me. I was wrong…"

Chapter Twenty-Seven

Delilah rubbed her temples. "Why not just arrest Augustus?"

There was a slight pause before Tyrone answered. "It would simply be your word against his. We have no evidence of his treachery. There is a possibility of having the marriage annulled however, as long as he…as long as you remain…"

Face burning, she said the word he seemed unable to. "As long as I am still a virgin?"

He cleared his throat before answering, and she grinned. "Yes, a virgin; however, I do not believe it will stop the baron from trying to get what he wants."

"If the marriage is annulled, he has no grounds to take control of my inheritance or estate."

"That is not exactly true, according to Deagan."

She pursed her lips. It seemed clear to her, but why did he hesitate? "What do you mean?"

Deagan shifted across from her. "I should tell her, my lord, not you."

"Tell me what?"

Her uncle's rough fingers cradled hers. "The night you were conceived was also the night the baron was."

"I do not understand."

Deagan sighed. "The night was crystal clear and warm. The wine, music, and opium flowed free and plentiful the night of the harvest moon. Your father and adoptive mother were not the only visitors to the encampment that night. The former baron and his wife were there, too. Your father and the baroness had been in love many years before and they indulged themselves freely, as did many couples."

Delilah gasped. "Are you saying my father slept with the baroness and Kata, and they both conceived that night?"

"Yes."

The world she constructed around her shattered and fell in jagged shards before her beliefs. *Augustus is my half-brother.* Disgust rolled in her stomach, pressing a wave of nausea to the back of her mouth. With effort she forced it back down, gulping great mouthfuls of air.

"Delilah, I am sorry. I did not know, or I would not have forced his suit on you. I was only trying to do what the king asked of me…I am sorry," Tyrone repeated.

She shook her head and turned away. "I…I do not know what to think, say, or…who I am."

"Delilah—"

"Please, Tyrone, just leave me alone. Please."

Deagan squeezed her hand. The stool beside him creaked. A draft of heavy air brushed the loose tendrils of hair about her cheeks as the door closed behind the earl.

"My little jewel, I did not mean to shock you. I wanted you to know your heritage. Perhaps I was wrong to tell you. Perhaps I am just a selfish old man. Please forgive me."

"I forgive you. Please, Uncle Deagan, leave me be. I need to be alone."

"I understand." After a soft kiss on her forehead he was gone.

A weaker woman might have cried, wailed, and uttered vengeful curses down on all their heads; instead Delilah examined the bits of her past with a calm detachment. *I am a gypsy's daughter, wild and free. I no longer have to conform to a normal life.* In exchange for annulling the marriage, she would give it all to Augustus with her blessings. *Let him be known as the bastard child of the squire. Let him face the shame of their pasts.* No longer would she be

Delilah Daysland—she would just be Delilah, the seer. She could disappear into a world of music and lightness with no cares. There was nothing stopping her from walking away. *Except Tyrone.* No, not even he would want to stop her, for she was a bastard, illegitimate and impure. An earl didn't marry the likes of her or fit into her new world.

Light strains of music carried through the open window. She was a gypsy and it was time she started living as one. Determined to embrace her heritage, she dressed in the dancing outfit trimmed by tiny jingling bells, pulling the soft blouse down to rest just across the tops of her breasts. *Time to live life to the fullest.*

Taking a deep breath, she opened the door and whistled for Jester. By the time she stepped onto the soft grass he was there, brushing against her tinkling skirt. "Fire, Jester. Tonight I shall end everyone's pursuit of me. No longer will anyone dictate my future but me." After tonight she would no longer be pure and therefore unfit to marry the Romo baro's son.

Her heart was pounding by the time they reached the fire. She could sense many eyes on her and fixed a bright smile on her lips to conceal her nervousness. Jester stopped near enough to the fire its welcome warmth caused her flesh to prickle. Someone pressed a thick wineskin into her hand as she released his harness. The pony moved off and she raised it to her lips, drinking long and deep of its sweet, potent nectar. It would give her the courage to dance with abandon tonight.

"Delilah?"

She waved Tyrone away and held out the half full skin. His fingers brushed hers as he took it, sending a little shiver up her spine. "Drink." She would have her way with him tonight, before she said good-bye. At least she would have a little of him to carry near her heart when he left to find a suitable wife. The music began to pick up tempo and she raised her arms to move with it. Closing her eyes she allowed the music free her soul, flashes of memories and bright colors stimulating her senses. Around and around she spun, undulating her hips and swaying in the most seductive way she could imagine.

A hand touched her shoulder. "Delilah, I think you have had far too much to drink."

She shook off the Tyrone's hand and pressed herself to him, smelling the wine on his breath. "Dance with me, my lord."

"You should come sit down."

Shaking her head, she rubbed her body down his, grinning as his manhood swelled and hardened between them. "I want to dance, my lord. Dance with me."

"Delilah, this is most unseemly."

"No, 'tis not, my lord. I am a wild gypsy, willing to share what is mine with you this night." On her tip toes she reached for his head, pulling it down until her lips found his. He remained stiff and passive under her caress until she ran her tongue across his lower lip. With a groan he opened and devoured her mouth with his. Her hands roamed his body and he began to move with her to the music. His response, the seductive moan of the violin and the sense stimulating skin to skin contact inflamed her desire. Heat seeped into her core, becoming like hot molten lava. She wanted him too much to be shocked or afraid when he pulled her from the fire. Kissing and stroking, they made their way into the shadows. When he made to pull away she wrapped her arms around his neck and explored his mouth with her tongue. With a strangled groan he eased her down onto a soft blanket.

"This is wrong."

"No. I am a gypsy. I choose to make love to you as is my right according to my birth," she lied. To prove her claim she maneuvered herself to straddle his hips. With a boldness she never before possessed she ran a hand over the bulge in his breeches, inciting another tortured groan from him. "I claim you as mine tonight to do with as I please."

"Delilah—"

"Shh. No talking," she whispered against his lips, her fingers stroking his rod beneath the restricting cloth.

"You are an innocent…don't know what you're doing…"

She chuckled against his lips, rubbing her heated core against him. "Nay, I know full well what my touch does to your body, for it is the same for me."

He groaned. Arms shaking, he buried his head against her neck, licking and nuzzling her heated skin. "I want you so much, to feel you, taste you, and make you cry out my name."

She sighed as his lips brought forth the most delicious sensations while he cupped her breast and teased the sensitive nipple through the thin fabric of her dress.

The simple gesture took her breath away. For many moments she was unable to string together any coherent words. Then he slipped his hand beneath her skirt and replaced his teasing fingers with his lips at her breast. "Oh, good Lord!"

He chuckled against her moist nipple and she arched against him with a primal howl of desire. "Make me your gypsy lover this night, Tyrone, for I can wait no longer."

Chapter Twenty-Eight

The steady pounding of his head and paper dry mouth was a rude awakening. Even more annoying was the cheerful prattle of a bevy of birds somewhere in the trees above. Tyrone rolled over on the soft blanket with a groan and reached for Delilah. He patted the emptiness once harboring a warm, sensual body. Frowning he opened his eyes and sat up. A whiff of smoke curled from the charred remains of the bonfire. *Where is everyone?* Alarm quickened his pulse. Rubbing the sleep from his eyes he scrambled to his feet. Did he dream it all? He sorted through the hazy moments of the night before. *Delilah, a seductive temptress, rousing my body into a state of almost painful eagerness.* Groaning he willed his manhood, already rising at the thought, to be still. How could he have permitted her to have her way with him? Disgust turned his stomach worse than the over indulgence of wine. *How could I have seduced such an innocent?* He frowned. Did he seduce her or had she seduced him? *Oh, what does it matter? Either way the king will have my head for it. What kind of cad have I become?* When he would have stomped across the clearing in search of his horse, his abused noggin protested. Putting a hand to his head, he took care to move slowly and carefully.

The animal was as he left him, dozing in the shade of the row of trees. After tightening the cinch, he stepped aboard and turned it back onto the path along the creek to the road. He needed to catch up with the gypsies. They couldn't have gone far. First he must see Delilah's marriage to the baron annulled, and then he could marry her. It was the right thing to do whether she saw it or not. If she refused him he could at least see she returned to her rightful place at Westpoint Manor until he could court and woo her properly. If she desired romantic gestures then that is exactly what he would give her.

Half slumped over the saddle in misery, he caught up with the slower moving wagon train a little over an hour later. Delilah rode on Jester next to her Uncle Deagan. At Tyrone's approach the older man excused himself and kicked his heavy horse into a lumbering trot.

"Delilah, what are you doing?"

She jumped, but kept her sightless gaze fixed above her pony's head. "I am traveling to the next town, my lord. It is what gypsies do."

He slowed his horse to keep step with her shorter legged pony. "You are not a gypsy."

A light snort escaped and her lips thinned. "I choose to be now."

Tyrone resisted the urge to sigh. Her mind was set; he could tell by her ramrod stiffness and determined expression. How was he to change it? It occurred to him he didn't have to change her mind. She was obligated to do as he commanded by the king's order. He glanced at her out of the corner of his eye. Perhaps attempting to force compliance out of her was not the way to go, at least not if he wanted her to marry him.

"Delilah, we need to talk about last eve."

Her jaw tightened. "There is nothing to talk about, my lord."

"I beg to differ. And please, could we drop the formality?"

"I see no reason for informality, my lord."

With growing frustration, he tempered his reply. "After sharing our bodies with each other last eve, formality seems fairly hypocritical, do you not think?" He reached down and grabbed Jester's headstall, yanking the pony to a halt.

Her sightless scowl unnerved him as no other able one could. "Why am I suddenly good enough to warrant such a display of gallantry now? Is it because your betrothed jilted you? Am I just a consolation prize?"

His breath hitched in his chest. "How did you know?"

"I am a seer, remember?"

"For God's sake, Delilah, you are not a gypsy and possess no such fictional powers."

"Did you not seek a seer last eve? If so, then how can you claim not to believe? Besides, I saw her jilt you in a ballroom."

His senses reeled at the idea she could have seen what she claimed. "I was not seeking a vision last eve, I was searching for you."

She turned her face away. "Why?"

The words he wanted to say clogged his mouth, choking him into silence. He cleared his throat. "I did wrong by you and wanted to make it right. I was concerned for your welfare."

"You can see I am fine, now unhand me."

"You call this fine? You are living the life of a penniless beggar."

She leaned forward, seeking his hand, and then snatched it from Jester's head stall. "Just because I choose a path different from yours does not make my life any less."

"I did not say it does—"

"I will never be like the rest of the ton; I never fit in their world and I never will. Now leave me be!" she kicked Jester into a rough lope, but not before he noted the tears in her eyes.

"Delilah!" He groaned as pain stabbed his liquor muddled head.

Helpless, he allowed her to go. What could he say? She believed she didn't fit into his world, nor he in her new one. Was she right? Perhaps he should just annul the marriage and leave her be with her own people. It seemed the kindest thing to do...for her anyway.

• • •

"To what do I owe this unpleasant visit, Lord Frost?"

Tyrone kept his face void of emotion and seated himself in the chair across from the baron's desk. "I have come to bring you the papers requesting an annulment of your marriage."

The baron scowled. "Now why would I want to do that?"

"Trust me, you want to." Tyrone fixed him with an unwavering stare.

"You cannot dissolve my marriage, Frost. Only I or my wife can."

"I know, March, which is precisely why you are going to be a gentleman and sign the paper." He placed it on the desk.

The baron leaned back in his chair with a smug expression. "Again, why would I want to do that?"

Tyrone sighed. "I know your secret, March, and I am sure the king would frown on incest." The slight tick starting in the baron's right eye was not lost on him.

"What nonsense are you uttering now?"

"Deagan told Delilah and I everything."

"You think the king will take the word of a lowlife heathen over me? You must be jesting."

Tyrone leaned forward. "Think you the king will doubt *my* word?"

Augustus blanched. "You have no proof."

"Would you like to wager on it?"

The silence hung in the air so hot and heavy, Tyrone couldn't breathe as he waited for the baron to call his bluff.

"Take your so-called proof to the magistrate, Frost, and leave me be. Be forewarned if you do though, for I think the king would not like you taking advantage of your vulnerable ward." The smug look returned to the baron's face.

How was it possible the baron could know what happened between him and Delilah the night before? Tyrone pinned the baron with a venomous glare. "To what are you referring to, March?"

The baron shrugged. "Since you arrived to look after the welfare of Miss Daysland, it has been rumored she has been repeatedly harmed and her estate pilfered away."

"Are you accusing me of something?" Tyrone leaned forward until he was scant inches from the baron. Only the desk checked his urge to throttle the man.

The baron met his gaze with a dangerous one of his own. "I am saying the king might find it a disturbing coincidence, do you not think?"

"The thefts began long before I arrived on the scene."

"According to you. How do you explain the attempts on my wife's life since you arrived?" The baron's gaze narrowed, his lips twisting into a grotesque sneer.

"How do *you* explain them, March? Which of the Westpoint staff is in your employ?"

With a smirk the baron stared him down. "Why, they all are, or are you forgetting all my wife's possessions are now mine?" His smirk broadened. "All of her possessions."

The urge to strike him was almost overpowering. He drew back his fist and then let it fall at his side, knowing no good would come of it. *Oh hell, it will feel good.* Before he could talk himself out of it, he punched the baron in the face. Blood spurted red and warm onto the desk before the baron covered his nose with his hand. Ignoring the baron's howl of indignation, Tyrone stalked from the room.

Chapter Twenty-Nine

There was an unmistakable feeling of festiveness in the night air as they made camp beside a shallow lake. According to Delinka, many other tribes were there, including the Romo baro and his son. Tonight she would meet the man everyone expected her to marry—and her mother. She both dreaded and looked forward to it. There were so many questions she wanted to ask Kata. But first Delilah would have to weather the anger directed at her once the gypsies discovered the truth of her betrayal. The door to her vardos opened, the light scent of smoke, herbs, and elderberry wine filling her senses. The smells were warm and comforting somehow, perhaps because it was part of her world these days.

"Belcher and I have come to ready you for your night, Delilah."

She shook her head as Delinka entered with the gruff herbalist. "There is no need, drabardi, for I am not the pure one required to fulfill the gypsy prophecy."

"Nonsense, I saw it in my visions. I have brought your ceremonial dress to wear."

A silky material was placed in her hands. "Your vision was wrong, Delinka, for I did lie with a man just this week under the stars. There will be no ceremony."

The woman gasped. "It is not true. You are afraid of the future and making up reasons to avoid your path."

"No!" Delilah dropped the material and turned away. "I laid with the earl the night he found me here."

Belcher released a groan filled with frustration. "Why, Delilah, why?"

"I do not want to be this leader of the gypsies. I want to be free."

Disappointment and disapproval colored Delinka's rebuke. "Your only hope of freedom laid within the circle of power. You have doomed yourself and our people."

Delilah's shoulders slumped. "I saw no other way. I do not love this Romo baro's son."

Delinka's heavy sigh hung in the air. "I should have seen the truth. It was the man in my vision, wasn't it?"

Without turning around, Delilah nodded. How angry would Uncle Deagan be when he learned of her betrayal? Would he cast her from the gypsy camp? Where would she go then? What would she do?

"Belcher, fetch Deagan."

Cringing, Delilah tried to ignore the finality in Delinka's command as the door closed. "I would like to see my mother."

"First you must say your piece to your uncle."

Delilah sat down on the narrow cot with a groan. She dreaded the meeting to come; there was nothing she could do except explain her position and hope her uncle would have mercy on her. In the tense silence she waited, washing each hand with the other. Just when she thought she couldn't stand the drabardi's quiet accusation any longer, the door opened. A heavy tread climbed the steps and stopped in front of her.

"What have you done, Delilah? Why have you forsaken your people?"

The heated anger sizzled from his censure, singeing her emotions. "I am sorry, uncle, but I saw no other way. You are wrong about my path in this life, for I have seen it for myself in the crystal ball."

"No! You see what you want to see!"

"Nay! I see with my heart, uncle, not with my useless eyes. I cannot be what you want and need. I am Delilah, not the great drabardi."

He slammed his fist down on the table, the vibrations covering the tremble of her hands as she flattened them against the surface. "You are right. You are no drabardi. You are nothing but a chuvihani!"

Hurt at his accusation of witchcraft tightened her chest. She had alienated the only family left in her world for what? For a man who didn't love her? Would her mother forgive her? The mother she never met.

"There must be a way to make things right." The desperation in Deagan's voice carried in the little room. "Belcher, lock Delilah in her wagon while I gather the Romo baro, drabardi, and counsel to decide what is to be done."

Delilah lowered her head to her arms as they shuffled out and the door closed behind them. A key scraped in the lock to confirm Deagan's order and then all was quiet. *Have I made a grave mistake?* There seemed nothing to do except wait and see what her punishment would be. Would their decision be swift and harsh or would they make her wallow in this discomfort for hours? It seemed the latter was the most promising as she cradled her head and waited. Yawning, she closed her eyes. Sleep eluded her of late, due to her own guilt she supposed. Though now was not the best time to slumber, she gave in to her body's need for rest.

...

Through her dream foggy mind a haze of noise began to register. Screams and the pop-pop of gunshots roused her to attention. *What is happening?* The thunder of hooves shook the little wagon as horses passed. The shrieks of women and children intensified until it was all she could hear. Terrified, she lurched to her feet and stumbled to the door. Jerking on the latch she found it still locked. "Deagan? Blecher? Delinka? Someone please let me out!"

A woman's scream, more blood curdling than the rest, echoed just outside the closed door. The hair on the back of her neck stood on end. Were the tribes at war over her betrayal? "Uncle Deagan!" Frantic, she pounded on the rough door with her fists, not caring when they bruised and became embedded with slivers. Her mind conjured all manner of evil outside happening to her family. After what seemed like hours the screams and gunshots faded. A strange roar took their place. Something snapped, crackled, and popped. The sounds grew louder and louder. Delilah sank to her knees in front of the door, exhausted. Cradling her injured hands in her lap, she leaned her head against it. Tears trickled down her face. The room grew warmer. The scent of smoke tickled her nose and she sneezed. Sneezing turned to coughing as the smoke grew thicker, until it choked her lungs. She drew back as the door against her cheek grew hot. *Fire!* Was the whole encampment on fire? A roaring filled her ears as flames devoured timbers. Sweat trickled from her brow and she wiped it away.

"Someone help me!" Scrambling back from the door, she huddled in the front of the wagon. *No one is coming. I am going to burn to death!* Her fingers skimmed the heated walls until they touched the water skin hung by the herb shelf. She jerked it down from the hook and rummaged through a basket by her feet for a piece of thick cloth. Snatching up a square of material, she held it to the mouth of the water skin to dampen it. After re-corking the skin, she pressed the cloth against her mouth and nose. Gagging and gasping she breathed through the material to minimize the smoke. Her eyes began to burn and water as the heat and smoke grew. Beads of sweat trickled down between her breasts, causing her clothing to stick to her like a second skin. The heat was almost unbearable now, even the coolness of the damp cloth was now warm and uncomfortable against her face. Hot sparks landed on the exposed flesh of her arms. Crying out in terror, she slapped at the sharp pricks burning her skin. The smell of singed hair and flesh rose above the smoke. There was nothing she could do but huddle there, afraid to move without knowing which direction to go to avoid the worst of the flames.

Above the roar of the blaze she thought a voice called. No, not a voice, but the whinny of a horse. She strained to hear it again over the fire consuming all around her. Again the faint sound reached her ears. Was it Jester calling her, or some other horse burning to death in its harness? The whinny came again, closer this time. Clutching the belief it was her guide, she called out, "Jester! Jester, come!"

A timber above her head creaked and then groaned. In a shower of hot sparks it collapsed. A fiery whoosh of air giving evidence it missed the corner she crouched in by scant inches. Another whinny, this time louder and unquestionably Jester's, claimed her attention. Summoning all the courage she possessed, Delilah crawled toward the sound. She let out a yelp when her hand landed on a burning splinter of wood and seared her palm. Skirting the wood she carried on and tried to block the sizzling pain from her mind. A gust of cooler air brushed her face before the floor disappeared beneath her searching hand. Screaming, she tumbled into nothing, coming to rest seconds later in a heap of smoldering timbers. The smell of burning cloth, hair, and the sizzle of her skin against heated coals made her scramble to her feet. Stumbling over debris she made her way from the worst of the heat. Something brushed her leg and then Jester's nicker greeted her.

"Jester, my friend." With tears of relief coursing down her flushed face, she flung her arms around her trusted guide's neck. He nickered again and rubbed her hip with his nose before he strained to move away. The crash of another falling timber encouraged her to scramble aboard the pony and urge him onward.

The sounds and heat died away as they wandered. Delilah couldn't fathom where they were headed and truth be told, she wasn't sure she even cared. Did the Romo baro defeat her own clan and leave her to burn as punishment for her betrayal? She was homeless, a lost soul. Did it matter where she ended up?

Her gritty eyes grew heavy and she closed them, leaning forward and wrapping her scorched hands around Jester's neck. The pain from hanging on was so great she smothered a sob. Despite it, she forced herself to hold tight lest she fall and get separated from the single thing anchoring her in the world. Delinka said Jester was her mate in another life. Was this true? Was his mission to see she was safe in her world of darkness because he sinned in his last life? If so, did it bother him she couldn't remember and was in love with another? She slid into a haze of pain and exhaustion, thoughts of Tyrone swirling about in her head.

Chapter Thirty

An insistent pounding permeated his slumber. Annoyed, Tyrone rolled over and opened his eyes. "Bloody hell, what is so urgent this early in the morn?"

"Come quick, my lord! The pony has shown up at Westpoint Manor with Miss Daysland aboard," came the valet's response from the other side of the door.

Tyrone sat up and flung off the bed covers. "Get in here. What is that you say?"

The connecting door to the valet's room flew open and banged against the wall. The valet rushed in and began yanking articles of clothing from various drawers. "Hurry, my lord. The mistress is in a bad way."

Tyrone scrambled to his feet and snatched a pair of breeches from the servant's hands. Shoving his legs into them, he hopped to the door. "Never mind the trappings, show me where she is!"

The servant darted out the door with Tyrone's boots, a shirt, waistcoat and great coat clutched in his hands. He led the way down to the lower floor of the inn while Tyrone hurried along behind buttoning his trousers. "How did you hear of this?"

"The maid, Teresa, sent the cook's husband here post haste, my lord." The butler crossed the public room that was empty of customers at such an early hour and rapped on the door to the innkeeper's private quarters.

"Why were the maid, the cook, and her husband in residence at Westpoint when they were let go?" Tyrone snatched his shirt from his valet as a sleepy eyed innkeeper opened the door.

The valet passed him his vest, coat and boots. "They refused to leave until they knew of Miss Daysland's fate, my lord." He turned to the innkeeper. "Lord Frost needs a fast horse saddled immediately."

With a nod the innkeeper scurried in the direction of the stables.

• • •

Upon entering Westpoint Manor Tyrone spotted Jester standing in the foyer. Miss Daysland was slumped across his back, filthy and tattered. He ran to the animal's side where the maid kneeled.

"Delilah?" When she moaned he reached for her and chastised the maid. "Why hasn't your mistress been taken above stairs?"

Tears streaked Teresa's cheeks. "She refuses to let go of the pony, my lord. I'm not sure she realizes where she is or who we are in her state."

With effort Tyrone steadied his voice and spoke with gentle persuasion. "Delilah, it is me, Tyrone. You are safe now at Westpoint. Jester has brought you home." The scent of smoke and burned flesh invaded his nostrils.

"Ty…rone?" Delilah moaned. "I'm not dead?"

"No, my little wood nymph, you are not dead."

Her lips quivered. "Jester…he brought me…home."

"Yes, he did. You are safe now, Delilah, I promise you."

"You never lie." A sob escaped her and her grip on the pony relaxed.

Despite the seriousness of the situation Tyrone could not help but smile. "Never." The smile slipped from his lips when he eased her fingers from around Jester's neck to lift her down and she cried out in pain. He scooped her up in his arms and looked over his shoulder at the butler. "Send for a physician."

"Yes, my lord."

Tyrone hurried upstairs to Delilah's former room. The light scent of flowers still lingered in the bedchamber, doing little to cover the stench of her burned flesh, hair and clothing. He placed her on top of the blankets. Her once shiny black locks hung limp and dirty, singed in some spots right to her scalp. Soot smudged the bridge of her nose and peppered her cheeks.

He leaned over her. "Delilah? Can you hear me?"

Her eyelids fluttered and then opened. The tip of her tongue slipped between her lips to moisten the cracked flesh before she mustered a hoarse whisper. "Ty…rone?"

"Yes." He brushed a strand of hair from her cheek.

She grimaced as if in pain and raised her hand to her face.

For the first time he noticed the bits of burned flesh hanging from the swollen, red appendages. "Your hands! What happened?"

"I'm…not sure. There were…screams. Gunshots. The fire… it burned…everything. I could not get out. Then…Jester came for me." She paused to cough, the sound raspy and dry. "Why are you here?"

He sat on the edge of the bed. "Teresa summoned me when Jester brought you home."

"Of course. Jester…" Her chapped lips twisted into a semblance of a smile. "He was my mate…in another life."

"What?"

Her lids fluttered and then closed. A soft sigh drifted from her lips as they parted and went slack. Concerned, he lay his head close to her mouth, relieved when her breath brushed his cheek. With great care he turned her hands palms up. Wet, painful looking blisters formed on the skin, oozing and seeping into the grime coating them. He recalled her reading to him in the library with her fingers and wondered if she would ever be able to do such amazing things again. The door opened and he turned.

The butler peered into the room. "The stable lad has taken your horse to fetch the physician."

"Good." Tyrone glanced back at Delilah and realized there was no household staff in attendance other than the maid, cook, butler, and stable lad. "When the lad returns send him to fetch back the rest of the servants but caution him and the rest of the staff to keep quiet about Miss Daysland's presence here, at least until I find out what happened."

"Yes, my lord."

The door closed with an abrupt click before he could ask if faithful Jester was taken care of. It occurred to him perhaps the stable lad couldn't be trusted. Who of the former staff could he trust? Teresa he believed was loyal and the butler, Aims, but the rest of them? A soft knock sounded on the door and he looked up.

The maid hurried in with an armload of towels and a basin of water. She didn't look surprised to see him perched there on the edge of the bed. "I brought some things to care for Miss Daysland, my lord."

"Thank you, Teresa." He nodded as she set the items on the bedside table. "I will take care of your mistress until the physician arrives."

She glanced at Delilah and opened her mouth as if to protest but wisely nodded instead. "Yes, my lord."

After the woman left Tyrone dipped a cloth in the warm water, wrung it out, and washed the soot and dirt from Delilah's face. She sighed and turned into the washcloth's caress, yet didn't wake. He rinsed the cloth and washed down her neck and along the burnt neckline of her soiled white blouse.

No other woman stirred him the way she did. Her lithe, white body squirming atop him while her hands stroked until he could take the pressure no longer haunted his dreams. Stifling a groan he returned his attention to washing. Angry red welts appeared along her arms where he wiped away the soot and bits of burned flesh. He hated the idea of causing her pain, but consoled himself with the thought that she wouldn't feel it in her sleep, and her blindness would prevent her from seeing the scars remaining from her ordeal. By the time he cleansed her face, throat, and arms the water was black and grimy. For lack of anything else to do he rang for more while he waited for the physician.

The maid returned with another basin of steaming water.

He did his best to smile with reassurance when she set the water beside him with a sniffle. "Is there a change of clean clothing about?"

Teresa stared at him wide eyed. "No, my lord."

"Ask my valet to fetch one of my night shirts then."

Her lips pressed into a disapproving frown no doubt thinking she was thinking he would attempt to undress the injured woman himself.

Tyrone suppressed a chuckle. "You may return here to change Miss Daysland after you dispose of the dirty water."

With a relieved look she took the basin of used water and left.

He soaked the clean cloth, wrung it out, and moved to the foot of the bed. He washed the grime from Delilah's feet and then made his way up along her legs until he reached the scorched hem just above her knees. Propriety halted his task, and he returned the cloth to the basin as the door opened again. When the maid entered with one of his soft, white nightshirts in hand, he excused himself and headed downstairs in search of the cook.

He found the woman stoking the fire in the kitchen, her long gray braid hanging over her shoulder. One look at her bleary eyed gaze was enough to convince him she was roused from her bed at Delilah's arrival. "Could you boil some tea, please, and send a thin porridge above stairs for Miss Daysland, in case she should wake hungry?"

"Yes, my lord." She wrung her hands, leaving him to believe her concern for her mistress was genuine. "Will Miss Daysland be all right?"

"I hope so. Who discovered her?"

"The gardener, my lord."

He frowned. "He was let go with the staff last week. What was he doing wandering the estate at four in the morning?"

She shrugged and turned to add more wood to the fire, over which a kettle of water hung. "I've no idea, my lord." When he cleared his throat she glanced back at him, guilt twisting her expression. "I risk my life, my lord, if I tell you what I heard and suspect."

"Who uttered such a threat?"

After looking around as if the walls sported ears she leaned close. "The butler suspected the gardener and stable boy of plotting against the mistress, but they were not working alone," she whispered.

"Who were they working with?"

"They were working for someone, I don't know who, but I suspect it might have been the baron, my lord."

Her words didn't come as a surprise to him, as more and more of late he suspected the baron was behind many of the suspicious incidents around the estate. He pondered her statement as she ladled hot water from the kettle over the fire into a delicate china teapot. The aroma of herbal tea leaves filled the room, reminding him of the gypsy encampment. What happened to the gypsies? Why did they fail to protect Delilah? Did something terrible happen to Deagan? He took the tray on which the cook set the teapot, cup, and bowl of heated broth and headed back upstairs, unanswered questions rattling about in his head.

Delilah was wearing the nightshirt and tucked under the covers. He set the tray with care on the bedside table lest he wake her and pulled a chair up to await the physician. The bedclothes rose and fell with her shallow, steady breathing. He focused on it for a moment to quiet his thoughts. Though her hair was still matted, he was glad to note some of the color returning to her face, at least as far as he could tell beneath the spotty burns. Guilt pricked his conscience. He'd failed to protect her. She stirred and moaned in her sleep. He brushed the hair from her forehead and mumbled soft words of comfort to her.

Her eyelids fluttered and then opened. Though sightless, her violet orbs locked on his. "Jester?"

Tyrone poured a cup of tea, sweetened it with a spoonful of honey, and leaned over her. "Jester is fine and resting in the stables, Delilah. Here, have some tea the cook sent up for you." He eased his arm around behind her head for support so she could sip the hot liquid. When she drank half of it and turned her head away he set the cup aside.

"He saved my life."

Jealousy reared its hideous head at the thought of a mere pony doing what he failed to. He pushed it back down into the dark recesses it came from. "I suppose he did. Can you tell me what happened?"

Her singed brows bunched and her pealing lips pursed for a moment before she answered. "We arrived at the lake and I told Uncle Deagan I could not go through with the ceremony. He was angry with me and locked me in the wagon. The next thing I remember were gunshots and screaming. The wagon caught fire." Her voice hitched with emotion and he stroked her hair, fearing his touch anywhere else would cause her physical pain. "I heard Jester whinny and followed the sound through the fire to him. He carried me away. I do not remember the journey here…" A sob bubbled from her despite her biting her lip to keep it in.

"You are safe now." He returned the cup to her mouth and she sipped the tea. When it was drained he set it on the tray. "What kind of ceremony did you refuse to take part in?"

A sigh, heavy with emotion escaped her. "Uncle Deagan said I was to marry the Romo boro's son during the harvest moon ceremony, to free the gypsies from their years of persecution. I could not though."

"Why not?"

"I am no longer pure."

Once again guilt stabbed him. "So your uncle tried to burn you alive?"

"No, at least I do not think it was his intention. I heard gunshots and women screaming."

Something disastrous had happened and he was inclined to believe Delilah was right in thinking it was not her uncle's revenge. Someone tapped on the door and he bid them enter.

Teresa opened it and a young man carrying a black bag stepped into the room. He pushed up his spectacles and cleared his throat. "I was summoned to see to Miss Daysland, my lord."

Tyrone stood. "I will wait in my study for your diagnosis, sir."

When the doctor nodded, Tyrone left the room and headed downstairs. In the study he rang for something stronger than his usual mint tea.

Chapter Thirty-One

Two days later a flash of lightning and the rumble of thunder drew Tyrone's attention out the window of the study. The last few days of rain and cool temperatures began to change the leaves on the trees to golden and orange hues, proclaiming the late start of fall. A gust of wind shook the window panes as the first heavy drops of rain splattered the glass. He supposed today was as good as any day to tell Delilah the fate of her gypsy family. Heavy hearted he left the study.

As he strolled down the hall he noticed the door to the library stood ajar. Pausing, he peeked inside. Delilah sat, legs curled under her on the window seat, bandaged hands in her lap and forehead pressed to the window panes. The deep rose colored gown she wore set off her dark hair, now cut to shoulder length and styled in ringlets to hide the few singed bits remaining. She turned from the window, and he knew she sensed his presence.

He stepped into the room. "Why are you sitting in here all alone?"

"I grew bored of being abed and wanted to play my pianoforte, but..." she trailed off.

He glanced at the bulky bandages smothering her fingers. "I see." He grimaced at his own choice of words and crossed the room to stand before her. "I came to speak with you about your family."

She tilted her head. "Have you found them? Is Uncle Deagan angry with me?"

He'd give anything to change the answer. "They are all dead, Delilah. I am sorry."

Her face paled and tears glistened in her eyes. "What happened?"

"No one is sure. It appears they were slaughtered by a group on horseback. No one seems to know who or why."

A single tear slipped from her eye, trickled down her pale cheek, and dripped onto the bandaged hands in her lap. "It is all because of me. I wanted what I could not have, what I was never meant to have, and because of it they all died. I should have heeded the gypsy magic."

He sat down beside her. "What are you talking about?"

"I wanted you. I did not want to marry anyone else. I purposely plied you with wine so you would lay with me and make my marriage to another impossible. Had I done as my uncle wanted, none of this would have happened." A strangled cry erupted from her lips and she covered her face with her hands.

He encircled her in his arms to comfort her as she sobbed. "Shh, Delilah. None of it was your fault. This gypsy magic you speak of does not exist."

"It does. I saw you in the crystal ball. I have seen a great many things in it from my past I know are true and real."

"I am sure you have." He soothed her with a hand stroking her back. "Even so, no supposed magical union could have prevented what happened. You are not a gypsy and none of their fight was yours to bear."

"How can you be sure?"

"I believe the baron is behind it all."

"What do you mean?" She wiped the tears with her bandages.

Tyrone settled back against the window seat and cradled her in his arms, knowing how inappropriate it would look to a passing servant, yet wanting to comfort her. "I believe it was the baron all along. At first he tried to frighten you into marrying him. When you resisted, he planted the idea it was I you needed to be afraid of. He intended to kill you shortly after your marriage to him and stage it as an accident. It would have been easy to make it look as if his blind bride simply fell down the stairs in an unfamiliar home." He squeezed her when she stiffened at his unintended slight.

"When you fought him off and ran away he was beside himself with anger. I thought you would be safe with the gypsies until I could prove what he was up to, but he must have found out where you were. I think he raided the encampment with the intention of killing you in the scuffle, but because you were locked in the wagon he did not find you. He burned the caravan to be sure there would be no one left alive to tell what he did."

At her sharp intake of breath he squeezed her again, wishing he didn't have to burden her with more terrible thoughts. "The baron was here today." She trembled beneath his hands. "He thought to take you back, except I let slip what I knew in hopes he would reconsider his position. I think he is noddy enough to push it to trial, Delilah. I have no desire to put you through such a farce, but I see no other way to keep you safe from him."

"A trial? A room full of strangers to hear all the sordid details of my life, of my father's indiscretions?" She shook her head, making her curls dance with mock cheeriness. "I cannot do it. I cannot."

He attempted to calm her fears with a light stroke of his hand across her hair. "Yes, you can. I will be there with you. For you."

Chapter Thirty-Two

"Are you ready?"

Delilah squared her shoulders and nodded as the carriage rolled to a stop.

The footman opened the door and Tyrone took her hand in his, squeezing it for reassurance. "I wish there was another way."

"I know." Taking a deep breath she favored him with a tight smile and submitted to him helping her down from the conveyance. Voices carried, whispering too low for her to hear the words, but she knew they were talking about her. Head held high she placed her hand on the earl's arm and he led the way. The voices seemed to follow them as a door opened on squeaky hinges and they entered a building. Despite the whispers, their footsteps echoed across what Delilah took to be a tile floor.

Tyrone paused. "I am Lord Tyrone Frost, the Earl of Merryweather, and this is my ward, Miss Delilah Daysland."

"Right this way, my lord, the council is waiting for you."

Covering her hand with his where it rested on the sleeve of his soft velvet coat, he moved forward down a long corridor. It was not long before they paused again and a soft whoosh of air indicated a set of double doors opened. The muffled conversations coming from within hushed when they stepped across the threshold. This time their footsteps were muffled by a thick carpet.

Delilah tried to quiet the rapid beat of her heart as she became the focus of dozens of eyes. She didn't need to see to know the room was full of people, their breathing and whispers were enough evidence. Her chest tightened, the breath squeezing from her lungs. Dozens of scents assaulted her sensitive nostrils. Strong cologne, flowered perfume, and musty cigar smoke made the room stale and warm. She struggled for air as dizziness over took her. Faltering, she clutched the earl's arm to keep from falling.

"Delilah? Are you all right?"

Though Tyrone voiced the question in a mere whisper, she recognized the concern in his tone. "Yes...no. Oh lord, I think I am going to faint."

"A couple more steps and you can sit."

True to his word after two more steps a chair pressed against the side of her leg. He helped her sit and forced her head down between her legs. A most undignified position she knew, but it couldn't be helped.

"Lord Frost, is there a problem?"

Tyrone placed his hand on her shoulder. "Yes, honorable sir. My charge gets ill in the company of a large group of people."

"Is she slow of wit?"

"Oh no, sir." He smoothed a hand on her shoulder when she tensed at the insult. "She is very quick-witted; it is only crowds make her uncomfortable. You see, she has spent most of her life sequestered in the quiet of her country estate due to her condition."

"And just what is this condition she suffers from that makes her so nervous amongst her peers?"

"She is blind, sir."

Delilah wanted to retch. She wished she could run and hide somewhere, anywhere to escape the pitying stares she knew were being directed at her.

"Would it be a kindness on my part to remove the bystanders?"

Relief flooded her when the earl answered, "Yes, honorable sir."

"Very well. Guards please remove everyone from my courtroom except for the defendants, the accuser, and their counsel."

Murmurs of discontent accompanied the shuffling of dozens of pairs of feet. Delilah's heart slowed as a set of doors closed behind the retreating bystanders with a dull thud. She took a couple of deep breaths to steady herself and clear her mind.

"Can we proceed now, Lord Frost?"

"Yes, sir."

"Good. I have been called today to hear a claim by Baron Augustus March, to the effect you have refused to return his bride to his residence upon her recovery from a despicable lot of thieving gypsies."

"Nay, they are a more scrupulous bunch than the baron is, sir!" Delilah clapped a hand over her mouth in dismay at her outburst.

"See here now, Miss Daysland, such outbursts will not be tolerated in my courtroom."

"Please forgive me, honorable sir, I was offended by the color with which you paint my heritage."

"*You* are a gypsy?"

She smiled at the note of astonishment in his question. "In part, sir."

"Do explain."

Knees knocking, she forced herself to stand and address him. "It began a long time ago, sir, and is a tale I myself just heard, though I believe Baron March was well aware of it and might have killed my father because of it."

"Murder and deception? This is a story I must hear for sure, Miss Daysland."

Delilah cringed at the high-pitched whine of protest from the baron.

"All bull cocky, honorable sir. We are here because Lord Frost refuses to return my wife, not to hear sordid lies said by people no longer alive to attest to their truths."

A gavel banged twice against a solid surface. "Enough! This is my court, and as such I will decide what to hear and what to dismiss as foolishness. Miss Daysland, please continue."

She launched into her story, beginning with her childhood memories and her father's death. By the time she finished her head throbbed and her mouth was dry.

"Here." As if sensing her thirst, Tyrone pressed a cool glass into her hand.

Raising it to her lips, she sipped the blackberry wine. The silence was deafening. Her hand shook as she held out the half empty glass. Tyrone took it from her, his warm fingers brushing hers in a way both unnerving and comforting. "You did just fine," he whispered. She tried to smile, but her nerves got the better of her.

The judge cleared his throat. "Well, that was quite a tale, Miss Daysland. If it is to be believed, then this baron is indeed quite the no-account scoundrel. Baron March, what say you to these accusations?"

"Pure hornswaggle, honorable sir. My wife has quite a vivid imagination you see, as she has nothing else to do but sit and think. Perhaps I should make a serious effort to rein in her ridiculous nature. Rest assured she will settle down once she is safely locked away in her room where she cannot injure herself, thinking of babes."

Delilah gasped. "How dare you!"

The judge banged his gavel again and she fell silent. Incurring his wrath might harm her case.

"Miss Daysland, I have allowed you to speak and refute the baron's charges. You must do him the same courtesy and give him the chance to defend against your claims."

She bit her lip, sickened by Augustus's righteous tone when he answered, "Thank you, honorable sir. I feel for my darling wife. I did promise her father I would look after her if anything were to befall him. I was doing my duty when I offered to marry her. The earl betrayed me when he helped her hide and took her as his lover in the midst of a gypsy celebration. The naive child mistook his lust for love."

An unladylike snort escaped Delilah's lips before she could prevent it. Tyrone squeezed her hand and she bowed her head to conceal her feelings.

"What say you to the charges she has brought against you saying you are responsible for her father's death, and are you indeed half brother and sister?"

Augustus snickered. "Preposterous, sir. I have here the announcement of my birth and hers to prove her claim false." Paper crinkled and she assumed said document was being examined by the judge.

After a moment the judge sighed. "So it would seem all in order. What say you to all this, Lord Frost?"

"I believe Miss Daysland and the gypsy Deagan's claim, honorable sir."

"Do you have any proof to back up these claims?"

"No, sir, but I was given the task to see her safe and happily wed by the king himself. The way I see it, Miss Daysland is neither happy nor safe in the baron's care. After all, she wandered away from his estate and all manner of dangers might have befallen her, if not for the gypsies who took her in."

"Ha!" the baron bellowed. "The gypsies did naught but fill her head with ridiculous ideas and she nearly burned to death while in their camp. Why I—"

"Enough!" The judge banged his gavel. "It seems clear to me since the king did order Lord Frost to see Miss Daysland safely wed, his duty is done. However, it is clear in this case she is not happy about the situation. I see no other alternative but to return her to her husband's care until the king himself can be consulted."

"No!" Delilah's scream reverberated off the walls of the little chamber, startling even her. She collapsed in the chair, and Tyrone wrapped his arms around her. Sobs wracked her body until she was no longer aware of anything except pure terror and profound sorrow.

• • •

Tyrone steadied Delilah as she sank to the chair sobbing. Was the judge deaf? How could he turn her over to a monster like March? "Sir, I beg you to reconsider leaving Miss Daysland in my care."

The judge shook his head. "Impossible, for who would chaperone her? Did you not have your way with her in a gypsy camp, in full view of any who happened by? I cannot understand what has become of the morals of you country folk."

"Honorable sir, I am not condoning what we did, but under different circumstances I would not hesitate to make an honorable match with her, at the court's earliest convenience and the king's blessing, of course."

"You had your chance to do right by your charge, Lord Frost. I hope the king punishes you for the misdeeds you have committed. To mislead such an innocent young soul is a terrible sin. You should be ashamed."

Delilah's heartfelt sobs pulled at Tyrone's heart more than he ever thought anything could. "Please, sir, consider what might happen to Miss Daysland in the baron's care if there is truth to her story. At least allow her to return to her own home under the protection of her most faithful servants."

"You cannot be serious." The baron hurried to the judge's podium. "It is sheer folly to allow an invalid to remain alone in a large house with no chaperone. In her distressed mental condition she might do herself harm—"

"Enough!" The judge banged his gavel and the room fell silent, except for Delilah's quiet weeping. The judge tugged at his wig with a heavy sigh. "In order to satisfy you both until the king can rightfully decide what is to be done with Miss Daysland, I have decided to release her to her home, in the care of two of her most trusted servants."

Augustus waved his fist in an agitated way. "See here—"

"Enough I say!" the judge growled. "If you persist in challenging my authority, Baron March, I will see you imprisoned until the matter is settled. Do I make myself clear?"

The baron glowered but nodded.

The judge turned back to Tyrone. "You are not to remain at Westpoint while Miss Daysland is present, nor is the baron permitted to press his nuptials until the king has his say. If there is any breech of my orders, I will come down hard and fast on both of you, understood?"

"Yes, sir." Tyrone glanced at the baron out of the corner of his eye. The younger man nodded, despite the anger sparkling in his dark eyes.

"Good. Now Lord Frost, I expect you to see your former charge back home safely. Repeat my directions to the servants, with the addition that if they fail to see to their mistress's care and protection they will serve the rest of their days in Newgate."

"Yes, sir."

The judge brought his gavel down one last time and then left the room, mumbling about the decline of propriety in the upper crust.

Tyrone placed his silk handkerchief in Delilah's hand. "Here, dry your tears before we must make our way through the throng of curious public to the carriage."

Sniffing, she raised the bit of cloth and dabbed at her eyes and cheeks. "The king will allow me to remain as I was before all this came to pass, will he not?"

"I have no idea what thoughts his majesty might have on the situation, but rest assured I will do my utmost to convince him to annul your marriage to the baron." And agree to my own suit, his consciousness added. "Are you ready to return home?"

Her chin raised in stubborn determination and she took a deep breath before nodding. Placing her still bandaged hand on his arm, he wished there were a way he could slip her away without exposing her to the morbid crowd of on lookers outside.

• • •

Once Delilah was returned to her home, Tyrone gathered his things and turned his horse back in the direction of town. He rode in worried silence for a while, his valet in the luggage coach trailing at an appropriate pace behind. What was to stop the baron from harming Delilah until the king arrived to make sense of the situation? Aims and Teresa were the most faithful of her servants, he was convinced, nevertheless the question still lingered as to which of the few servants remaining were not. Though he was sure Delilah was safer in her own home than the baron's, the fact remained she still could be in danger. Could the butler protect her from an unseen, unknown enemy?

Unease made him rein in his mount when they came to the little trail to the pool where he first encountered his wood nymph. Perhaps he should stay hidden in the secret place, to be nearby in case Delilah should need him. He wouldn't be disobeying the court's order; after all the pool spanned on the edge of Westpoint and the baron's land. Yes, he would camp out here to keep a watchful eye on his ward until the king arrived.

Turning in his saddle, he summoned the coach to draw up alongside. He leaned in the window to speak with his valet. "Take all my things, except a small satchel of the basics to the inn in town and rent the best room and meals. I am going to stay behind and watch over Miss Daysland. You will stay in the room in my stead, careful to keep your presence a mystery in case the baron should send a spy there. When the king arrives in a few days' time come fetch me here." He tossed a sack of coins through the window and onto the valet's lap. The servant filled a satchel from the items in one of the trunks stacked inside the conveyance and handed it to him. With a nod of thanks Tyrone tapped on the roof to signal the driver to carry on and then turned his horse down the path in the woods.

Chapter Thirty-Three

Delilah tossed and turned, unable to quiet her restless mind. Would the king see fit to permit her to continue on as she was before, or would he insist she return to Augustus? Perhaps he would again decree that Tyrone find her a suitable husband. Her heart pinched at the idea of being married to any other than the earl. She sighed and rolled over onto her other side. Tyrone didn't really want her, did he? Could his offer of marriage only be a way to atone for their sin of passion at the gypsy camp? Her heart cried out against the falseness of her thoughts. He felt something for her, perhaps not love, but at least a fondness of sorts. Groaning at the idea she rolled back over. The room was stuffy and uncomfortable. Never did she experience such a warm, dry fall.

Flipping back the tangled covers, she swung her legs over the side of the bed and felt for her slippers with her toes. After locating them, she slipped them on and rose. Stretching she made her way to the window, fumbled for the latch, and opened it. A slight breeze tickled her cheeks as she leaned against the windowsill and took a deep breath through her nose. A hint of crispness, mixed with musty leaves and dried grass made her long to be outside. She turned away from the window as an owl hooted and reached for the thin cotton servant's frock at the foot of her bed. It wouldn't hurt to go for a short ride, for she was confident she was safe enough until the king came to set down his ruling.

Once dressed, she crossed to the door and twisted the knob. It opened without sound as usual and she slipped out into the hall. The stale house air was so still it was almost eerie. After a moment's pause she made her way down the hall to the stairs, trailing her fingers along the familiar walls. Once she descended the staircase, she stopped at the base to listen. The tiniest of noises reached her and a chill of alarm raised the fine dusting of hair on her arms. Was someone there, in the dark, watching and waiting for her? She strained to catch the sound again over the thumping of her heart. Nothing but silence. She shook off the feeling. *Damn the baron for making me ill at ease in my own home.* In disgust she carried on, groping her way to the kitchen and the back door to the herb garden.

The door squeaked as she opened it and she froze lest anyone heard and came to investigate. When no footsteps sounded in the hall or on the servant's stairs, she stepped out of the house. Something warm brushed her outstretched hand and her heart leaped into her throat before she giggled, realizing it was her guide.

"Good eve, Jester." The pony nickered and she stroked his velvety soft muzzle. "I cannot sleep either, old friend."

She grasped the harness, pulled herself onto his back, and then clucked for him to walk on. A sense of peace radiated from the pony. Her stressed mind soaked it in and she began to relax, focusing on the rocking motion of the animal under her. As Jester plodded on at his ever steady pace, she gave thanks to her deceased Uncle Deagan for providing such a trustworthy guide to see her through life's obstacles. The gypsy leader meant well, despite his actions.

The rush of the waterfall reached her ears before its dampness touched her with icy fingers. The water would be too cold now for a swim; just to sit upon the banks and savor its calmness would be enough this night. As the twigs brushed her legs a different scent reached her. *Smoke.* The faintest trace, as if a campfire burned down to coals. Did a roving band of gypsies come to camp here? She was sure they wouldn't harm her if she told them she was of

Deagan's blood. Jester stopped and altered his course to the right, his unexpected shift in direction jarring her.

Delilah became aware of the sharp essence of mint before the leaves rustled as he rose from the ground before her. "Tyrone? What are you doing here?"

"I might ask you the same thing."

The pony came to an abrupt halt, leading her to believe the earl now held him by the headstall. "I could not sleep."

"Nor could I." He chuckled. "The water is far too cold for a swim, you know."

She smiled at the light admonishment. "I know, I just thought to sit upon the bank and bask in the serenity of the place."

"Allow me help you down."

Even though she didn't need his help, she permitted him to guide her to the forest floor. "You have not answered my question of why you are here, my lord."

"I came to watch over you, Delilah."

For a moment she pondered the soberness of his answer. He was worried about her, which meant he cared for her at least. "How did you know I would come here when the water is so cold?"

His warm hand slipped around to cradle the small of her back as he guided her to the pool's edge to sit. "I didn't. I was waiting to be sure the manor was asleep before I set up a watch on the property."

"Oh." With a grin she sat on the fabric he spread upon the bank, glad in the dark he wouldn't be able to see how much his care pleased her.

He chuckled. "It pleases you."

She let the smile slip from her lips. "How do you know?"

"I can sense it. You have taught me well to see without my eyes, Delilah."

"Have I?"

Again he chuckled. "Most assuredly. I find my senses sharpened where you are concerned."

She allowed the comment to pass and drew her knees up to rest her arms across them. "Soon it will be winter and I will not be able to venture very far from the house."

His arm brushed hers as he sat beside her. "Then what will you do when your mind is too restless to sleep?"

"Other things." She shrugged and rested her head atop her arms. It was nice here, with him. Comfortable and easy.

"Such as?"

The lightness of his tone told her he was teasing and she smiled. "Read, play my pianoforte, and dance."

"Will you dance as you did at the gypsy camp?"

The idea of dancing again with wild abandon thrilled her. "Perhaps, though to dance by one's self without music might be seen as a little noddy to the servants."

"Indeed." He shifted beside her. "Perhaps I shall dance with you."

Her heart constricted at the idea of his embrace, knowing it would never be. Her sigh of despair lingered over the water. "If it could be. I suspect the king will seek to have me wed to some proper gentleman of his choosing before the snow flies, if he releases me from my agreement with Augustus."

Silence stretched between them for many moments before he answered. "I will make him see the wisdom of an annulment, Delilah." The cricket's chirping mingled with the rustling leaves and tumbling waterfall. Delilah closed her eyes and her mind wandered back to dancing with him.

"Would you have me if I petitioned the king for your hand?"

Startled by his question she gasped. "What?"

"Would you marry me?"

Her heart soared. She would like nothing more than to be near him every day, yet doubt about his feelings made her temper her reply. "If I have to marry, I would choose it to be you."

He was too quiet, and for a minute she wondered if he regretted his offer. "Then I shall ask the king when he arrives. Come, it is time you retire to the safety of your room."

Though she didn't want to return to her solitary room, she didn't resist when he helped her aboard the pony and led the animal back along the trail. The silence stretched between them, thick with unsaid thoughts and feelings. Did they have a future together?

• • •

The next night found Delilah again unable to sleep, and in frustration she slipped down to the kitchen in hopes the cook left her a snack. She found the treat as easily as the cook intended and took it to sit on a stool by the rough table. With a deep sniff, she savored the sweet smell of apples and spicy hint of cinnamon. *A slice of leftover apple pie, my favorite.* She giggled, disturbing the silence. *All foods are my favorite.* The tastes and textures thrilled her senses, making every snack and meal an adventure. Breaking off a generous chunk with her fingers, she popped it in her mouth, savoring its stimulation of her taste buds. The flaky pastry all but melted on her tongue, the tangy bits of apple and spices making her moan. She smothered a second giggle as the seductive sound echoed in the room. There was much joy in the simple things. A shuffling noise made her turn toward the doorway. "Forgive me, Mrs. Smith, for interrupting your sleep. I was just enjoying the pie you so thoughtfully left me."

"Enjoy it while you can, Miss Daysland."

The sinister male voice made her freeze, her hand halfway to her lips. She choked on the crumbs left in her mouth. "Who are you and what are you doing here?"

"I am here to deliver a message," the man answered.

She set down the pie. "From the earl? Has the king come already?"

"No. The baron sent me to fetch the beast and advise you to change your tale."

Icy fingers of fear clawed her chest. "Jester? What have you done to him?"

"Nothing yet. If you recant your gypsy story and agree to let your marriage to the baron stand, he will be returned to you unharmed."

"The baron will kill me regardless."

"No, he has decided to let you live, but he'll kill you both the first chance he gets if you decline his suggestion."

There was no doubt in her mind Augustus meant his threat. Could she live looking over her shoulder? Could Tyrone protect her forever and keep watch for her sightless eyes? No, no matter how able the man, it was not possible. One day there would come a time when he would fail. She nodded, knowing there was no other choice. She owed it to Jester to protect him, as he protected her all these years.

When the door closed behind the mysterious man she pushed away her forgotten snack, laid her head on the table, and cried for the man she loved, whom she would never marry.

Chapter Thirty-Four

Tyrone rubbed a hand over the two days' worth of stubble on his chin and blinked to refocus his bleary gaze. Two nights he had sat here in the shadows of the garden elm tree and seen no one, other than one man enter the kitchen from the stable and then exit a short time after. He presumed the fellow was a stable hand after a late night snack and found something to tempt his appetite in the cook's pantry.

He glanced up at the sky. The horizon was showing a lighter strip of blue to mark the coming of the sun. The king sent word of his arrival this morning, a fact Tyrone both dreaded and welcomed. Would the king see the truth and take his side in the situation? He couldn't be sure, but he needed to believe the monarch wise enough to see the evils of the baron's words. Jamming his hat back on his head, he got to his feet and stealthily made his way back through the bushes to the forest. It was time to go to the inn and clean up before they all met with the king.

...

A quick glance in the mirror proved a bath, shave, and change of clothing erased most traces of his two days spent in the woods, except for the lingering dark circles under his blue eyes. Tyrone turned away and waited as his valet knotted the lacy cravat at his neck. When the piece of material was fastened as it should be, he shrugged into his deep blue waistcoat and dove gray overcoat. As much as he took pride in cutting a dashing figure, he would give it all away if it meant marrying Delilah.

Taken unaware by his own thoughts he frowned. Did he love her? Yes, there was no doubt in his mind his feelings were far beyond admiration for the raven haired beauty. Did he ever feel anything but appreciation for the woman whose hand he once sought before he met his violet-eyed gypsy? It was apparent he didn't, for the woman fled his thoughts the moment he met Delilah, and he was never been able to go an hour without wanting to see her fascinating gaze.

The urge to whistle was strange and out of place considering the serious nature of the meeting to come, but he allowed his whim to take flight. Whistling a jaunty tune he headed for the coach waiting to take him to the courthouse. With any luck he would be returning to Westpoint this day with a wife-to-be.

The journey to the courthouse in the village took less than five minutes. Upon arriving he discovered a large crowd milling about in front of the building. Knowing Delilah's paranoia would get the best of her if she must brave the gawking bunch alone, he waited on the steps for her carriage. The crowd began to mumble as her conveyance, pulled by a modest two-horse team of bays, came around the corner and drew up at the base of the steps. He hurried to the door, opened it, and took her hand in his to help her down.

She was a sight to behold as she stepped from the carriage. A rose-colored silk dress draped her slender frame, showing off her tiny figure to perfection. The frilled neckline gave a tantalizing glimpse of her ample breasts and showed her flawless skin and swanlike neck to perfection. A light white fur stole nestled her shoulders, disappearing beneath rows of shiny black ringlets. Except for the palms of her hands, still wrapped in white bandages, one would never have known the elegant miss before him was ever in a fire, let alone danced before the flames in a gypsy camp with wild abandon.

He tucked her hand in the crook of his arm, wanting to tell her how beautiful she looked, but knowing now was not the time. Her fingers bit into the sleeve of his dress coat, her face pale and her breath coming in tiny gasps. She wobbled as they passed the onlookers and walked up the steps. By the time the door closed behind them and they crossed a less crowded foyer, she was shaking. He patted her hand and they followed a footman to the judge's private chambers. She showed no sign of being aware of his support. They entered the chambers and found King George III already in attendance. Tyrone leaned close to whisper in her ear, "The king is here, just in front of you."

A strained smile formed on her lips as she curtsied. Knowing how terrified she was, he bowed without releasing her hand. The baron rose from his seat against the far wall with a sneer when the king addressed them.

"I have been called here today to settle a dispute over the marriage of my ward, Miss Delilah Daysland. Is this correct?"

Tyrone cleared his throat. "Yes, Your Majesty. You requested I go to Miss Daysland's home and see her properly chaperoned, cared for, and suitably married before the snow fell."

The king frowned, his thick white brows bunching above his cold, blue eyes. "And I hear tell you have done just that, so what may I ask was so urgent to bring me out in the country during the last week of the London season?"

"The marriage was entered into under false pretenses on both sides, Your Majesty."

"These pretenses, are they not something that can be rectified among yourselves?"

"No, Your Excellence, we thought the court could decide, but I believe your appointed judge has failed to see the seriousness of the claims."

The monarch released a heavy sigh and then sat in a chair behind the judge's desk. "Very well, do explain and do not take all day about it, Lord Frost, for I am a very busy man."

"Yes, Your Majesty." Tyrone took a deep breath, grateful to be permitted to tell Delilah's side of the story.

Delilah released Tyrone's arm and stepped forward. "Your Majesty, if it pleases you, I would like to withdraw my petition for an annulment of my recent marriage."

Tyrone stared at her in shock. Did she know what she was saying? He glanced at the baron, who stood there with a smug look on his face.

The monarch's brow rose. "God's thunder! Are you saying you have no qualms about your marriage to Baron March, Miss Daysland? Have I been deliberately misled?"

She twisted her hands in her lap. "No, Your Majesty, after careful reflection I see it was nerves making me regret my decision."

The king turned to Tyrone, bright spots of red forming at his temples. "Were you aware of this, Lord Frost? Is this some kind of jest?"

"No, no…Your Excellence, I was not aware…of this," Tyrone stammered. Something was not right. Why did Delilah change her story?

She dropped her head. "Please, Your Majesty. Lord Frost knew nothing of my feelings. He did not deceive you, I did."

The king looked back and forth between them, his eyes narrowing. "The story I was told was all made up then?"

Tyrone grasped her hand. "No."

"Yes!" she refuted.

Augustus shot him a triumphant leer. "Yes."

"I am very disappointed in you, Lord Frost. You have deceived me and wasted my valuable time."

"Your Excellence, I did not deceive you. For some reason I do not understand, Miss Daysland has changed her story. Since I have never known her to be anything but honest and trustworthy, it alarms me. Please, press her further, for I know she is desperate to withdraw from her union with the baron. The marriage was not consummated and therefore it is not too late to undo it."

The king studied him for a moment. "Ah, Lord Frost, I do see what is going on here. You fancy yourself in love with this innocent you seduced; however, her good conscience has made her see reason and honor the vows she took—"

"Nay! 'Tis not true, sire! He has done or said something to make her change her mind. They are half brother and sister and therefore to allow them to marry would be a sacrilege."

"Enough," the king bellowed, his face turning an alarming red tincture.

"But, Your Majesty—"

"I said enough! There is no proof to your claim. You embarrass yourself, and me, with your ridiculous imaginings."

A despair he never experienced before took hold of Tyrone and clouded his judgment. In desperation he jerked Delilah back against him. "I will not allow this to happen!"

The king stepped back wide eyed. "Guards!"

A dozen royal clad men burst into the chamber and surrounded Tyrone with guns drawn. It was over. Hopelessly, he released his hold on Delilah. "Why, Delilah, why?"

The guards subdued him and dragged him from the room. The last thing he registered was Delilah, weeping.

"I am sorry, my lord."

•••

A dream. It is all a bad dream. Numbness enveloped her body and senses. She registered the baron's lips on hers. The king's praise of her choice. The baron's steadfastness in the face of her waiver. It made her want to retch. She moved in a haze. *It does not matter. I did what I needed to do.* The hurt and bewilderment in Tyrone's voice stung like thousands of nettles stabbing her flesh. She would have run if she thought she could escape the sound of his pain, but it would ring in her ears forever. *I am going to die. Not now, but soon. At least Jester is safe. I have repaid your kindness in this life, my friend. I hope to see you again in the next.* Her mind succumbed to a filmy dreamlike state, not sleep, an empty place where she didn't have to think or feel.

••••

It was quiet and still when her mind slipped back to her. She was lying on a bed. Was someone with her? She listened for any indication of movement or breath. Deathlike silence made her shudder. *I am alone. Or dead. And cold.* It was not a bone-chilling cold, just cool enough for goose bumps to form along her arms. *Why has Teresa not lit the fire?* A clock ticked somewhere nearby, its steady tick-tock lending an eerie and otherworldly feel to the room. She drew a deep breath through her nose. *Musty.* There was no doubt she was not at home at Westpoint in her own cozy room, which always smelled of vanilla and citrus. *This must be the room I occupied before at Augustus'.* Bile rose in her throat and she would have retched if she was not too nervous to eat in the morning.

Bits and pieces of the meeting with the king surfaced. *Oh God. Jester. Where is he?* She forced her sluggish body to sit up. How long did she lay there? Was it day or night? An owl hooted outside her window answering her unvoiced question. A vague memory returned of a glass being held to her lips and the command to drink the bitter brew it contained. Was she drugged to keep her quiet? Sliding from the bed, she tried to recall the setup of the room. *Chairs in the center. Fireplace on the far wall. Window… across from the bed?* She held out a hand, shuffling forward until she met a wooden ledge and then cool glass. Turning left, she carried on, trailing her fingers along the wall to guide her steps. Two dozen and she came to the corner, another dozen steps and her hand touched a wooden frame. She smiled. *The door.* Lowering her hand she groped for the knob, finding its brass surface with ease. It didn't budge when she tried to turn it.

Imprisoned to await death. I never even got a chance to meet my mother. What words of wisdom would she have shared with me? Did she too possess the power of past, present, and future sight? Tears she didn't bother to brush away trickled down her cheeks. What would happen to Jester after her murder? Would he be turned loose to fend for himself, or sold at market to pull a coal cart for some cruel master somewhere? Why did she not confide in Tyrone? Perhaps he could have taken her far away where Augustus couldn't harm them. Would the king have believed her? Maybe not since the first judge doubted her story.

Chapter Thirty-Five

Why did she do it? As callous as any butcher, Delilah ripped his heart out and stomped it into the dirt. Did the woman have some kind of death wish? It was only a matter of time before the baron would find a way to "accidentally" rid himself of her. Until then the despicable lecher would make her pay, make her sheltered life a living hell. No matter how many times Tyrone rolled her refusal to have her marriage annulled around in his head, he couldn't come up with an explanation for her about-face.

He shifted on the lumpy prison cot. Locked in here there was no way he could protect or save her from the baron's evil. Though part of him wondered why he still cared. It was obvious she had no feelings for him. It was all a lie. Served him right for falling in love with a deceitful gypsy. *A beautiful gypsy.* He shook his head. Maybe she put a spell on him, made him think he was in love with her until she no longer needed him. Groaning, he sat up. It didn't make sense. She needed him more now than ever. He swung his legs over the side of the cot and stomped to the little barred window in the door.

"I demand to be released!" He slammed his fist against the rough wooden surface as his voice echoed down the narrow passageway beyond. It was futile. No one was going to come along to hear his ranting. Who knew when he would be set free? Did his message reach Perry? Even so, he doubted Perry would be able to secure his release. For all he knew the king left orders to leave him in the dingy little cell until he rotted. He paced the tiny confines of his prison for lack of any other way to vent his frustrations.

Why did this happen to him? He did what the king commanded. Well, a little more than the king asked. Though he didn't regret deflowering Delilah, not entirely anyway. What was the baron doing to her now? For the first time in his life Tyrone experienced helplessness. Unable to stop loving the little wood nymph, understand her motives, or do anything to save her.

Footsteps echoed down the corridor outside his cell, mixing with the steady drip, drip of water. These were the constant sounds for the two days of his incarceration. He pulled his fob watch from his pocket. A glance proved it too soon for supper. The footsteps slowed and then stopped. He focused on the cell door as a set of keys jingled. The loud click of the tumblers heralded its opening. He shielded his eyes at the intrusion of light from the guard's lantern.

"Lord Frost?"

"Yes?"

"Come with me." The guard stepped back, allowing him to exit into the dank corridor.

He followed a second guard down the narrow passageway. "Where are you taking me?"

"Your release has been secured."

Tyrone heaved a sigh of relief. Good old Perry did get his message. He could always count on his childhood friend. They paused at the end of the corridor and waited while the door was unlocked and opened from the other side. At the end of a second passageway he was shown into a small office. Sure enough Perry sat, in all his finery, in a crude wooden chair facing the warden across the desk.

He raised his eyebrows and gave Tyrone a crooked smile. "You look like hell, Ty."

"Thanks. I feel like hell." He sat in the chair next to his friend. "What took you so long to spring me?"

"That is gratitude for you." Perry grinned. "I was out of town and just got your message."

Tyrone surveyed his friend's appearance. "And you dressed to the nines to come bail me out?"

Perry tossed a sack of coins on the desk. "Nope, unfortunately your untimely arrest interrupted my betrothal ball."

"Damn, sorry to be such a trial, my friend."

Perry shrugged. "No matter, as long as we get out of here before anyone notices my absence." He cast a meaningful look at the warden, who was testing the gold pieces in front of him with his teeth. When the man nodded his ascent Perry got up. "Come on, let's get out of here. This place makes me nervous."

Tyrone laughed as they left the room. "Why? Have you done something you are not proud of you might have failed to tell me about?"

His friend shrugged as they stepped onto the dark street and hailed a passing hackney cab. "No, but I have the feeling I am about to. You have ten minutes to tell me what we should do about your lady love."

"Delilah?"

Perry raised an eyebrow and they climbed aboard the coach. "First name basis. I see you have it bad, my friend."

"Is it so obvious?" Tyrone settled back against the worn cushions.

"It was already painfully obvious when your intended betrothed left you at the ball and you did not call out her new suitor." Perry leaned out the window and gave the address of Tyrone's townhouse before sitting down opposite him. "I have booked passage on a vessel bound for France for my sister's grand tour at the end of the week." He fished a paper from his pocket and handed it to Tyrone. "Here is the extra ticket. We will sneak into the baron's house, rescue your lady love, and ship her to France as my sister's spinster companion before the baron realizes she is gone."

Tyrone shook his head. "She will not go. She chose to stay with the baron of her own free will. Besides, she will not leave the pony, claims he is her protector from her past life or some such nonsense."

"Do you believe it?"

Tyrone snorted. "I do not believe in any of that past lives drivel."

"No, I mean do you believe Miss Daysland returned to the baron of her own free will?"

Doubt ate at Tyrone. "No, but I have no idea what he might have held over her head to make her go back."

The interior of the coach was cloaked in silence while both men contemplated the situation.

Even if Delilah wanted to flee to France she would not go without Jester. Jester. No one visited Delilah while I was on watch, except a stable boy the one night. Could the baron have held the pony as hostage to ensure Delilah's cooperation? He turned to Perry. "I think I know what happened. Before we rescue Delilah we have to find the pony."

They pulled up in front of his London townhouse. "I will come by tomorrow afternoon and we can plot our rescue mission." Perry placed a hand on Tyrone's shoulder. "Find the pony and leave the rest to me."

"I hope I can repay your kindness one day, Perry."

Perry grinned. "Just try to stay out of trouble, all right?"

Tyrone nodded and stepped down from the coach. One couldn't ask for a better friend.

• • •

Tyrone rode into the clearing surrounding the little pool a day after his release, surprised to find a shaggy piebald horse hitched to a gypsy vardos. A small fire burned underneath a black kettle

216

hanging from a structure. The fragrance of stewing vegetables mixed with herbs and spices reached him, and he savored it with appreciation before announcing his presence.

"Hallooo, the wagon."

At his call the door to the vardos swung open. A middle-aged woman peered out, an old musket in her hands. She leveled the piece at him with a frown. "Who are ye, and what do ye want?"

He raised his hands to show he was unarmed. "The name is Tyrone Frost, Earl of Merryweather. Who are you and what are you doing on Westpoint land?"

Her gaze narrowed. "Ain't Westpoint land. What do ye want with me?"

If she knew this side of the pool was not on Westpoint land, she was familiar with the area. Tyrone lowered his hands. "I did not expect anyone to be here."

"Me neither." She lowered the gun. "Yer welcome to share my meal."

"Thank you for your kindness." He dismounted and led his horse into the clearing, securing it to a tree a short distance from the gelding. The woman stepped from her wagon and crossed to stir the contents of the pot. When he approached she nodded to one of two stumps nearest the fire and then set her weapon on the ground at her feet. After he sat she dished up a wooden bowl of the hearty stew and handed it to him.

He dug in as she helped herself to a bowl and sat on the other stump. "Why is it you are here all alone?"

She darted an uneasy glance at him. "Never said I was alone, did I?"

"No, you did not," he admitted. "I just assumed, since I have not seen any other."

"My Meeko is out waiting." She turned back to her meal.

He paused, a spoonful of delicious stew halfway to his mouth. "What is he waiting for?"

"My daughter to return to Westpoint."

His spoon clattered to the bowl and he stared at her. "You are Delilah's mother?"

Her head snapped up and her startled gaze fixed on him. "What do you know of my daughter?"

"You are Kata then?"

She nodded.

"If only I'd found you a week ago."

"Why were you looking for me?" Her gaze slid to the weapon at her feet.

"You are the one who can save Delilah from her fate." Tyrone set his bowl down. "She returned to the baron, though I believe the choice was not hers. I think he used Jester to convince her to go with him."

Her eyes widened. "She is with March's boy?"

"Yes, and she is in grave danger, for now that all her lands and inheritance are in his greedy hands he will do away with her at the first chance to make it look like an accident. We have little time to save her."

"But he is her half brother. What kind of person would allow such a marriage to exist?"

Tyrone rubbed his jaw. "The king, but without you we had no way to prove either of their parentages. I believe March had Deagan and the rest of his clan murdered."

Kata sighed. "I, too, believe it was the baron's men who burned our camp that night. My mate, Meeko, and I helped birth a farmer's babe and by the time we returned to the camp all that was left were a few smoldering wagons and charred beasts. I was supposed to see my daughter for the first time in fourteen summers. She was to marry the Romo baro's son and be the new leader of all the clans."

"You said your mate is at Westpoint waiting for Delilah's return? How did you know she survived the fire?" He pierced the woman with a suspicious stare.

"I saw it in my dreams."

He frowned, unwilling to believe in such nonsense. When the woman returned his look with steadfast determination, he decided she was telling the truth. "I do not believe Delilah will be returning to Westpoint on her own. I came here to wait until dark to attempt to steal her away from March."

Kata's lips thinned. "Meeko and I will help you."

He nodded. "The first thing we must do is find Jester, for I do not think Delilah will come with us without him."

She smiled. "It will take a gypsy to steal such an item from under someone's nose without his knowing."

Chapter Thirty-Six

Delilah rolled over in bed to face the door as a key scraped in the lock. It was too late for the woman who cared for her to be entering. It was far past dinner and she was already abed. The door opened and heavy footsteps crossed the carpet. "Wake up, *dear* wife."

She scrambled into a sitting position. For days she had been locked in this room and her husband had never come to see her. Why was he here now, and at such a late hour? Easing off the bed, she stood, clutching the blanket to her chest, and forced herself to remain clam. "What do you want, Augustus?"

"I have everything I want, Delilah." His evil laugh raised the hairs on the back of her neck. "We are going for a little swim, you and I."

"Swim?" She stepped back when his fingers clamped around her wrist.

"You like to swim. I saw you there with the earl the night I pulled you from that horrid little beast of yours." His sadistic laugh reverberated off the walls of her prison.

"I do not understand."

He dragged her along behind him, jostling her against the door jam on their way by. Delilah cried out as her shoulder glanced off it. "You may yell the house down if you want, my dear, but all the servants have been given the night off except for two who are most loyal to me."

Frightened, she struck out at him and he pushed her back into the arms of another who smelled of horse sweat and manure. Her wrists were pinned behind her back and she was shoved forward in the direction of the stairs. Were they going to push her down them to her death? "Help! Someone help me. Jester!" They reached the top of the stairs and to her relief she was guided down them instead of being thrown from the top.

"You can scream all you want, but your simple-minded beast is not here."

Terror squeezed her chest. "You promised you would not hurt Jester if I came to you willingly. What did you do to him?"

"I did nothing to the filthy creature. He is being sent to the market as we speak to find a new position, perhaps as a vendor's mule. Or, maybe I should have returned him to your lover as a rug, a reminder of his failure to protect his ward." His cruel chuckle sent a shiver down her spine. "Either way, you will not need him to go for a swim. As your loving husband, rest assured I will guide you safe and sound to the pool you love to visit each night."

She gasped. "How do you know my habits?"

"One learns the movements of their prey, if they observe them long enough. Hurry up, I have not got all night, my dear. I will need all my strength to act the grieving, distraught husband on the morrow when your body is found floating in the pool where you drowned."

Their footsteps echoed as they crossed the tile foyer, reminding Delilah of how alone she was at the moment. She was left with little choice but to try to fight back on her own. The hands securing her wrists tightened as if the person holding her was privy to her thoughts. She knew the way to the little waterfall and could swim the length of it by memory. There was a chance she could outwit them and find help. It was a small chance, but one she was willing to take.

The door opened and a brisk fall breeze nipped at her cheeks, bare feet, and arms as she was guided down the icy marble steps. They didn't walk five minutes across the frosty grass before her teeth were chattering. The wind picked up, rustling the remaining leaves in the trees, its chilled fingers plucking at the fabric of her thin nightdress, flapping it about her shaking knees. In hope Jester might be nearby, she puckered her lips, stiff from cold, and whistled long and low.

"Whistle all you like, Delilah, your guide will not come for you," Augustus needled.

She strained to hear any noise Jester might make over the howl of the wind and rush of dying leaves set loose from the trees. A faint sound made her turn her head. Was it the telltale whinny and light tread of the pony reaching her desperate ears? "Jester?" She listened for it again, but heard nothing. *It must have been the wind. It is up to me now.* The faithful animal guided her most of the way through her life—now she must fend for herself in the biggest test she ever faced.

Their footsteps crunched over the dried leaves blanketing the ground and poked her bare feet, stirring up the scent of mold and decay. On foot the path was not so familiar to her and she fought to make sense of their journey. A lone owl hooted above. She wondered if it was the same one who always roosted in the big, knotted tree at the side of the path she usually took with Jester.

To occupy her panicked mind she pictured Jester as a colt, the two of them frolicking around the flames of the gypsy fire. It was one of the last visual memories remaining before the sickness came with its high fever and took away her sight. *To bask in the heat of a fire at this moment would be welcome. To wrap my arms around Jester's furry neck would be heavenly…* Shaking the thoughts from her head, she tried to focus on something other than the cold. Her feet and toes became numb, causing her to stumble. The man who held her grunted and hauled her back to her feet. *I cannot walk much further.* As luck would have it they pressed through the thicket surrounding the little pool and the spray from the waterfall dampened her cheeks. She stumbled again and fell to her knees on the bank. The light scent of smoke registered as she huddled there on the wet moss. Was Tyrone still camped out here? Hope flared in her breast. Who else would be here? "Tyrone!"

"Calling for your lover, are you?" Augustus snickered. "'Tis a little late now, my dear."

A sob caught in her throat. *He is right. Tyrone will be long gone back to London. Why would he wait for me when I wounded him so?*

A pair of hands pulled her upright. "Get in the water."

Without waiting for her to take a step, the stable boy shoved her off the bank into the icy pool. The shock of the temperature drove the air from her lungs. Her captor released her hands, and she floundered for purchase on the slick rocks. Then when she gained her footing someone grabbed her by the shoulder and propelled her deeper into the water. When the frigid blanket reached her chest she was yanked to a halt.

"It is deep enough there. Drown her now and be quick about it. It is damned cold out here tonight."

She fought with everything she possessed, fingers clawing and scratching. Twisting she tried to get free of the hands pressing her down. Water flowed over her head. Her scream was cut off in a choking bubble. In terror and desperation she struggled. *No! Jester, Tyrone, where are you? Help me…please.*

Chapter Thirty-Seven

The three of them crouched in the bushes lining the path to the baron's stable. A gust of wind made Tyrone wish he brought his greatcoat, but the garment would have flapped and crinkled, perhaps blowing their cover. He shifted. "What is taking so long?" he whispered to Perry, who hunkered beside him on the damp leaves.

Kata jabbed him in the ribs. "Shh, Meeko will not fail you."

Tyrone resisted the urge to criticize the reliability of gypsies in general. Instead he focused his gaze on the small square of light spilling from the narrow opening in the barn door. Five minutes passed and there was still no sign of Kata's mate. Perhaps he shouldn't have trusted the mission to the gypsy. Just as he was about to crawl out of their cover and retrieve Jester himself, the man poked his head out of the doorway, looked both ways, and then slipped from the barn, leading the shaggy pony behind. Breathing a sigh of relief, Tyrone took the halter shank from Meeko and passed it to Perry as the gypsy ducked into the brush with them.

"Easy as stroking a honey bee as it gathers nectar from a flower," Meeko boasted.

Perry snorted. "Now that is a risky thing to try, unless you enjoy being stung, Meeko. All right, are you ready, Kata?"

"Aye."

Tyrone slipped from the bushes and jogged along the trees until he reached the back garden gate. He waited for Kata to make her way to him before he lifted the latch and pushed it open. A slight squeak was all the noise it made, but in his mind he cursed the sound as they squeezed through the gap. Once Kata was inside she would find Delilah's room and wake her daughter. A candle in the window was the signal for Perry to bring Jester into the open lawn. With any luck the pony would respond to Delilah's whistle and whinny in return to prove he was alive and in their possession.

A door opened and voices drifted from the veranda at the back of the house. Tyrone stayed Kata with a hand on her shoulder. Curious, he crept through the herb garden to the corner of the house. He pressed himself up against the wall and peered around the corner. Three figures approached in single file, the middle one wearing a flapping white gown of some kind. As they passed he got a better look at the three and concluded it was the baron, Delilah, and a servant.

He cringed as the pony nickered. If Perry didn't silence the animal, their plan would be foiled.

"Jester?"

Relief flooded him when the pony remained silent despite her call. The group kept walking across the lawn toward the fringe of forest bordering the estate. As quiet as possible, he made his way back to Kata and signaled for her to follow him back out the gate. As soon as the trio disappeared into the woods he hurried across the lawn to where Perry, Meeko, and Jester still hid.

"March and a servant have Delilah. They went into the woods at the end of the lawn."

Perry groaned and released his grip on the pony's nostrils. "What do we do now?" The animal took a deep breath and shook his head.

"We follow them. There is only one reason they would take a walk in the middle of the night." Tyrone didn't bother to give the reason torturing his mind, knowing by their silence they reached the same conclusion.

Single file they made their way to the woods. They came across the path the others took with little difficulty. The wind picked up, covering any noise they made as they followed the party ahead of them. The path turned, joining with a wider one. Even in the dark, Tyrone recognized it as the path to the little waterfall Delilah loved. A few moments later the apparitions ahead disappeared in a rustle of branches. He signaled for the others to hold up and crept forward. On his hands and knees he crawled beneath the boughs. Voices cut through the darkness as the three figures tarried upon the bank above the pool.

"Tyrone!" Delilah called, her voice pinched with fear.

The baron said something and laughed.

"Get in the water," the second figure growled.

Tyrone realized the servant holding Delilah was none other than the stable boy he had fired that first day for fornicating on the job. The man shoved Delilah in the water and she screamed. Tyrone leaped into action. With a warlike cry, he sprinted to the water. Rushing the stable boy he knocked him off his feet and together they tumbled into the icy pool. They wrestled each other as they scrambled for footing on the slick bottom. Something bobbed to the surface sputtering and splashing just beyond his elbow. He hoped it was Delilah as he tried to dodge a blow from the stable boy. It glanced off his head. Ears ringing and head pounding, he threw a punch of his own. It connected with enough force to topple the slighter lad backward. The boy went down with a splash. Tyrone held him under for a moment to leave the servant breathless enough to be unable to gain the upper hand.

Panting and out of breath he yanked the lad to his feet and dragged him to the bank. The boy flopped on the sand gasping and throwing up water as Tyrone turned to find Delilah. The click of a pistol made him freeze and look to the bank.

"Stop right there, Frost." The baron braced his feet, his arm around Delilah's neck, a pistol muzzle to her temple. She shivered as she clutched his arm, water dripping from her sodden hair and nightdress and her teeth chattering loud enough for all to hear. Meeko and Perry stood to one side, their hands in the air.

"Ghastly timing, Frost. Now I have to find a way to dispose of you and your friends before I can drown my half sister." The baron sighed as if it were a boring task to be performed.

Tyrone raised his hands. "How will you make all our deaths look like an accident, March? You will never get away with it."

The baron's brow furrowed. "I admit it will take some doing; however, I shall rise to the challenge."

Out of the corner of his eye Tyrone noticed Jester saunter onto the bank behind the baron. Maybe he could use the pony to distract the man and get the gun away. "Perhaps we can make a deal, March."

"A deal?" The baron's eyes narrowed. "What kind of deal?"

Tyrone glanced at Perry and rolled his eyes toward the pony before he stepped to one side to divert the baron's attention. With any luck Perry would get his hint and spook the pony into the man, distracting him long enough for Tyrone to make a move for the gun.

"Stop." Augustus glanced between him and Perry. "Jeb, get your arse up off the ground and watch that one over there." He jerked his head in Perry's direction. "If you try jumping me, Frost, the girl dies."

Left with no other choice, Tyrone stepped back toward the group. "Release Delilah and you can have the estate and her inheritance."

"Yeah, right." Augustus shook his head. "How dull-witted do you think I am? As soon as I let go of her I will be floating in the water."

"Please, Augustus', I promise I will give you all of it," Delilah pleaded, her voice shaking with the force of her fear and the cold. "I beg of you. Let me take Jester and disappear with the gypsies."

At the mention of his name the pony's ears flickered.

"Stubble it," Augustus growled tightening his grip on her windpipe.

Delilah's strangled cry made the pony pin his ears. Without warning he leaped forward and bit the baron on the arm. Augustus dropped the pistol with a shriek so loud it drowned Delilah's cry as he released her. Tyrone sprang forward and tackled him, rolling over and over on the bank until Perry helped him pin the baron to the ground. When he looked over his shoulder he saw that Meeko had secured the scrawny stable boy in a headlock.

Delilah dropped to her knees and wrapped her arms around Jester's neck. Tears streamed down her wind-chapped cheeks as she sobbed.

Tyrone eased off the baron, who was whining about "the damned beast trying to eat him," picked up the gun, and handed it to Perry. He crossed to Delilah's side and knelt beside her on the muddy bank. "Delilah, everything is all right now." Jester nuzzled him with a soft nicker as he patted the pony's head. "Good boy, Jester. I owe you a bucket full of apples, my friend." The pony nodded his head as if in agreement and blew through his nose as a light rain began to fall. Tyrone chuckled and pried Delilah's frozen fingers from the animal's tangled mane. "Come on, we need to get you home."

Kata appeared at the opposite edge of the pond leading the piebald hitched to her wagon. "My lord, bring my daughter here where it is warm."

"My mother is alive?"

Tyrone touched Delilah's cheek. "Yes, Delilah, your mother Kata is here. She and her mate Meeko helped us rescue you. Come now, there will be time to explain all when you are warm."

Delilah sniffled and allowed him to scoop her up into his arms. She tucked her face against his neck as he carried her, her tears warm compared to the rain. Once she eyes tucked in a big down quilt on the narrow cot in Kata's care, Tyrone climbed aboard the vardos and turned the horse to the main road. After securing the baron's and his servant's hands behind their backs with pieces of stout rope, Perry and Meeko marched them along behind.

Chapter Thirty-Eight

Delilah contemplated the woman perched on the edge of her bed, wishing she could see her. Did her mother still look as she remembered as a child? Was her former nursemaid still a great beauty, or did age strip her of all her youthful luster? The light scent of cinnamon surrounding her mother made Delilah think of cozy fall nights and apple pie. There were so many questions she needed to ask. Would Kata be forthcoming with the answers?

"You are wondering how to ask me all you wish to know."

"How did you know? Do you have special powers, too?"

Kata laughed. "No, my daughter, I do not. It seems safe to believe you would want to know everything we denied you since your birth."

Taking a deep breath, Delilah asked the question she both dreaded and needed to know most. "Why did you leave me when my mother…my father's wife died?"

A sorrowful sigh filled the room. "Ah, I am not surprised it is your first question of me, Delilah. I left because I had no other choice. Your father and I continued to share our passion after his wife adopted you. I suppose she knew about it yet was so complete with her joy in you she turned a blind eye to it. Everyone was happy for a time, and then the fever came. It was strange, but the fever attacked only you and her. You were strong and I used every herb and spell I knew to keep the sickness from claiming you. Instead it claimed your eyesight. We took you back to Deagan in hopes he could cure you, but nothing could be done."

"Then your father's wife took ill. He begged me to save her. He said it was God's punishment for our sins. I gave him the same herbs I used for you, but I refused to leave your side to administer them to her. She died within hours. Your father never forgave me, for he still loved her, you see. Once you were well enough he sent me away. He said the way to atone for his sins was to never lay eyes on me or any other gypsy witch again."

"Are you a witch?"

Kata gave a hollow laugh. "No, my child. I am a simple caregiver."

"Why did you not take me, too?"

"I could not, for as you know English law gives the sire all rights to a child."

Doubt fueled Delilah's mind. "You could have stolen me away. He would have never found me hidden among the gypsies."

"Yes, but the squire could give you so much more than a vagabond life. He looked after you well and gave you everything you desired, did he not?"

"Yes," Delilah was forced to admit. "Except I did not have my mother."

"For that I am sorry. Deagan did the one thing he could to make up for it by gifting you with Jester."

"Uncle Deagan says Jester was my mate in another life. Do you believe such things?"

"It matters not what I think, child. What do you think?"

Delilah replayed all the times in her mind Jester came to her rescue, seemed to know what she was thinking, protected her, and somehow knew when she was heartsore. Did she believe he was her mate reincarnated? No, she supposed she was too practical for such nonsense, but she couldn't deny their unusual connection. "No. He and I are tied with a special bond though, one I cannot explain or understand."

"Then that is all you need to believe in." A soft hand covered hers where it rested atop the bedcovers.

Delilah sighed. "Am I a squire's daughter or a gypsy?"

"You are both those things. You cannot deny your heritage or your upbringing. To find your perfect balance you must combine the two and listen to your heart."

Listen to her heart? Her heart was too sad and wounded to speak to her. She hurt Tyrone to the core with her betrayal. He would never forgive her. She could never forgive herself. Why did love hurt so much? He was going back to London to find himself a suitable bride after the king rewarded him for rescuing her. The king would appoint someone else to see to her estate until a suitable husband could be found, she was sure. How could she combine her two lives when one was now no more than an empty house? "I am a gypsy. I will sell the estate and travel as you do, telling people of their futures, in the crystal ball."

"Mine is a hard life, Delilah. You are better to stay here where you are warm and protected."

A tear slipped down Delilah's cheek and she brushed it away. "Here I am all alone. If you will not approve my coming, then stay here with me."

Kata patted her hand. "You are not alone, you have Jester. I would not be happy here living as a poor relation. I am a free spirit, a wanderer who calls nowhere and everywhere home. I cannot stay more than a few days. It will be winter soon and I must join up with another gypsy clan before the snow flies." She wiped a second tear from Delilah's cheek. "Rest now, my child. If you still want to be a gypsy when I return from London, then I will take you with me."

The bed shifted and Kata was gone, the door closing with the softest whisper behind her.

Alone. Again. What was she to do? If Tyrone returned after speaking to the king, would he believe her if she professed her feelings for him? She lied to him once, would he think her deceitful now?

Chapter Thirty-Nine

Delilah placed her fingers on the keyboard. Her scared hands changed the feel of the ivory. The cool keys were smoother now somehow. Would she still be able to coax the sweet melodies from the instrument? *There is no time like the present to find out.* She was alone so no one would hear the notes if they were sour. Taking a deep breath she pressed down. The first notes were stilted yet in tune. With bated breath she entered into the first few bars of one of her favorite, simpler pieces. Her fingers fumbled, though she suspected it was more from not having played in a while than the thin layer of scar tissue. The more she played the looser and more sure of the notes her fingers became. A smile of genuine happiness spread across her face as she relaxed and swayed to the music.

She sensed Tyrone's presence as the last notes died away. "You came back."

His footsteps crossed the plush carpet with a whisper of sound. "Of course I did."

Turning from the pianoforte, she tried to glean something of his encounter with the king from his tone but failed. "Has the king seen fit to annul my marriage to Augustus?"

"Yes." He stopped in front of her, his breath brushing the top of her hair.

Why was he back? Would it not have been easier for him to send a missive advising her of the change in her marital status? She frowned. "Have you come back to finish the task the king assigned you?"

"Yes, I have been sent back to see you wed."

Anger at his nonchalance made her slide from the bench and face him arms akimbo. "I relieve you of the duty, my lord, for I have decided to go with my mother and learn the gypsy ways."

"You cannot be serious. Why?"

Did she detect a hint of hurt in his question? "There is nothing for me here. I do not wish to be married off. I am a gypsy and choose to live wild and free like the rest of my clan."

"Kata has agreed to this?"

She raised her chin with stubborn resolve. "Yes, before you went to see the king."

His voice was soft. "The king will not be pleased. Is there nothing I can say or do to change your mind?"

There was, but she was not about to lead him into an admission he didn't make of his own accord. She wouldn't force him to lie just to soothe both their offended honors. "No." Saying the word was like slamming a door that could never be opened again.

• • •

Tyrone shoved back his chair and got up to pace the squire's study for the umpteenth time. The beads of sweat formed along his hairline, trickling down his face and under his limp cravat. Would this infernal heat ever cease? He tugged the limp material from around his neck and tossed it to the desk top. *Unusual weather for this time of year.* By now a morning frost was the norm with temperatures comfortable in wool clothes. Except for a day or two of cooler temperatures, the weather seemed to have reverted to summer conditions. After wiping his brow with his sleeve, he strolled to the window and looked out over the garden.

What would the king say when he informed him Delilah declined marriage to join the gypsies? He still didn't understand her reasoning. Was marriage so bad she would give up her comfortable life just to avoid it? Perhaps it was him she detested.

A movement in the garden below caught his eye. Was it Jester out for a midnight stroll among the gardener's prize hollyhocks? A shape formed out of the shadows in a light colored billow of fabric. The material floated around the wearer, lending a supernatural feel to the apparition. He shook his head. *Not again.* Why could the blasted woman not stay put in her room where she was safe? Though there was less danger with the baron and his servant locked in Newgate, the fact remained that wandering the countryside at night was risky whether the wanderer were blind or sighted.

The woods were cooler than the house and he welcomed the slight breeze cooling the sweat on his brow. It was easy to understand why Delilah slipped from the house on such nights and took refuge in the woods. Leaves crunched beneath his feet and he grimaced. Would she detect his pursuit? He paused to listen. The pony's steady thuds over the dry vegetation was louder than his own tread, and he felt sure enough to continue. Taking a heady breath of damp ground, dry leaves, and overripe apples he smiled. It was easy to experience the world as Delilah did in the darkness surrounding him. Lost in his newfound sensory perception, he was startled to find himself at the narrow thicket bordering the pool. After stepping through it he waited for his eyes to adjust to the moonlight reflecting off the shimmering water. He scanned the pool for her and then swung his inspection to the bank. Delilah crouched there, splashing water over her face and neck.

She froze, head cocked to one side, and then turned to face him. "Why do you insist on following me?"

He grinned, not surprised she heard him. "I would not want anything to happen to the lovely wood nymph who visits this pool."

Her little snort broadened his grin. "I am no wood nymph, as I have told you before. Why can you not leave me in peace to enjoy my last night of the pool?"

The smile slipped from his lips. "I fail to see why this must be your last night, Delilah."

"For one so well sighted you fail to see a great many things, Tyrone."

She turned back to sit cross-legged on the bank, and he was taken by the sight of the moon's glow on her dark hair. Oh yes, she was indeed a magical creature who wove a spell over him the first night he spied her here. "For one so well tuned to the world around them, I think it is you who fail to see."

"A coup, my lord, for pointing out the obvious."

The bitterness in her reply made him bite his lip. She missed his meaning. He sat down beside her, close enough to catch her familiar scent of honey and oranges. "Why are you leaving?"

"You should know the answer," she snipped.

He grunted. "The king will be most upset, I suspect."

"I shall send a note to him explaining I ran off to spare you his wrath."

Was she angry at him or the king? "I am not worried about the king. I am worried about you."

"You should not be. I have my mother and Jester. Besides, I can look after myself. I did so before you barged into my music room." She tossed a pebble into the pool. It landed with a plop, the moonlight accenting the ripples melting into the churning spray of the waterfall.

He wanted to shake her, make her see what she was giving up by running away. "Damn your ridiculous pride! Why will you not stay and permit me to see things made right?"

Anger sizzled in her voice. "And let you marry me off to soothe your masculine sense of duty? I suppose I cannot blame you for doing the king's work when he is dangling a political appointment above your head as an incentive. "

"No! Delilah, I no longer care about the king's agenda. I want to marry you and spend the rest of my life with you." He looked away, afraid he would regret laying his heart out there for her to stomp on and throw back in his face.

She gasped. Silence lingered, broken only by the sound of the falls and the rhythmic slosh of water against the bank.

What was she thinking?

"You want to marry me? After I returned to Augustus and… hurt you?"

He almost laughed at her shocked tone. "Yes, is it so hard for you to fathom?"

"Yes," she whispered.

"I love you, Delilah."

Her response was harsh. "Nay, a match between us would not further your political aspirations. People see me as a pitiful excuse for a woman. You need someone with connections, whom people will respect and admire, someone who enjoys being in the public eye and attending balls and such. I hate crowds. I have nothing to offer."

Tyrone drew her stiff form into his arms. "You have many things to offer, wood nymph. Every day with you is an adventure, from reading and seeing with your fingertips to the astounding melodies that flow every time you sit at your pianoforte. I have begun to see the world as you do, and I am a better person for it. I love you, Delilah, and I want to explore your world every day for the rest of my life. I do not need a political career to be happy, I see that now. No well-connected milk and water miss could ever make me as happy as you will."

Her posture softened and she exhaled a deep breath. He reached up with a hand to cradle her jaw and bring her lips to his. The dampness of her tears met his fingertips. His lips covered hers as her arms wound around his neck. Their simple kiss, gentle, caressing, and sweet, brought him so much joy he thought his heart would burst. She pulled back, the act filling him with dread. Was she going to refute his love?

Her fingers traced the plains and peaks of his face.

"What are you doing?"

"I want to see the face of the man who loves me."

He frowned. "Why? You have seen me before with your fingertips and I have not changed in so short a time."

A grin formed on her lips that puzzled him. "Ah, but I would like to be able to picture his reaction when I tell him I love him, too."

She laughed as he hugged her to him. "Will you consent to be my wife?"

"Nothing would make me happier, Tyrone."

"We shall wed right here by the pool where I was first captivated by my wood nymph as soon as the bans can be read." He pulled back and cradled her hands in his. "We will have a small ceremony, only Kata, Perry, and a minister."

Jester whinnied and ambled over from his spot beside the bushes. Delilah laughed. "I think you are forgetting someone."

Tyrone chuckled and patted the pony's head. "It would not be official without you, Jester, to guide Delilah to the alter."

A Sneak Peek from Crimson Romance
(From *A Rogue in Sheep's Clothing* by Elf Ahearn)

With a bang, Ellie Albright burst into the hall and slammed shut the oak door to the study. The windowpanes of the massive Tudor mansion rattled from the blow. Her three sisters poked their noses around the parlor entrance, then, at the sight of her, quickly retreated. Even the dogs scattered in alarm. Ellie turned to the empty hallway and shouted, "He simply won't listen to reason!"

Her mother, Lady Albright, hastened down the corridor, shutting doors as she approached. "Hush, the servants will hear."

"He could sell anything, anything but my horse, but that fool Lank told him to do it, so he won't listen to me." Ellie seethed at the thought of the estate steward filling her father's gullible mind with false information. "Why does Papa believe that scoundrel?"

Her mother patted her arm as if stroking a pinecone. "Oh dear, we mustn't upset Papa. He's a brilliant man who's trying to do his best."

"Do his best!" Ellie jammed her fist against her mouth until the stricken look in her mother's eyes registered. It was too unbearable to witness; the girl turned away and fought to douse the fire of emotion burning through her self-control. But her frustration could not be tamed. "Rahhhh," she growled, hands shaking at her sides. "Rahhhh." Her mother reached to touch her again, but Ellie bolted out of the house and into a pelting rain.

The black bellies of clouds sagged against the treetops on a distant hill, splitting the sun into anemic rays. Taking great gulps of raw air into her lungs, Ellie slapped away a trickle of water that dared blur her vision. She'd hoped the cold would numb her mind, but over and over again she saw her father's index finger pointing at the numbers on a ledger sheet. "Mr. Lank," her father said, giving the estate manager's name the same reverence due a scholar, "Mr. Lank says selling Manifesto is the only way to pay our debts."

Ellie ran further into the rain. The wind tore spring leaves off the trees. It freed her soaking hair from the last of its pins and whipped tendrils across her eyes. The downpour coursed over her cheeks cooling her tears before she felt their heat, and because her body was no match for nature, she lost herself in its fury. Then her mother's voice pierced the storm's comforting blanket. "Come back in, Ellie!"

But Ellie couldn't. Instead, she ran against the gale, out toward the moors where the storm promised solace.

• • •

It seemed hours later, though Ellie had no idea how much time had passed when she drifted back toward home. The rain had ceased and the clouds had gone white. Her sister Claire met her as she stumbled through a water-soaked field of barley.

"Poor thing," Claire said, wrapping a cloak around Ellie's shoulders. "You're wet as a fish. I'll be dosing you with Sydney peppermint and mustard plasters if we don't get you warmed soon."

"I won't get sick," said Ellie, not bothering to hold her skirts above the wet grass. "I'd welcome a fever to let me forget."

Claire patted her shoulder. "Poor Papa. He'd do anything to be left alone with his copy of the Rosetta Stone, a Greek dictionary, and a set of hieroglyphs. Perhaps if you speak to him tomorrow…"

From the set of her father's jaw, Ellie doubted it. He was a kind, absent-minded man, a man who usually gave in to the entreaties of his wife and daughters, but this time…This time something was different.

She and Claire entered the house and Ellie plodded up the stairs toward her bedroom. Her mother watched as she went by, but said nothing, eyes deep with sorrow. Sisters Snap and Peggity stood at a respectful distance and were quiet as well.

In Ellie's room, Claire silently stripped her sister of her drenched clothing. "Manifesto is the greatest horse bred by centuries of Albrights," Ellie said, her voice hollow. "What financial difficulty could be so bad we'd sell our most valuable asset?" Though she'd thought she'd shed the last of them, tears pricked her lids. "I was there the day Manifesto was born. I've raised him, trained him, cared for him. He trusts only me." Suddenly furious, she brushed the tears from her cheeks. "This is Lank's decision. He's reduced the mares to bone and hair. He's stealing the money for grain…"

Taking the hem of Ellie's wet chemise, Claire pulled the soaked garment over her sister's head. "But can you prove it?"

Ellie shook her head. "No. No, I can't."

"Mrs. Lank isn't buying goods from Finchy's anymore," Snap, Ellie's six-year-old sister, announced, racing into the room and hurling herself on the bed, the pack of hounds trailing. "Mr. Finchy's boy told me no one likes her because she's wearing air."

"You mean she's putting on airs," Peggity, the eldest of the four Albright sisters, corrected, coming in behind Snap. She joined her little sister on the bed and watched Claire towel Ellie dry. "If only Papa would let you run the estate," Peggity said, plumping a pillow behind her. "You're so wonderful with horses."

Ellie took the towel and scrubbed her wet hair. "I'll tell you the first thing I'd do—I'd fire that Lank and kick his fat wife back into Finchy's."

Claire winced. "A civil tongue…"

Lady Albright swept into the room, a hot water bottle tucked under her arm. "Oh dear, dear me, come sweet darling." She pushed the bottle under the bed linens and wrapped a blanket around Ellie's shivering shoulders, then tucked her under the covers. "I wish your father told you the truth up front. It does no good to leave loved ones in the dark." She sighed, lifted Snap off the bed, then put the child on her lap. "This is very serious, my darlings. We have true cause for alarm. Your papa says Uncle Sebastian, God rest his soul, gambled with Baron Wadsworth and left a debt of three thousand pounds. The baron..." Lady Albright's voice went faint with emotion and she bit her lip, "He's a very dangerous man. Your Papa said the baron slashed a young woman's face on High Street in the middle of Exeter. Cut her with his sword, and not a man went to her assistance. Everyone was too afraid. The baron said he'd do the same to Papa and then to us if the money wasn't delivered."

Never in her life had Ellie seen a tear leak from her mother's eye. The sight frightened her more than Baron Wadsworth's threat. She and her sisters went still, the dogs stopped fidgeting, and a pall weighed the air.

Pressing a corner of Snap's pinafore to her eyes, Lady Albright continued, "I would rather sell the Fitzcarry pearls than tear your heart this way, my darling Ellie, but your papa absolutely forbids it."

Ellie swallowed hard, a lump growing in her chest. "I don't mean to be selfish, Mama, but without Manifesto we will go bankrupt. That horse is our future."

Her mother plunked Snap back on the bed and took Ellie's hands in her trembling fingers. "Oh sweeting, I wish you could understand. It's terrible news, we'll all miss Manifesto, but he isn't *your* future." She turned to address all of her daughters. "My darlings, you're no longer the offspring of a respected scientist— you're the daughters of an earl. The best way to avoid bankruptcy is to marry well, and that means pretty dresses and Almack's in London."

"What!" Ellie exploded, pulling away from her mother. "The Albrights can't give up breeding horses!"

Lady Albright's hand caught Ellie's arm and gripped it tight. "Nineteen-year-old daughters of earls do not gallop astride on stallions. That must end, Ellie, and perhaps selling Manifesto is the best way to make that change. Your sisters wish to marry, and for that to happen we must maintain our reputation."

Ellie's mouth dropped open. "But Mama!"

Her mother abruptly stood and interrupted before Ellie could say more. "Tonight let's forget our troubles and get ready for the Mortimers' assembly. Wash your faces and put cucumbers on your eyes. My girls must eat asparagus to eliminate puffiness, so the bachelors find them attractive."

Ellie jumped to her feet, but her mother held up a hand to hush her. "Snap, would you ask Cook for cucumbers? And Claire, add some of your special herbs. Peggity, could you help? I'd like a word with Ellie, alone."

With her sisters gone, the room seemed dark and cold. Ellie climbed back into bed and moved her toes under the hot water bottle, but felt no warmth from it. Lady Albright smoothed her skirts, and took Ellie's hand. Against her palm, she felt her mother shaking. "I'm sorry you and your father fought today. You're a passionate girl, my darling, but when your father asks you to do something, you must obey."

"I'll apologize to Papa," Ellie said, removing her hand from her mother's and pressing her fingers to her brow, trying to tamp down the pain in her heart.

"This has been such an awful day," her mother continued. "Why don't you wear the Fitzcarry pearls tonight? You'll look beautiful in them."

Stunned, Ellie lowered her hands. No one but her mother ever wore the pearl necklace. A series of white beads, each the size of a fingernail, the strand could wrap three times about the throat. It fastened with a black pearl surrounded by diamonds. Her mother's great, great grandfather, Walter Fitzcarry, had bought, gambled, and killed for each pearl during years of adventure in the Orient. Queen Elizabeth had so admired the necklace, she'd offered thirty-five thousand acres of Scottish soil for them. Walter Fitzcarry refused. Each bead, he'd said, represented his great love for his wife.

"I don't much feel like going to the ball tonight," Ellie choked. "Claire and Peggity can find rich husbands. I don't know how to give up horses, and no man would marry a hoyden who rides astride."

As if she weren't listening, her mother pulled the covers over Ellie's bare shoulder. "All the same, wear the pearls tonight and help your family. It's every young lady's duty."

Her mother was right, of course, and Ellie knew it. Brokenhearted or not, she must do what she could for the sake of her sisters. And she had to admit, wearing the pearls would be exciting. She threw her arms around her mother's neck. "Thank you for giving me something to look forward to, Mama. You're the nicest person in the world."

"Your Papa is pretty nice too, sweet darling. He would never sell Manifesto unless he absolutely had to."

"I understand…I just…don't know who I am without my horse."

• • •

Leaning against a white panel in the Mortimers' ballroom, Ellie tried to catch her breath from dancing. The party elated her. Tomorrow, when her father'd had a night to think, she'd convince him to sell something other than Manifesto. Uncle Sebastian had left them plenty of valuable things. And the evening was so lovely, it was impossible to feel blue. Mothers and chaperones lined the walls in a colonnade of damask, silk, satin, and jewels. Young ladies floated in clouds of muslin—their faces flushed with excitement, their hair swept high and fastened with glittering combs. The Mortimers had decorated with garlands of pine strung around the ballroom, offset by sprays of silver birch at every pillar. Lit by candles, perfumed by pine, the ball was too beautiful for tragedy.

And there was the attention of the men to distract her, too. The moment Ellie and her sisters arrived, a phalanx of eligible bachelors pounced. She felt radiant, graceful, and tinged with sadness—a combination the male sex seemed unable to resist.

As she fanned her brow, Howard Fastham spied her through the crowd. Ellie ducked behind the fan's folds. *Would Mama want me to marry Howard Fastham?* The thought made her queasy. He'd paid her no heed at last year's ball. Haughty, inaccessible, Howard seemed powerful then. But with the soil still fresh over Uncle Sebastian's body, Howard led the pack of men who'd sniffed around Fairland like dogs looking for a cozy spot. His grandeur had crumbled before her eyes.

"Lady Ellie," Howard cried. "How lovely you look this evening." He tipped the front of her fan down and focused a broad, yellow-toothed smile.

"Why thank you, Mr. Fastham." The magic of the night died as Howard's eyes rested on the Fitzcarry pearls.

He stood on tiptoe and rocked toward her. "The Mortimers outdid themselves this year."

"Yes, the ballroom is splendid."

Rolling back on his heels, he added, "And how is your eldest sister, Lady Peggity, this fine evening?"

Of course he wanted to know about Peggity. She would inherit the pearls. "La, can't you see her on the dance floor, Mr. Fastham? I'm afraid she'll be without a partner in a moment. Perhaps you'd better rescue her."

Howard smiled ingratiatingly. "You'll excuse me then."

Cruel, really, to foist him off on Peggity, Ellie thought, *but could he be a more obvious fortune hunter?*

Tony Binge Harper, another dog in the pack, caught her eye as he elbowed through the crowd. *This is just too much*, she thought, twisting her fan. *And just when Howard Fastham's round rump finally disappeared.*

She pushed off from the wall, intent on escape. Before she'd taken a step, however, someone's heel landed on her foot. "Ouch, you beast!" she said.

"Good gracious. So sorry," said the "beast," turning swiftly and splashing her with white wine.

Ellie eyed the splattered front of her gown. "Now look what you've done. I'm a mess."

The beast yanked a crumpled handkerchief from his pocket. "Use this," he said, accidentally brushing her breast.

Ellie shied from his touch. "My heavens, sir, cease and desist! Now, give me your handkerchief, slowly." As she took the linen square, her hand halted in mid air. The sour look she intended for her assailant melted. *La, what a handsome man.* And then she realized she'd seen him before, but where? Dark eyes, nearly black, met her own, a hooked curl bisected his forehead, meeting the edge of a scar that crossed the ruddy crest of his right cheek.

I'm staring. Quickly she pretended to swab a spot of wine at her waist. Her breath went shallow and her thoughts scattered, but a smile tipped the corners of her lips. She'd had the great good fortune to be trod upon by one of Devon's most elusive bachelors, Hugh Davenport, Earl of Bruxburton—one of the few gentlemen who'd failed to call at Fairland. A pulse of pain reminded her of her foot. "I…I think I need to sit down," she told him.

"Ah yes…" said Hugh, searching for an empty chair.

Putting the tiniest bit of weight down, Ellie received a powerful jolt. "I'm afraid I'll not be dancing again this evening."

Hugh's back straightened and a hard look seeped into his eyes. *Is he annoyed?* she wondered.

"Well, there must be a chair here somewhere." He moved off on the hunt.

Ellie took a few limping steps after him. "I'll need your assistance." He came back and eyed her suspiciously. "Your arm, in fact," she told him.

His lips hardened, but he looped her arm through his. As they passed a row of seated grande dams, every eye watched with envy.

At an alcove, Hugh stopped to let her pass. "In here," he said.

"I can't go in there alone with you."

"Did you see a free chair on the floor?" he said. "Because what I saw was a row of plump sugar plums, and none of them likely to abandon her seat."

"People will say I've been compromised."

"Nonsense. I couldn't possibly compromise anyone in an alcove shielded by a simple palm tree. A young lady compromised in such a manner either wants to be or wants to pretend she was. Which one are you?"

"Neither," snapped Ellie.

"Then sit." He whacked back the palm revealing a gilded bench by the wall. "Besides," he continued, following her into the alcove, "your reputation will swell in direct correlation to the amount of time spent in my company."

As she sat, she rolled her eyes. "La, what an extraordinary view of oneself," she said, just loud enough for him to hear or ignore, as he saw fit.

Hugh cocked an eyebrow. "I tell you nothing but the truth."

"But we haven't even been properly introduced."

"Are you implying that you don't know who I am?"

A burning pricked her cheeks.

He folded his arms. "I thought so."

Unable to think of a retort, Ellie straightened her skirts. "Well, as long as we're here, would you be so kind as to bring over that footstool?"

With stunning grace, he lifted the stool and placed it in front of her. She caught his eyes on her trim ankle as she rested her foot on the upholstery.

"Are you comfortable?" he asked.

"Yes, just fine." She tucked her skirt tight around the leg. He stepped back, assuming an air of indifference.

She unlaced the ribbon affixing her slipper and massaged the damaged crown of her foot. A red bump had formed.

"Not such a bad wound," he said. "You'll be dancing the next jig."

"It is swollen and throbbing," she replied. "I may be confined to this alcove all evening."

He threw a haunted look over his shoulder at the ballroom.

Ha, thinking of escape, are we? She smiled. "Are you back in Devon to stay?"

"I am," said Hugh. He peered through the palm fronds again. He wouldn't look at her.

Well, if he's going to devastate my foot, I'll jolly well make him suffer a bit, too, she decided. She twirled the magnificent strand of pearls about an index finger. "Lovely weather we're having," she said, reveling in his discomfort.

A hand went through his hair, the picture of agitation. "Yes, rather."

"It already feels like summer."

"Exactly like summer—I was thinking the same thing."

"Were you, Lord Davenport? When?"

"When…when?" He paced the alcove as if searching for the exact moment he realized it felt like summer. "When I was in the garden the other day."

"Ah, in the garden," said Ellie. *Was he sweating? Very possibly he was sweating.* "Would you like your handkerchief back?"

"Perhaps that would be best." Snatching the crumpled cloth from her, he ignored his dewy brow and stuffed the linen in his pocket.

Does he think I'd want to keep his silly handkerchief because of the insignia? The conceit of the man. "The spring foals will have a fine time of it with the warmer weather."

"I say, you're an Albright, aren't you?" he said, as if struck by a revelation. "Your family owns Manifesto."

Misery swept through her at the reminder of her father's decision. "We do," she said, swallowing.

"He's a speedy animal."

"Very fast, and he jumps like a winged angel."

"My guess is his offspring will be toppers."

"You predict correctly."

"Amazing luck, your father putting him up for auction—I'm planning to bid on him tomorrow."

Ellie's throat went tight. "I beg your pardon?" she choked.

"Yes, at the horse fair. You must have known. When else was he going to sell?"

"I…I suppose I wasn't thinking properly."

"You seem upset."

Ellie scarcely heard him. "Yes," she said.

Hugh flipped the tails of his coat and sat on the edge of the bench next to her. "You didn't know Manifesto was on the block tomorrow, did you?"

"Funny, no. I thought we'd have him a bit longer."

"Sorry for springing it on you."

Ellie couldn't respond. Her thoughts were like the noise of a coach and six tearing through her brain.

"Are you disheartened? Maybe I should get you something to drink. It could help."

She looked at him, and the sympathy in his eyes sliced at her last vestige of control. She turned away and blinked back tears.

"I'm afraid I don't want anything," was all she could say. Silence filled the alcove like thick fog.

Hugh blew out a long breath. "How's your foot?"

"It's better," she said, struggling to squeeze out the words.

"That's good. Are you sure there isn't anything I can bring you?"

Shoving agony to the farthest reaches of her heart, she said, "That's all right. Would you mind leaving me alone?"

"No, of course not," he replied. "I suppose I'd feel the same way if Manifesto were my horse. But we've got some prime mares that will make him happ—"

"Could you fetch my chaperone?" she interrupted.

"Are you quite sure you're all right?"

"I'm fine, my lord. Thank you for asking, but a moment alone is all I require."

Hugh hovered, backed toward the alcove's opening. "If you'll excuse me," he said, and slipped through the palm.

Seconds later he reappeared. "How will I know which chaperone is yours?"

Ellie closed her eyes. She hated this man, this man who dared to try to take her horse. "According to your own self-assessment," she hissed, "my chaperone will be the one paying closest attention to this alcove."

•••

Feisty thing, Hugh thought, scanning the room for anxious chaperones. Ach, God help him, his mother had an approving look in her eye. She must like the Albright girl.

Another set of eyes fed on him. By the near wall sat a woman so large she seemed to have taken the chair into her flesh and consumed it whole. *The chaperone.* On the verge of approaching, he realized his mother would think he was inquiring about the Albright wench. Though the girl had looks, with her blue eyes and white hair, she was…well, entirely too appropriate. Gad, every biddy with an eligible chit had her net out for him. Aristocratic pimping—the whole thing disgusted him.

"Jake, take care of the young lady in the alcove for me, would you," he told a bewigged footman in velvet livery. "She needs her chaperone. Do you see the woman sending that chair to its death? She's the one." He slipped the man a shilling, and caught the attention of a second liveried servant. "Give me a glass of that stuff you're carrying." Hugh tossed back the champagne in a single gulp. "Wait, Willy, another."

The footman grinned. "Lord Davenport, you're a bit out of breath."

"A close call with a damsel in distress."

"Would you want a third, my lord, or will that glass hold you?"

Hugh clapped the footman on the shoulder. "I'm good for now. I'll hunt you down if I have any further frights."

It was a point of pride with Hugh that he knew most of the servants by name in the grand estates around Exeter. People of the lower classes were kind and generous. Whenever he'd had difficulties it was the serving class that came to his aid, not his mother, and certainly not the neighboring gentry.

When his mother had scandalized the family name, the eyes of the upper classes went to slits as if studying him for signs of infectious disease. That is, until his father died, leaving him sole heir.

As he strode through the ballroom, he could see the question on the lips of every doe-eyed girl and rapacious mother. Had he chosen the Albright girl? *Do something before the gossips hit their stride!* he told himself. Hortense, Lady Mortimer's comely kitchen maid, popped into mind. With her fizzy hair and fleshy breasts, Hortense was always ready, willing, and able to rescue a gentleman in need.

"My fellow revelers," he said, joining the well-tailored Eton ne're-do-wells he called his friends, "did you happen to see Hortense slopping sauce down someone's cravat tonight?"

"Why, are you in the market for a stain?" asked Poultney Bigalow.

"A blot on the family crest?" added Algernon Swift.

"A saucy piece to wrap around your neck?" Poultney added, raising his eyebrows.

"Bawdy bunch," Hugh said. "Our Hortense may have a giddy hand with a platter, but she's unmatched at extracting a fellow from a parson's mousetrap."

Algie saluted. "Godspeed, man. I believe I spied your protector feeding trays to the footmen."

•••

Hortense's pert behind led the way directly into Hugh's groin as she backed through the kitchen door balancing a tray of oysters in one hand and a magnum of champagne in the other.

"Can you help me out of a tight spot?" Hugh said, pushing her back through the door.

"Blimey, let me hand over me oysters, at least." Hortense giggled. "Now here's a first—Lord Davenport finally takin' advantage of me charms."

"You're a generous doxie," said Hugh, his eyes twinkling. "Always there for a man when he needs her."

"Oooo, you're a wicked one, my lord. Remember, I don't have a lot of time. I got me oysters."

"Follow me closely," he told her.

Hugh sauntered through the ballroom with Hortense trailing behind. As he passed his mother, he swung behind the maid, giving her a little pinch on the bottom. Hortense skipped and giggled as his mother's lips tightened.

"You were perfection," Hugh said, outside the doors to the ballroom, beyond his mother's view. "That pit of cunning baggage would have me shackled and married by morning."

"Poor lad," said Hortense. "You're a fine treasure for the ladies."

"And they are an unseemly lot of tricksters," he replied.

"We can duck into the closet near the lady's retiring room," Hortense said, pulling Hugh down the hall.

"Nay Hortense, you've already served your purpose."

The maid's shoulders slumped in disappointment. "But I've always had a longing for ye. You talk to us nice in the kitchen—as if we was friends."

"Well, you are my friends," said Hugh. "Which is why I can't stuff you in the closet outside the lady's retiring room. You've done me a favor, so let me give you a token of gratitude." He fished around in his pocket, producing a shiny gold guinea.

"Lawkes, my lord, a guinea! All's I did was walk you from the ballroom."

"And saved me from the Devon marriage market—truly a worthy service."

Overcome with excitement, Hortense threw her beefy arms about his neck. "Any favor for you, my lord, is a favor to me."

A strangled "Oh!" interrupted the embrace. Hugh disengaged from Hortense and looked full into the horrified eyes of the damsel he'd led limping from the dance floor.

• • •

Shock rocketed through Ellie. She couldn't move. Mouth open, she stared at Hugh, deep in the arms of the Mortimers' kitchen maid—face buried in her breasts—a golden guinea glinting like a beacon in the wench's wash-reddened hand.

"Like to join us?" Hortense said. "Three's welcome company." She threw her frizzed head back and gave a full-throated laugh.

Ellie backed away from the pair. Forgetting her hurt foot, she turned and ran into the ballroom—straight into her sister Peggity.

"Ellie, you look as if you'd seen a ghost."

"No," she replied. "I have seen the devil."

In the mood for more Crimson Romance?
Check out *One Moment's Pleasure*
by Rue Allyn
at *CrimsonRomance.com*.

About the Author

Killarney is a mother of five who lives on a ranch in the Canadian Prairies. She divides her time between her family, writing, gardening, music, and her thoroughbred stallion Stamp de Gold who she affectionately refers to as "Love Monkey." When asked why she pens romance her answer is simple, "Because love makes you believe."